LOVE ON TAP

What Reviewers Say About Karis Walsh's Work

Blindsided

"A jaded television reporter and a guide dog trainer form an unlikely bond in Walsh's delightful contemporary romance. Their slow-burn romance is a nuanced exploration of trust, desire, and negotiating boundaries, without a hint of schmaltz or pity. The sex scenes are sizzling hot, but it's the slow burn that really allows Walsh to shine."—*Publishers Weekly*

"Karis Walsh always comes up with charming Traditional Romances with interesting characters who have slightly unusual quirks."—*Curve Magazine*

Sea Glass Inn

"Karis Walsh's third book, excellently written and paced as always, takes us on a gentle but determined journey through two womens' awakening. …The story is well paced, with just enough tension to keep you turning the pages but without an overdramatic melodrama."—*Lesbian Reading Room*

Improvisation

"Walsh tells this story in achingly beautiful words, phrases and paragraphs, building a tension that is bittersweet. The main characters are skillfully drawn, as is Jan's dad, the distinctly loveable and wise Glen Carroll. As the two women interact, there is always an undercurrent of sensuality buzzing around the edges of the pages, even while they exchange sometimes snappy, sometimes comic dialogue. Improvisation is a true romantic tale, Walsh's fourth book, and she's evolving into a master romantic storyteller. "—Lambda Literary

Wingspan

"As with all Karis Walsh's wonderful books the characters are the story. Multifaceted, layered and beautifully drawn, Ken and Bailey hold our attention from the start. ...The pace is gentle, the writing is beautifully crafted and the story a wonderful exploration of how childhood events can shape our lives. The challenge is to outgrow the childhood fears and find the freedom to start living."—*Lesbian Reading Room*

Visit us at www.boldstrokesbooks.com

By the Author

Harmony

Worth the Risk

Sea Glass Inn

Improvisation

Mounting Danger

Wingspan

Blindsided

Mounting Evidence

Love on Tap

LOVE ON TAP

by
Karis Walsh

2016

LOVE ON TAP

ISBN 13: 978-1-62639-564-0

This Trade Paperback Original Is Published By
Bold Strokes Books, Inc.
P.O. Box 249
Valley Falls, NY 12185

First Edition: February 2016

CREDITS
Editor: Ruth Sternglantz
Production Design: Susan Ramundo
Cover Design By Sheri (graphicartist2020@hotmail.com)

CHAPTER ONE

Stacy Lomond stared out the store window while she mechanically folded a lime-green polo shirt. Someone had made a mess of the neat, rainbow-colored stacks she had made when she first came on shift, and she let her mind wander while she sorted the shirts by size and color. The old-fashioned storefronts of Walla Walla's Main Street faded out of sight and were replaced by the memory of the forest path she had followed on her hike last week. She mentally retraced her steps from Hurricane Creek to Sawtooth Peak in Oregon's Wallowa Mountains. Even in the busy months of summer, the wilderness area was quiet on weekdays, and Tace had felt the buoyancy of solitude as she scrambled up a talus chute to an alpine meadow ringed by larches and mountain hemlock. She'd had two glorious hours alone on the peak, looking over the Wallowas and the Seven Devils Mountains in Idaho and planning her next hiking conquest, until a trio of climbers had come into view and she'd started her descent before they noticed her. The night before she summited, she'd even managed to find a quiet spot for her tent not far from Falls Creek, and the baying of coyotes had lulled her to sleep.

Tace went into the fitting room and gathered an armload of clothes someone had left behind. She dropped them on a table next to her register and put the garments back in order—turning sleeves right-side out and smoothing wrinkles—while her surroundings dimmed again. She needed to buy another journal before her next hike since she'd filled the last pages of her old one with sketches of birds and plants she saw, notes on the ones she hadn't been able to identify on the spot, and pressed leaves and pine needles. She had a whole shelf full of bulky notebooks from her treks outdoors. When she had first started her solo hikes, she hadn't known the names of many of the birds and trees, but now she was familiar with most of the ones crossing her path, and the thrill of discovering some new-to-her species was less common but no less exciting.

She walked through the store on autopilot, hanging blouses and cardigans in their places while wishing she could replace the hum of the air conditioner with the sound of wind rasping through pine branches. As beautiful as the sights had been on her trip, the sounds had been even more noteworthy this time. She had started her hike to the summit just before dawn, with her tent and bottles of water stuffed in her backpack. Her arms were laden with field guides, her journal, and a mechanical pencil, and she'd been trying to balance her breakfast granola bar and a flashlight while she looked up the difference between blue and spruce grouse. A sudden grating, honking sound had erupted directly over her head, making her drop everything in surprise. She picked up her books and granola bar out of the dirt while what sounded like a dive-bombing pterodactyl alternated between a nasal cheeping sound and the gruff honk. It had been too dark to see the bird, and she couldn't find anything large enough to be so loud in her field guide, so she hadn't been able to identify it until she got home and did some research.

She shook out a pair of jeans and folded them in thirds. Hard to believe the prehistoric sounds she'd heard were the *peent*s and booms of a common nighthawk. Once the sun had come up, she'd seen the slender birds flying overhead, with distinctive white stripes on their tapered wings, but she hadn't connected them with the echoing calls that had seemed to come from only inches above her head.

A piercing metallic chime broke Tace out of her daydreams. A young woman was standing by the register, tapping her fingers next to the service bell. Tace hurried over before she rang it again.

"Sorry to keep you waiting," she said. She didn't get an answer and didn't really expect one since the girl pulled out her phone once Tace started ringing up her purchase. A student from Whitman College, most likely, given her age and the store's proximity to campus. One of the least desirable aspects of Tace's undesirable job.

"Did you find everything you needed?" Tace asked mechanically. She had just cleaned out the girl's dressing room. Most of the store's inventory had been tried on in her attempt to find what she needed.

"Uh-huh."

"Would you like to save fifteen percent by opening an account with us today?" Tace scanned the last item and asked the requisite question even though she wanted to retreat into her wilderness fantasy—so temptingly willing to whisk her thoughts away from reality.

"Hm-mm." Tace's customer mumbled a negative with a brief shake of her head, not bothering to glance up from her phone.

A fluttering movement in the petite section caught Tace's attention, and she looked up and saw her friend Allie waving her arms in greeting. Tace managed to control her grin enough to make it seem like merely a friendly and professional smile. She and Allie had grown up together in Walla Walla, townies floating through a constantly changing—yet never really changing—sea of Whitties. Tace was older now, and no one called a thirty-one-year-old woman names or threw things at her from passing cars. Allie had gone on to get her associate's degree in nutrition from Walla Walla Community College, and she worked in Whitman's cafeteria. They'd each risen above the types of harassment they'd experienced as kids, but the memories didn't fade completely.

Tace gave the total of the purchase and put the clothing in a large bag while the girl swiped her debit card and entered her PIN. "Thank you for shopping at Drake's, and have a nice day," she said with a bright, practiced smile.

"Thanks," the girl said with a bare glance in Tace's direction. She left the store with her bag in one hand and phone in the other while Allie took her place in front of the register.

"How can I serve you, ma'am?" Tace asked with exaggerated subservience in her voice. "Can I open an account for you? Cater to your every whim? Give you a pint of my blood?"

Allie laughed. "You're awful," she said with a shake of her head. "You stand here looking so professional while you help people. If they only knew what was going on in your mind."

"I'd be fired for sure," Tace said with a grin, relishing the thought. "No severance package, just leave my name tag on the counter and get out."

Allie pushed a strand of pale red hair behind her ear. "The rude and entitled ones are the exception, not the rule, you know. Most of these college kids are really great. I love working with them."

Tace sighed. She had felt a momentary elation at even a joke about being fired, but she couldn't give up this job. She depended on the money she got from waiting on uncaring customers for her home and for her family's future. The inevitable path her career—such as it was—would take made her stomach tighten like a spasm. Move into a lower management position. Possibly, once her obligations and mortgage were under control, transfer to another store in a different, bigger city. She loved her home, though, and doubted even that small step forward would be taken before she retired at age...what, eighty-five?

"I'm not thinking of applying to Whitman, so spare me the recruiting speech," she said. Her gloomy thoughts were reflected in her tone, and she gave Allie's upper arm a quick squeeze. "Sorry. It's been a long day."

"I understand. But maybe if you engaged with them a little more, you'd find they're friendlier than when you act so detached."

Tace tilted her head and glared at Allie. She'd spent eight hours cleaning up after strangers. She wasn't in the mood to feel charitable toward them. "She was having a more meaningful connection with the apps on her phone than with me. Was I supposed to slap the thing out of her hand and ask about her childhood?"

Allie held up her hands in laughing surrender. "Maybe I should take you out for a drink instead of lecturing you on the joys of talking to college students."

Tace had to join in her laughter. Allie's impish smile—made more so by the freckles splashed across her cheeks and nose—showed she was undeterred by Tace's crankiness. A drink was exactly what Tace needed. And maybe a stranger to share her bed for the night? Always a good way to dispel the haze of monotony from her job.

"That's a much better idea," she said. "I just need to clock out and I'm ready to go."

"I'll wait for you outside. It's a gorgeous day."

Tace hurried to the back room and signed out before changing out of her stiff white shirt and black polyester pants. The natural feel of soft khakis and a faded green cotton T-shirt against her skin erased the sensed residue from the artificial fabrics she had worn all day. She shoved her work clothes into her backpack, glad to get them out of sight. Was Allie right about her being emotionally detached from the people she saw at work? Tace shook her head. Of course Allie was correct, but that didn't mean Tace needed to change. She was polite and tidy and she spoke to her customers as much as necessary. Even if she became suddenly more effusive or cheery, nothing would change. She'd still be treated like an extension of the register. No one talked to an ATM or the credit card machine. Why talk to the robot putting clothes in a bag and handing out credit applications?

Tace left the store at a brisk walk. Whatever. At least work was behind her for the day. She'd made some money, she had great benefits, and once her shift was over, her job was out of her head. She didn't envy the people who were married to their careers and couldn't leave their cares at the office. Maybe she'd like to feel that sort of passion for her work, but it didn't seem likely to happen here unless she had a partial lobotomy.

Allie was in the shade of the store, leaning against a wrought-iron lamppost—another of the annoyingly charming fixtures on Main Street. Tace inhaled deeply when she stepped outside and felt the heat slam into her like a solid force. After six, and it was at least ninety. Summer was Tace's favorite time of year, when the air was warm and most of the students had deserted the town. A few stayed, of course, and with the next semester only a few weeks away, others were beginning to invade her hometown. She'd milk the most pleasure she could out of the waning days of the season.

"Where are we going?" she asked. "The Blue?"

"Of course. Let's walk."

The tavern—named after the nearby Blue Mountains and probably just as old—was over a mile away, but Tace welcomed the movement. Although she'd been on her feet all day, the freedom of being outside with no shirts to fold and no mandatory phrases to say was sweet. She listened while Allie talked about her own work in the cafeteria. During the month leading up to the students' return, she and the other dieticians researched and tested new recipes. Tace had a freezer full of dishes in disposable tins. She never had to cook during the month of August.

"What did you think about the food I brought last week?" Allie asked while they waited to cross Isaacs Avenue.

Tace started walking across the street during a lull in traffic, before the walk signal came on. Allie jogged to catch up to her.

"I liked the casserole with broccoli and rice, and the Salisbury steak with grilled onions. The meatloaf thing made out of lentils was gross."

"Yeah, that didn't pass the taste test. We have more and more vegetarian students every year, and I want to give them options besides cheese. Maybe we could make a veggie version of Cajun red beans and rice…"

She started listing ingredients, and Tace joined in. She wasn't the best cook, but she got interested when the conversation turned to blends of spices and herbs. She'd even considered joining Allie at the community college to study culinary arts—one of the many subjects in which she had a passing interest—but the thought had never been a serious one. Tace had been lucky to find the time to graduate from high school. Anything beyond that had never been a possibility for her.

Talk about college food stopped when they entered the dimly lit bar. Dark wood paneling and stained-glass windows gave the room a gloomy, nighttime feel even when the sun was shining like today. Tace felt the familiar cling of her shoes to the sticky cement floor, its peeling red paint covered with a layer of spilled beer. Without needing to speak, each went her separate way once they got inside. Allie went over to stake out a tall round table near the dartboards, and Tace got a couple of Bud Lights and a handful of darts from the bartender. The familiarity of their routine was comforting, and Tace tapped her bottle against Allie's in a silent toast before taking a long swallow.

Nothing spectacular, but the beer was ice cold and helped wash away the rest of Tace's day at the store. She set down the bottle and picked up her three darts to take the first turn. The barrels were dented from years of use, but she managed to land two of them in the double ring.

"Very impressive." A woman's voice made Tace pause while she was writing her score on the chalkboard. "Are you always so accurate?"

"In everything I do," Tace said. She turned around with a smile. She hadn't even had a chance to scope out the night's prospects from among the bar's clientele, and the brunette in front of her seemed to have saved her the trouble. "I'm Tace, and this is Allie."

"Lynn." She set down the beer she was holding and shook hands with both of them, giving Tace a chance to check her out. She was pretty, with long legs and enough buttons undone to give Tace a hint of full breasts.

Allie put her darts on the table. "Why don't you take my place, Lynn? I'll go keep your friend over there company while the two of you…play."

She left just enough of a pause between words to make Tace laugh. "What do you say, Lynn? Want to play?"

"Definitely," Lynn said. She stood in place for a few seconds and then slapped her forehead with a playful gesture. "Oh, wait. Do you mean play darts? Well, okay, I guess."

She bumped her shoulder against Tace's on her way to the line and took aim. The first dart missed the board completely, but the second landed in the triple ring.

"Either that was an extremely lucky shot, or I've just met a hustler. Which is it?" Tace rested one elbow on the table and took another swallow of beer. The evening was going exactly as she needed it to, apparently. Lynn was playful and nice looking, and she'd taken the pressure off Tace by approaching her first. A promising start to a rare fun and carefree night.

Lynn paused before throwing her third dart. "Care to bet on which one I am?"

"I'm game." *For anything.* "What's the wager?"

"If I make less than thirty points on this next toss, I'll buy the drinks for the rest of the night. If I make more, I get a kiss from you."

Tace was beginning to like this game. "Deal."

Lynn took her time aiming, and she dropped the dart in the double ring again. "Ha! Eighteen and eighteen, if I'm not mistaken, make thirty-six. Pay up."

Gladly. Tace put her beer down and walked slowly over to Lynn. She cupped Lynn's cheek with one hand and leaned down to kiss her gently on the lips. She lingered there a moment, not pushing further, but with a hint of desire in her firm pressure.

Like the beer, Lynn's kiss was nice and refreshing. Nothing earth-shattering, but Tace didn't want fireworks. She wanted a break from normal for one night.

"Another impressive skill," Lynn said. She retrieved her darts and wrote her score on the board. She made an extravagant show of checking out Tace's ass when she got up to take her turn. "You seem to be a woman with many assets."

Tace laughed and her shot went wide of its mark. "You're distracting me on purpose." She took careful aim and made a better throw.

"I'll behave. For now," Lynn said. "Say, are you here for the seminar, too? I thought I recognized you from registration."

Tace threw her last dart without much care. She had a sinking feeling about the sudden turn her evening seemed to be taking. How easy to simply go along with the story. *Yes, I'm here for the seminar. I noticed you, too.*

She couldn't pretend, not even for one night. "No, I live here in town. What seminar?"

"I didn't know there were others going on at the same time. Mine is on curriculum planning for philosophy programs. Are you on faculty here?"

Tace frowned. When she had been younger, she had been easily recognizable as a townie. Now, she was often asked this same question, and she wasn't sure what had changed in her to make the difference. So Lynn was a philosophy professor. What would they have to talk about? Not that Tace had been planning on lengthy conversations tonight. But what would Lynn say when Tace told her she worked at Drake's department store? That she had scraped by to get her high-school diploma, but nothing more? Tace wasn't about to stick around and find out.

She tugged her darts out of the board one by one and returned to the table. She stuck out her hand. "Lynn, it was great meeting you tonight. I hate to run off like this, but I just remembered something I have to do."

Not exactly a graceful exit, but Tace couldn't think of another way to get out of the bar fast. Lynn shook her offered hand with a look of confusion on her face. Tace stopped by the table where Allie was chatting up Lynn's friend.

"I need to go," Tace said. "Early morning tomorrow." She walked toward the door, but Allie followed and caught her arm before she could open it.

"What's wrong, Tace?" Allie's expression was concerned, but when she glanced over at Lynn, she seemed to read the situation all too well. "Tace, you don't need to go. You're worth more than any degree—"

Tace stopped her with a wave of her hand. "Don't, Allie. And don't say anything to them."

"Of course I won't. Okay, you can go. But wait for me to get my purse and I'll come with you."

"No. Stay. Have fun." Tace sometimes envied Allie's confidence. She got along as easily with tenured professors as with the janitors at the college. She didn't seem fazed by any differences between her and anyone else, but Tace couldn't do the same. She couldn't bear to be pitied for any reason.

She walked outside and took a deep breath. The sun was starting to set, and the sky to the west was washed with oranges and pinks. Tace walked in that direction and pulled out her phone. She hit speed dial and waited five rings until Christiana answered.

"Tace? What's up?" Chris's voice sounded cheerful and carefree. Exactly how Tace wanted her to sound.

"Nothing much. I just wanted to check on you. Did you register today?"

"I did. I got all the classes I wanted. Even the medieval lit class I thought might be full."

"Great, Chris." Tace stopped at a crosswalk on Isaacs and smacked the button for the walk signal several times. "Do you have enough cash for books and everything?"

"I'm good. Tace, are you sure everything is all right?"

"Everything is fine. Look, I'll call you later this week. E-mail me your schedule so I can see what classes you'll be taking."

"I will. Take care, sis."

"You, too," Tace said even though Chris had already ended the call. She was working on her master's at Oregon State. Tace felt a muddled mixture of emotions every time she thought of Chris and what she was doing. She'd be the first Lomond to get a college degree of any kind, let alone an advanced one. Tace was enormously proud of her sister, and admittedly a little envious when she allowed the feeling to rise. Mostly, she never wanted Chris to experience the sense of being insignificant or unworthy that Tace felt when she met someone like Lynn. She wanted Chris to be proud and accomplished, and she'd make it happen no matter how hard she had to work.

Tace turned right on Hobson Street. She was climbing the steps leading to her yellow-and-white Craftsman-style house when her phone buzzed again. Kyle. Great—just what she needed tonight. She sighed and answered.

"Hey, Kyle. What do you want?"

"I've got some exciting news, sis! When are you working tomorrow?"

"Five to close. What's the news?" Tace had no doubt it would be exciting, but probably not in a way she'd think was positive.

"I'll tell you tomorrow. Can you meet me about ten?"

He gave her an address on the outskirts of town, and she reluctantly agreed before hanging up. She unlocked her front door and entered the dark and silent living room. One thing she knew for sure. If her brother was involved, she'd better bring along her checkbook.

CHAPTER TWO

B erit Katsaros wove through the temporary city of tents and tarps on her way to the tin shack that served as the dig's HQ. She stopped to rest for a moment and mopped her sweaty forehead with the corner of a red kerchief she had tied over her short blond hair. She was accustomed to the desert heat of Europe, Asia, and North Africa, but the combination of high humidity and near-constant rainfall here in the tropical lowlands of Peru sapped her energy. Since her first experiences with field school back in the summers of her undergrad days, she had learned to remove her attention from physical discomfort and focus on the work she was doing. She had gotten too soft, too acclimated to a certain set of conditions. She had come to South America for a change of pace while she was between jobs—unable to sit still and be idle for long—and she was glad she had. Since she had first stepped off the floating piece of timber that had passed as a boat in Yurimaguas, she had felt the conflicting swing between the exhilaration of being in a new place with a new project and a weariness settling deep in her muscles and tendons.

Work. Work would eventually ease her troubling lack of energy. She had been fighting a sense of ennui for months now, and the oppressive heat at this archaeological site was aggravating her emotions. She quickly covered the last few yards to the hut and opened the corrugated metal door, clenching her teeth at the squeal of rusty hinges.

"You must be Jim. I'm Berit," she said, crossing to the young man and shaking his hand. He was an inch or so taller than her five-eight height, with dark-framed hipster glasses and wearing black jeans and a plain white T-shirt. He still smelled like a newcomer. She inhaled the scents of detergent and shampoo and felt an almost physical longing for a shower of her own. Clean hair and freshly washed clothes, using all the chemicals the big detergent companies could supply. Heavenly.

Give him two days using the shared latrine and bathing with a bucket of cold river water, and the olfactory remnants of civilization would be gone. She wondered whether his interest in this career would fade as quickly. His expression was one she remembered from her early days—eager and anticipatory. Certain he was about to uncover a find equivalent to the lost city of Troy. She had agreed to let him join the dig here as a favor to a friend, but she was hoping his enthusiasm would help rejuvenate her own. She always got energized by introducing young students and budding archaeologists to her world, although not all of them were able to sustain their own interest for more than a week or two on the job.

"Thank you for having me here, Dr. Katsaros. I'm thrilled to be able to work with you and I can't wait to get started."

"Call me Berit. And we're glad to have you here. We're very short-handed at the moment." A phrase that usually didn't need stating on any given dig—when were they ever *not* short-handed? "Come along and I'll give you the tour. Bring your bag and we'll stop by the dorms first."

Berit led the way to the two large tents set up behind the headquarters building. She pulled back the flap of one of them and pointed at a vacant bunk. A few of the other cots were occupied with sleeping workers who were taking a quick siesta during the heat of the day. Because of the heat and the number of underground sites, a lot of the archaeologists did their work during the cooler nights, with the help of large floodlights. Berit had discovered that when she needed time alone to refresh and recharge, she had to seek refuge in an excavated tomb or building or take a walk in the thick forest. At any given time, the sounds of snores filled the tents.

Jim put his duffel bag on the cot and looked around. Berit could see his already disconcerted expression. She understood, and she'd gone through the same range of emotions herself. The transition from being an idealistic and unrealistic archaeology student—when too many of their future dreams and hopes were based on movies and television—to living in the actual dirty and uncomfortable world of a site was a wrenching one. What happened next, once disillusionment gave way to the reality of life in the trenches, either created or destroyed a career.

"I guess when you called this a dorm, I was expecting something more like a...building," he said once they were outside again. "Where are the, um, facilities?"

Berit pointed toward the tree line. "A few hundred yards in that direction. Don't worry, you'll be able to smell your way to the latrine."

Jim smiled. "Doc Martinson said you weren't one to sugarcoat life out here. I guess she wasn't joking."

Berit returned his smile, with fond memories of her friend. She and Kim Martinson—Kim Price at the time—had entered grad school together at UC Berkeley. She had gone on to specialize in Classical Archaeology, while Kim had focused on the textual side of Classics. Kim had stayed in the States, married, and was now a tenured professor at Whitman College. Berit's journey had taken her to far-off and ever-changing places, but the two had remained good friends. When Kim had promising undergrads with an interest in archaeology, she tested their resolve by sending them to work with Berit for a few weeks before they applied to graduate school. *Why have them waste years of their lives and thousands of dollars if they aren't going to cut it in the field? If anyone can dishearten the brave but foolhardy, it'd be you, Berit.*

Kim had meant her words to be a compliment, and Berit had taken them that way. Sharing her beloved work with fresh, young minds was rewarding, but giving them a dose of reality was even more important. She felt as if she was initiating them into an elite club. Anyone who wanted could join, and she helped students figure out if they were willing to commit to the lifestyle she had chosen. The dues were steep—often uncomfortable and primitive living conditions, and little pay relative to the amount of schooling and unpaid fieldwork necessary to gain a foothold in the discipline. The work was always intense. Intensely and earthshakingly boring at times, intensely mind-consuming and thrilling at others.

Berit ducked under a piece of loose canvas doubling as a door to the excavation site and shook rainwater out of her hair. She and Jim stood in the spacious entryway to the burial site beyond. This area had long ago been cleared of artifacts, and now it was the center of activity at the dig. Textbooks and albums full of photos taken of earlier finds covered makeshift shelves that were carved into the walls. Long tables were covered with remains and pottery shards. Most cleaning, sorting, and cataloging took place here, along with the collaborative brainstorming Berit enjoyed with her coworkers. Questions were raised and answered around these tables, strengthening the sense of family she felt with her colleagues as they all worked together to decipher the past.

"Kim said you had photography experience."

"Um, sure."

Jim was frowning. He had probably been expecting to be in the trenches with trowel and brush, unearthing incredible riches. Well, his romantic ideas were about to be squashed. Berit took a tripod and digital camera off one of the tables. "Your main job while you're here will be as camp photographer. We need general shots of each dig site. Most are tomb chambers, but there are some outdoor trenches as well. We had a plastic sheet somewhere"— Berit held up a crinkly piece of clear plastic she found under the table—"for the rain. Anyway, you'll also be taking find shots. The tripod is rigged so you can use it like normal, or you can suspend the camera underneath and take pictures from above bones in situ."

"Okay." Jim took the camera when she handed it to him. He looked so disappointed, she felt compelled to reassure him.

"I know it isn't the most glamorous job, but it's very necessary to what we're doing here. Not only will you have access to all the trenches and tombs, you'll also be able to observe a variety of archaeologists doing fieldwork. If you keep your eyes open and ask some good questions, this could be an extraordinary experience for you. Besides, since you'll be viewing the finds from all angles, at each step of the process, you might be the one who figures out the use or meaning of an object. Something we might miss if we don't have all the pieces of the puzzle like you will."

"I wasn't complaining," he said in a rush, as if hurrying to reassure her of his willingness to work. "I'll do anything just for the chance to be here. It's just…well, I think Dr. Martinson might have slightly exaggerated my photography abilities."

Berit bit her lip to keep from chuckling at his worried expression. Had she ever been so earnest and eager? She didn't feel either one right now. "Exactly what is your experience with cameras?"

"I can use the one on my phone to take selfies."

She burst out laughing and was glad when he joined her. A sense of humor always came in handy in the field. "The manual for the camera is in the case. How fast can you learn?"

"I'll have it memorized by tomorrow."

He said it with a grin, but she had a feeling he wasn't lying. She'd need to have a little chat with Kim about padding her students' résumés, but she understood why she had wanted to give this student a chance to prove himself. He reminded her of her younger self, and the comparison made her sad somehow. She couldn't quite figure out why. Maybe she was just tired. She'd been working hard for the past two years, and for her first free month in ages she'd chosen to come here to Peru.

She took the camera from Jim and put the whole kit back where she had found it. "We'll finish the tour and pick up the camera and manual on the way back."

She was about to lead him through the tunnel at the far side of the room and into the tombs when a man and a woman came through the opening with a gurney. Another of the skeletons. Berit felt the familiar prickle of excitement.

"Is this the one?" she asked. She hurried over to the table. Introductions were made in the form of orders since she felt an urgency to get the body settled, even though the woman had been dead for centuries. "Jim, help Mark hold the stretcher and Lisa and I will move her."

Berit and Lisa each held two corners of the plastic sheet and lifted it off the gurney and onto the table. The bones had been carefully and precisely returned to the position they were in when discovered, and Berit was anxious not to disturb them during the relocation. She stood back and looked at the unusual positioning of the eroding skeleton.

"Female, post-adolescent," Mark said. "We have no idea why she's the only one curled on her side, when every other body we've found has been supine."

Berit walked slowly around the table while the three made their formal introductions. Jim asked the same questions she and the other archaeologists had been asking since the find, two days before. *Was she buried apart from the others?* No. *Did she seem to be either royal or wealthier than the others, or maybe of a lower class?* No, neither seemed to be indicated. They had hoped to have more answers once the body was fully and painstakingly exhumed, but they still only had questions.

The voices of the other people in the room faded from Berit's consciousness as she concentrated on the woman. *Who are you?* Why was she on her side with her knees bent? Berit followed the curve of the bones, letting the shape fill her mind. Strangely familiar, edging into the corner of Berit's memory.

She jumped up on the table and stared down at the motionless form beneath her. A question mark without the dot. Why hadn't she noticed this before?

She leaped off the table, ran over to the shelves, and started pulling down albums. "Where are the pictures of the houses? The ones with symbols over the doors?"

Mark and Lisa came over and wordlessly started searching with her. Like her, they recognized when someone was grasping for a solution to something. Instead of peppering her with questions about what she was thinking, they gave her space.

"Here," Mark said. He plopped a heavy album in front of Berit and she shuffled through the pages. They'd found and excavated the heart of the little town early in the dig—before Berit arrived. She'd only come once they had discovered the cemetery, but she had pored over the albums as she familiarized herself with the ancient community they were unearthing, piece by piece and bone by bone.

She found the page she was looking for. A symbol carved over the door of a hut. A question mark *with* a dot. They hadn't yet identified the marking, whether it indicated the home of a healer or religious leader or some other occupation.

"A baby," she said, looking up at Mark and Lisa. "This must be the sign of a midwife, or someone who delivers babies. This woman is in the same position as the symbol, and she probably died in childbirth."

She watched their expressions shift as they followed her train of thought. No one had thought to search for more bones in the burial plot since every other one had only held one person.

"The interns are clearing out the rest of the plot now," Lisa said, giving voice to Berit's worries. "We need to get down there before they excavate and possibly damage the infant."

Berit jogged after them as they rushed back into the tunnels, with Jim close on her heels. She felt the months of tiredness fall away like a dropped cloak as she ran. These moments of pure discovery, of figuring out an ancient and challenging riddle were the moments she lived for.

They crossed a bridge made of dirt and clay before entering a tight passageway. The tombs were located underneath them, and they were heading for the access chute where a rope ladder served as a two-story staircase for people and a lift for removing artifacts. Mark skidded to a stop near the edge, but the ground seemed to crumble under his feet. He was dropping out of sight when Berit flung herself on her stomach and reached for his hand. She felt his fingers grasp hers for a moment before he lost his grip and fell. She scrabbled for purchase but couldn't keep from tumbling over the side after him.

CHAPTER THREE

Tace drove out of town the next morning, through the gentle, undulating hills surrounding Walla Walla. She passed signs pointing to wineries at regular intervals, and the buildings containing tasting rooms and reception areas looked very similar to pictures she'd seen of Tuscany. These fields had been planted with crops like corn, wheat, and peas when she was younger, but now they were covered with grapevines.

The booming wine industry in Walla Walla had changed not only the landscape of the surrounding areas, but also the town itself. Every other store downtown seemed to be either a wineshop or a wine bar, and buses full of tourists came for the spring barrel openings and the numerous tasting tours. Tace's life was hardly touched by the industry, thank God. She made the same money whether she waited on one customer or a thousand, and she rarely shopped where the wine enthusiasts did. She knew where college students and tourists tended to go, and she avoided both. Unless she was riding her bike along these winding roads or buying a bottle of wine for one of the rare times she had a date over for dinner, Tace stayed well outside the exclusive world of high-end wines.

She lowered her car window and let the hot breeze riffle her hair. She had to admit the scenery was beautiful here, with the rolling foothills of the Blues and the stone wineries covered with creeping vines. She loved to ride out here for the exercise she got while pedaling up the sometimes quite steep hills, but mostly because the views were captivating. Even in the heat of late summer, the carefully maintained gardens of the wineries were filled with flowers in a rainbow of colors, and peregrine falcons would often perch on fence posts near the tidy rows of grapes while they hunted for field mice.

Today, however, she wasn't here for sightseeing. She held the page of printed directions flat against her steering wheel, alternately watching the road and glancing at the paper as it flapped in the wind. She drove into a small valley and found the dirt road leading off the highway. She tossed the paper aside and drove her ancient Chrysler along the rutted path. The little powder-blue car was almost as old as she was, and she hoped it didn't shake to pieces before she got to the mysterious place her brother wanted her to see. She figured she must be close to the Walla Walla River down here since the vegetation grew more thickly than on the more barren, vineyard-covered hills.

Kyle's black Camaro was parked near a metal warehouse. Tace stopped beside him and got out of her car, noticing a new dent in Kyle's fender. All three of the siblings had gotten a small inheritance when their father passed, and Tace had tried to encourage the others to invest or save the money. Instead, Kyle had bought a brand new car, and he had been steadily gambling away the rest of it. Chris had been a bit more sensible—buying a Mustang instead—and Tace had convinced her to put the rest in an investment account. Tace was paying for her schooling, and Chris would graduate with no loans and with some money of her own. She'd have choices. Kyle had choices, too, but he tended to make the least responsible ones every time.

Tace looked around. The yard was in a sad state, with rusted barrels and overgrown weeds surrounding the small gravel parking lot. A scrawny black-and-white tuxedo cat peered at her from behind a weed-covered woodpile, and she knelt on the ground and tried to call it to her. The kitten vanished, so Tace stood up again and resumed her gloomy appraisal of the place. She didn't see any sign of a house, but the area was dense with trees so she wasn't sure what else might be hidden from sight. The tan shed with brown eaves and spouts looked to be in decent condition, and a door stood propped open a few yards from her. She sighed and walked toward it. She didn't have a good feeling about this.

"Hey, sis, you made it! Isn't this a great place?"

Kyle came out of the door and swooped her up into a big hug before she could get a glimpse inside the building. His overly effusive greeting didn't ease her worries. She returned his hug with affection, though. She hadn't seen him for months, and irresponsible and undisciplined as he was, he was still her baby brother. She disentangled herself from him and held him at arm's length. He looked well, with his bright, charismatic grin and thick, wavy dark hair that was characteristic of all the Lomonds. He was twenty-four, nearly seven years her junior, but he looked like a naughty fourteen-year-old who had just broken a neighbor's window with a baseball and didn't feel guilty about it at all. He had been only three, and Chris was two, when Tace's mom had left the family. Her dad had worked overtime to support them and to cover her mom's gambling debts, so Tace had been part parent, part sister. Despite her best efforts, Kyle had become a younger version of their mother.

"Sure, Kyle. It's a great place. A great big mess." She punched him playfully in the arm. "What did you get tangled in and what do I have to do to get you out of it?"

He put on a hurt expression, but it didn't last long and his mouth naturally curved into a smile again. "It's nothing like that. Come inside. You're going to love this."

He pulled her through the door and spread his arms wide. "Ta-da!"

Tace let her eyes adjust to the dim light inside. The difference between the ratty outdoors and the spotless interior was striking.

Large gleaming metal vats filled the space, and the copper and steel looked like they'd been recently polished. The concrete floor was swept and clean, and there didn't seem to be an ounce of dust in the place. Someone apparently cared for this enough to keep it in good condition. No one seemed to care about the outside.

"Please tell me you didn't buy a meth lab," she said, glaring at her brother.

"Jeez, what kind of guy do you think I am? I don't do that crap and you know it. It's a brewery. Isn't it cool?"

Tace sighed. She wanted the whole story, but Kyle shared a snippet at a time. What she needed to know was what he expected her role to be. "What are you planning to do with a brewery?"

"It's a moneymaker, for sure. All the equipment is here and in good condition. With a small amount of marketing, this place could be a gold mine. Just think of all those frat parties at the college—this stuff will sell itself."

"You should be selling used cars to strangers, not trying to sell me anything. I'm not buying you a brewery. End of story."

"Seriously, you need to relax. I'm not asking you to buy it for me. I bought it for *you*."

Tace rubbed her temples and took a deep breath. "Kyle, tell me the whole story. Now. And please don't let it start with the phrase *I was playing poker with these guys*..."

Kyle flashed his put-out expression again. "Give me some credit, Tace."

"Blackjack?"

He crossed his arms over his chest. "No. You were right with poker."

Tace ran a hand through her hair. She didn't understand how she could be irritated with Kyle and suspicious of his motives, but still want to laugh at his boyish grin and enthusiasm. "Of course I was. So you lost a bet?"

"No. I won a huge bet." Kyle spread his arms again, in a grand gesture. "I won this place."

"And how do I fit in?"

"It's yours. I had him sign it over to you. Don't worry, it's all legit."

Sure it was. Tace put her hands on her hips and didn't respond. She had bailed her brother out of trouble enough times to know she hadn't yet gotten the whole story, and she was tired of asking questions and trying to drag it out of him. She didn't for one minute believe his actions had been anything but self-serving. Besides, why the hell would she want a brewery, least of all one you could barely see for all the weeds and debris surrounding it?

"Look, sis," he said, using the same beseeching gesture with his hands that she'd seen countless times when he was about to explain something that seemed entirely logical to him, but would be costly and illogical to her. "I'm a little short right now. When I made the bet, I was thinking we could run this place together. You know, a real family business. You'd put up the capital, and I'd take over as manager."

Tace couldn't hold back a scoffing laugh. Put Kyle in charge of a brewery? She might as well invite the local fraternities to guard the stills on a Saturday night.

"Don't make fun. I thought it'd be cool to work together. We make a great team."

"Yeah, you get in trouble, and I pay to get you out."

He ran a hand through his dark hair, and she saw the moment when his expression lost its false animation. She saw the truth coming before he opened his mouth. "I need your help, Tace. I owe some money. Gambling debts. I thought this poker game would be an easy way to get some quick cash, but turns out the other guys weren't any better off than I am. I don't have time to wait until I can sell the property, so I had him put your name on the deed. I thought you could float me the cost up front. You'll make your money back and more when you unload this place."

His earlier enthusiasm hadn't fooled her, but his honest look of fearful entreaty scared her. "How much do you need?"

He told her and she felt her knees tremble. She never was going to get out of the hole her family had dug for her. She'd thought she might have a reprieve once Chris was finished with school. A chance to make some changes, see some new places. But she didn't share Kyle's belief that she'd recoup the amount he was asking for when this weed-infested property finally sold.

"I have to talk to a banker or a Realtor or someone," she said, feeling the weight of her responsibility settle so hard on her shoulders that her feet seemed to sink into the ground. She was already resigned to her plans even as she made them. Second mortgage. Give him the money he needed. Sell this place and hopefully make enough to get back near the level of debt she had had at the start of this fiasco. "Let's get out of here."

❖

Three days later—days of wasting her free time filing paperwork at the county office and consulting with loan officers at the bank—Tace was back at the hateful brewery. She had been planning on another hike in the cleansing wilderness of the Wallowas during her days off, but instead she was waiting to meet a real estate agent. She was wearing her work uniform because it was the most professional outfit she owned, and she felt the chafe of the polyester and the whole situation rubbing her raw.

She'd arrived a few minutes early to look around the place. *Her* brewery. What the hell did she know about beer? Nothing. Not a damned thing. She gingerly walked through the long grass to the woodpile and put an orange plastic bowl on the ground. She popped open a can of cat food and dumped it out, hoping it would be eaten by the cat she'd seen before and not by a family of rats.

As flaky as her brother was, he'd somehow managed to find a pretty decent guy to beat at poker. Tace had contacted the previous owner, and the deed he'd signed over to her actually was in good order. He was a recent Whitman graduate who'd bought the place on a lark, wanting to avoid entry into real life after college. He had spent a few months drinking the product he was making before realizing no one else wanted to buy it. He'd lost interest in the venture and hadn't seemed to mind losing the business his parents' money had bought him. Tace felt sympathy for these unknown parents. The three of them had been nothing more than chips in a poker game. Played by their relatives and left to cover the tab.

Tace picked her way back to the warehouse and fished in her pocket for the key her brother had given her. She inserted it in the lock, but the door swung open. She sighed and walked inside. Kyle must not have locked it before. She squinted in the dim interior, lit only by the wedge of sunlight streaming through the door. She had no idea if anything was missing, but the room looked the same as it had when—

"You the new owner?"

Tace yelped and whipped around to face a hairy young man wearing a plaid shirt and overalls. He stood between her and the door, and she could barely discern his features since he was backlit by the sun. She tightened her grip on the empty cat-food can she still held. Could she slit his throat with the sharp edge of the lid?

"Um, yes. I guess so. Who are you?"

"Your brewmaster."

Her brewmaster? No one had told her the property came complete with a brewer who looked more vagabond than skilled craftsman. "I'm sorry, but I'm not planning to keep the place. If you want to leave your contact information, I can pass it along to whoever buys the brewery."

He stepped toward her and she got ready to start carving him up with her tin can, but once he was away from the patch of sunlight she saw he was holding a tall glass of beer in each hand. He held one out to her.

"Is this…did you make this?" He nodded and waited in silence while she considered the odds that he'd go through the trouble of poisoning her. Eh, what the hell? She reached for the glass and felt its icy chill against her palm. She took a tentative sip, expecting as appealing an experience as licking beer off the floor of a frat house. Instead, she let the liquid roll over her tongue with an appreciative slowness. She was accustomed to the cold blandness of cheap bottled beer, and the nuances of flavor in this ale were surprising. Sharp and tangy, but with a honeyed aftertaste and hints of something floral. She had a larger swallow. "Hey, this is really good. What kind is it?"

"IPA."

She heard a car door slam before she could ask more questions. She looked at the door and saw a woman who must be the Realtor she'd found in the phone book. She was wearing a navy suit, complete with silk blouse, pencil skirt, and high heels. She looked as out of place in this weedy backwoods brewery as Tace felt. She came over and offered her hand. Tace put her glass of beer and the cat food can on the floor and shook hands.

"Hello, I'm Joan from Bridgewater Realty."

"I'm Stacy Lomond, and this is…"

She turned toward her brewer-masquerading-as-a-lumberjack to ask his name, but he was nowhere to be seen. He seemed to move without making a sound. A ninja? Or the ghost of some long-dead brewmaster who was haunting the stills? Creepy. The sooner Tace got rid of him and the property, the better.

"This is…the brewery." She finished her sentence with an awkward wave of her hand, pointing out the obvious instead of introducing the invisible.

"Let's have a look around," Joan said in a cheerful voice, as if she were about to tour a piece of prime real estate. She led the way through the maze of vats and ladders. Tace hoped she wouldn't ask too many questions about the operation since she had no idea what anything was. "How large did you say the property is?"

"One point six four acres." Tace looked up and saw the brewer standing on a metal platform next to one of the large copper tanks.

He ducked into the shadows, and she shook her head. He was a weirdo, but he made a great glass of beer.

The tour through the metal building was soon over, and Tace and Joan walked back to the parking area. Joan surveyed the weeds around her with the competent air of someone who could accurately pinpoint the value of the land to the nearest dime.

"Honestly, your best option would be to have the building removed and sell the land as a residential plot. The zoning is right. You could develop it yourself and put a house or two on the property, but you probably wouldn't recoup the expenses."

She gave Tace an estimate of what she'd make on the land alone. Tace kept her face relaxed, but she felt her heart shrink inside her. The price was barely half what she had given Kyle. Not nearly enough to repay the second mortgage.

Tace stared at Joan. She'd expected to sell a brewery, not an unattractive piece of land. "But the equipment is well-maintained, and it's producing good beer. Why wouldn't someone want to give the business a chance?"

Joan gave her a smile that verged on condescending. "If this land were…well, more attractive, this might be a suitable location for a new winery. But anyone in the market for that type of property will want enough acreage for some vineyards, a place for receptions or weddings, and a large enough building to accommodate wine tasting tour groups. Something in the hills would be preferable to a valley like yours. I'm sure you could make some money selling the equipment to other microbreweries."

Tace looked around. Late-blooming wildflowers dotted the variegated greens of grass and weeds. The skinny little cat was crouched near the woodpile and gobbling the food she'd left. She couldn't see the bearded brewer in the shadows of the building's interior, but she was sure he was lurking there and watching her and Joan.

Above all, the beer tasted great. Wasn't that the most important thing? "What if the brewery was making money? Wouldn't someone want to buy it then?"

Joan shrugged. "I suppose if it were a viable business opportunity, you'd have the potential for finding a buyer." She glanced around again, her attention seeming to rest on the parking lot. "But operating costs will be expensive, and I'd advise against investing any more money if you aren't certain you'll get it back."

Joan had assessed her car, the brewery, *her* and had found them lacking. Tace felt a surprising desire to prove her wrong. She wasn't sure why—she usually didn't care what other people thought of her or her financial situation. As long as she was getting by and helping Chris with school. But something about this place...

She could do most of the maintenance work herself. Spruce up the property and bring in some tourists to taste—and buy—the beer. How hard could it be to sell beer in a college town? God, she sounded like Kyle, the dreamer in the family. Not like herself at all.

Besides, Joan was right. No matter how much mowing and trimming she did on her own, there'd be expenses involved. A salary for the brewer, state and federal licenses, at the very least. She could add more hours at the store, but her wages were too low and wouldn't make it worthwhile, especially since she'd need to spend time here. She'd be crazy to even consider it.

"Shall we go back to the office and sign the paperwork?" Joan asked, her voice clearly confident that Tace would listen to her and unload the property as soon as possible.

Yes. Say yes. But all she could see was an imagined picture of the two tiny rooms in the attic of her old house. They had originally been her and Chris's bedrooms, but when her father passed and she moved downstairs, she had gotten the small bedrooms and the Jack and Jill bathroom painted and cleaned. They were empty now, but the rent from two boarders ought to be enough to get the brewery up and running. She'd have to share her kitchen—yuk— but it wouldn't be permanent. And where did one find temporary boarders, only interested in leasing a room for a semester or two? Tace sighed. The college.

"Thanks for your advice, Joan, but I think I can get the brewery going. Maybe I'll contact you when I'm ready to sell it as a functioning business."

But probably not. She wouldn't let Joan profit from her hard work if she managed to make the brewery a success. And she sure as hell didn't want to give her a chance to gloat if she failed.

CHAPTER FOUR

Berit sat slumped against the door of the taxi. She'd just endured a long twelve hours on planes and in airports, and her back ached with a ferocity she'd never experienced before. She was accustomed to being uncomfortable, but over the course of this day she'd been humiliated, undignified, and helpless. Now she added cranky to the list.

If she survived this year and managed to walk again, she'd do so with a newfound appreciation of and sympathy for anyone needing a wheelchair for mobility. The airports had been completely accessible, of course, with ramps and elevators and cloyingly helpful porters, but the actual experience of using them had been much more challenging than she'd anticipated. She'd had airline attendants pushing her from gate to gate calling *Excuse us! Wheelchair coming through!* She'd had those same attendants stand outside her bathroom stall every time she'd had to use a toilet. Seeing their feet stationed just on the other side of the half-door had been worse than sharing an open-air latrine with a jumble of other archaeologists. Far, far worse had been when she'd lost her balance in the handicapped stall in the Denver airport bathroom and pushed her chair out of reach. She'd nearly had to ask for help, but she'd managed to catch herself with the guardrail and had used her foot to pull the chair close enough to grab with her free hand.

Her doctors and therapists had warned her against doing too much too soon, but she hadn't seen how coming to this tiny, godforsaken town and teaching a few classes could possibly be considered doing too much. On the last leg of her flight, though, from Seattle to Walla Walla, she'd sat stiffly in the tight seat on the Bombardier turboprop and wondered if she'd made a huge mistake. She could barely stand the trip to get from Florida, where she'd been since her return to the States, to the backwoods of Washington State. Over the course of her career, she'd spent hundreds of hours in rickety little planes, a few with nothing more than a canvas tarp as a door and more than one without a working radio, and the seventy-some seat plane would normally have seemed luxurious as the Concorde to her. Instead, she'd shifted and winced and wished she hadn't thrown out the pain pills her doctor had prescribed. The scenery below offered little distraction. Fields and barren hills. Deep gouges and steep basalt ridges left behind after millennia of glacial and volcanic activity. Boring. She could dig all day and probably find nothing more than rocks.

After a tedious day of travel, the taxi ride to her new lodging was much too short. She wasn't prepared to meet her landlord and have to ask for help getting settled in her rooms. She was also uncomfortably aware that she hadn't mentioned her injury when she'd e-mailed this Stacy person about the space she had available. She'd hoped to be more mobile by now, although it had only been a few weeks since her accident and the surgery to fuse her two cracked vertebrae. She was still wheelchair bound, however, except for brief forays to the toilet or into bed. She'd been warned repeatedly about the serious damage she could do if she pushed herself and injured her back again before it was fully healed. Paralysis. A permanent limp, constant pain, and a lifetime in her wheelchair. She wasn't sure if her doctors were merely being thoroughly pessimistic or not, but she had to resist her usual blasé attitude toward health-care providers and actually listen to what they were telling her.

Except for this job. She couldn't stand to sit still for months, with nothing to do. Kim's offer of an academic-year-long job at Whitman sounded dull, but at least it was something to do. She could use the time to write another book, do the minimum required to skate through her classes, and give her spine time to recuperate. She looked at the quiet residential neighborhood passing by outside the taxi window. As soon as she had the go-ahead from her doctors, she was out of here.

The cab parked outside a yellow- and white-trimmed house. Old by American standards—practically brand new by Berit's— the home looked tidy and cared for. Walking or wheeling distance from the campus. Two rooms and a private bathroom—heavenly, considering the accommodations Berit had left in Peru. A shared kitchen and living space with one person. Delightful. But right now, Berit would give just about anything to be back on the dig, hiking to the stinky latrine and trying to muffle the snores of her bunkmates with a questionably clean pillow held over her head.

The cab driver got Berit's chair out of the trunk and came to her door to help her get out. She was carefully transferring her annoyingly fragile body from car to seat when she noticed a woman standing on the front porch. At the top of a flight of wooden stairs. Of course she'd have stairs—how many houses had Berit seen with them in her lifetime? Now, something she'd taken for granted and barely gave any attention to loomed before her like an insurmountable obstacle. And at the top of them, unreachable as a goddess, was—she presumed—her sexy new landlord. Damn. Long legs shown to perfection by khaki shorts. *Short* being the operative word. A snug teal V-neck shirt revealed small breasts and a thin waist. She looked muscular and slender at the same time. Outdoorsy and down-to-earth. Exactly the kind of distraction Berit needed during her months in purgatory. Unfortunately, vigorous sex was off the table for the time being.

Berit wheeled up the path leading to the door and met her landlord as she descended the stairs.

"Are you Stacy Lomond?" Up close, she was even more beautiful than her gorgeous figure had led Berit to expect. Her mouth turned up in the corners, as if she were perpetually about to smile, and her eyes were a clear spring green. The openness implied by these two features was contradicted by the shape of those crystal eyes. Almond-shaped? Cat's eyes? Neither phrase did them justice. The enticing slant of her eyes and brows gave them an exotic look, and Berit pictured them gazing at her over the edge of a silky, gold-filigreed veil. Hiding a mystery. Berit wanted to dig her fingers deep into Stacy's short, thick hair and kiss her until she gave up all her secrets. She gripped the arms of her chair instead. She was apparently addle-brained after an arduous day of traveling.

Stacy hesitated a moment before approaching Berit and shaking her hand with a firm grip. "Everyone calls me Tace. You must be Berit Katsaros? I wasn't expecting…Did you mention you were…?"

"In a wheelchair? No, I seem to have forgotten to tell you. It's a new experience for me."

"Oh, I'm sorry."

Berit hated the look of sympathy she saw in Tace's lovely eyes. She'd seen it over and over since her accident. She had never been in this position before, and she knew she wasn't handling it with as much dignity and grace as she should. Usually at this point she made some joke to break the tension and keep herself from buying into the self-pity she felt rising within her. *You should see the guy I landed on!* It was only funny because Mark had come out of the fall with a bodysuit of colorful bruises, but nothing more serious. She had managed to land on her back on the edge of a worktable before rolling off it and coming to rest on top of Mark.

Berit didn't feel like joking now. The sun was already starting to set, casting a pinkish glow over them, and she was exhausted. She could normally curl up in the corner of a trench and take a nap, but now she craved a soft bed and warm blankets. And the comforting arms of someone like Tace Lomond. She'd usually be flirting by now, confident in her ability to get a woman in and back out of her bed with equal ease. Instead, she was looking up at Tace, seeing the pity and doubt in her expression, and feeling—yet again—completely helpless.

"I'm sorry, too," she said, with a biting snap in her voice. "I wasn't even supposed to be on that dig, but I thought I'd help some fellow scientists while I had a break between my normal jobs. Stupid rain seeped in and eroded the shelf between the levels, and we fell through. My injury will heal, but for now…I really don't want to be here"—Berit pointed at her lap—"or here." She gestured around her, indicating the whole damned town.

She half expected Tace to respond to her angry tone and yell back at her. The thought was oddly appealing. Berit wasn't afraid to speak her mind, but she never actively sought out debates or arguments. She felt tightly wound after her trek across country, and her futile attraction to Tace exacerbated her anxiety.

"I haven't made any preparations," Tace said, "and your rooms are on the second floor, in what used to be the attic." Instead of responding to her provocation, Tace's voice and expression remained calm and irritatingly aloof.

"Then I guess I'll need to find somewhere else to stay," Berit said. She pushed hard against the wheels of her chair and backed over the toes of the cab driver who had come up behind her with her duffel bag. He swore and stepped back, dropping her bag.

"Jesus," Berit said, her anger dissipating and leaving her deflated and ready to drop. "I'm sorry. I didn't know you were right there."

"Just came to get my money," he said, sounding as if he'd absorbed her negative emotions.

Berit frowned. She was spreading joy everywhere she went. "You'll need to drive me to a hotel, I suppose. I'll find a new place to rent in the morning."

He looked about as pleased by the proposition of stuffing Berit and her belongings back into his cab as she felt about being stuffed in there. He sighed and picked up the bag. "Won't be able to find a hotel room in town this week."

"He's right," Tace said. "With school starting next week, everything will be booked. And finding another place to rent won't be easy, either. Maybe we can work something out."

"Like what? Do you want to just wheel me into the garage?" Berit asked, waving toward the gentle slope of the driveway. On second thought, it might not be a bad idea. She could park in a quiet corner and let herself fall asleep…

"I hope this isn't rude or insensitive, but…can we help you up these few stairs? You can stay in my room, and tomorrow I'll move my stuff into the attic. Until…for as long as you need."

Berit looked at Tace and felt the fog of self-absorption fade. Tace seemed almost desperate to keep her there. The house was decent, and the neighborhood nice enough, but maybe she needed the money from rent as much as Berit needed a place to rest.

"I don't know. You can't be here every time I come in or out of the house." Berit wanted to help both of them by staying, especially Tace. Her own weariness seemed to ease when she saw the worry lines appear on Tace's forehead when she frowned. She'd either stay, or have Kim help her find students to lease the rooms she was leaving vacant.

"I can get a ramp installed out here," Tace said. "The stairs to the attic rooms are too steep to maneuver even with a ramp, so getting upstairs would be impossible. Although you could get down easily enough, as long as you didn't mind using the kitchen island as a brake."

Tace's mouth turned up in a smile, fulfilling the promise of its natural shape, and Berit felt her breath hitch in her chest. The thought of being in Tace's bed, between her sheets, was enticing, even though Berit couldn't do much beyond sleep. And she desperately needed to sleep. The sky, once it had started moving toward dusk, was darkening rapidly.

"Okay. We can give it a try."

Tace hadn't realized how tense she was until Berit's words made her relax with a sigh of relief. She'd been dreading the invasion of her home by a college professor, but she needed the money enough to make her disregard her personal concerns. She slung the duffel bag over her shoulder and carried it inside, then walked back out to meet Berit as she wheeled herself toward the stairs.

Tace had been torn when Berit answered her ad about the rooms for rent. She'd been planning to have two students, but Berit wanted one room for a bedroom and the other for a study. Tace's age would have given her a slight advantage over college kids, and they'd be unlikely to care much about her or her education. A professor, an adult, might be more patronizing toward her, but less likely to have parties or a constant stream of drunken friends over to visit. In the end, Tace had gone with the numbers. Berit was only one person, as opposed to two students. Plus, she'd offered more rent money since she wanted to occupy the entire suite. A win-win for Tace.

When Berit got to the bottom of the stairs, Tace held her arm out and supported Berit as she stood up. The cab driver came along to help, albeit with a reluctant expression—probably still angry about the run-in between his toes and the wheelchair. Berit waved him off, however, and gave him the cab fare. He seemed happy to go, and Tace had a feeling Berit didn't want more people than necessary to see her awkward ascent of the stairs.

She wrapped her arm around Berit's waist and tried to ignore the suddenly heated sensation in her left side where their bodies were in contact. She'd come out to greet her tenant and had been stunned by her beauty. Short blond hair, cut in a pixie style with wispy ends, and big blue eyes were common enough, but Berit had the timeless look of someone who could have been a movie star in any decade. Her beauty spanned generations. Her nose was gracefully slender, and her skin flawless. A slightly square jaw kept her from being too perfect and made her look unique instead.

Tace had been so enraptured she hadn't noticed the chair until she herself was walking down the stairs toward Berit and she realized her house wasn't accessible any other way. The back entrance had just as many steps.

Tace felt the contours of some sort of brace under her arm. Berit's voice had been angry when she spoke, but Tace heard something deeper. Pain, weariness, frustration? More emotions than simple surliness. So Tace had not only insisted Berit come in—instead of accepting the reprieve and letting her go somewhere else—but she'd offered her own rooms as well. Partly because she really did need the rent money. Mostly, however, she wanted to help erase the tension and hurt on Berit's face.

Berit kept one hand on the railing and held tightly to Tace with her other one. They climbed slowly up the five steps, and Tace left Berit leaning against the doorway to rest while she jogged down the steps and retrieved the chair. She carried it across the threshold and helped Berit sit down again.

"Are you hungry?" she asked as she hesitated just inside the house.

"I just need a bed," Berit said. She sounded smaller somehow as her voice dimmed with exhaustion.

Tace shouldered the duffel's strap again and pushed Berit's chair down the hall. Luckily, the halls and doorways had been widened when she refurbished the house after her father died. Instead of the maze of small rooms, the house now had an open floor plan and two bright downstairs rooms instead of four tiny, dark ones. Tace's bedroom, a bathroom, and a den opened off the short hallway. Chris and Kyle slept upstairs when they came to visit. Tace had done a lot of the demolition work herself, as well as some of the finishing touches like paint and laminate floors. Anything to save money, but she'd also felt a real sense of accomplishment while doing the project and she'd enjoyed her new rooms since she'd done so much on her own. Now she was giving them away to a stranger.

She set the duffel within easy reach of Berit on her king-size bed with its blue and gray comforter. "The bathroom is right through here," she said, opening the door leading into her master bath. "Do you need help?"

She was as embarrassed to ask the question as Berit seemed to be about answering it.

"No, thank you. I can manage."

Tace busied herself by gathering a tank top for sleeping and clothes for the next day. Once Berit came out of the bathroom, Tace went in and quickly scooped up the few items she'd need for an overnight stay upstairs.

When she came out, Berit was already in bed and looked half-asleep. Tace left the bathroom light on and opened the door just a crack so the room wasn't in total darkness.

"I'll get the rest of my stuff moved out tomorrow, and I'll clear out my den for you to use as a study." Tace made sure the wheelchair was close enough for Berit to reach, and then she turned off the overhead light.

"Major inconvenience," Berit mumbled. "I'm sorry...not for long."

"It's okay. Good night," Tace said. She closed the door, guessing that Berit was already asleep before the latch clicked shut. She got a few books out of her den and went through the kitchen and up the steep staircase to the attic rooms. Her few belongings made the white rooms look even more barren than they had when they were empty.

Tace sat on her childhood bed and thought about her reaction to Berit. She was attracted to her, but that was understandable. Berit was beautiful, and she was sleeping only yards away, in the bed Tace had been in just last night. The intimacy of the situation was naturally and explicably discomfiting. What bothered Tace was her willingness to completely uproot her life for someone she didn't even know. Was this her purpose in life? The only role she was suited for? She took care of Chris and Kyle just as she had when they were kids. Now she was taking care of Berit.

As much as Berit claimed the inconvenience wouldn't last long, Tace saw the reality of the situation. She didn't know the details of Berit's injury, but she would undoubtedly need help even as she got stronger. Tace, working at her retail job and spending every free moment at the brewery, would be the one Berit relied on for help with shopping, cooking, whatever. Tace was finally getting a small taste of what it was like to run a business, to do work that mattered to her financially, at least, and Berit's presence threatened her newfound occupation.

She couldn't possibly have said no to her tonight. Not just because of her obvious interest—although it played a part in Tace's decision—but also because she felt drawn to her. She was clearly a strong and intelligent woman, someone unfamiliar with her present circumstances. Unwilling to ask for help, yet needing support and assistance. Tace had been compelled to help her, by what force she didn't know.

She got in the narrow bed and tossed restlessly. She was sure of one thing—Berit would likely be an inconvenience to her for a very long time.

CHAPTER FIVE

Tace was up early the next morning, easy to do since she had barely slept after leaving Berit in her bed. She showered and went downstairs quietly, trying to avoid the squeakier steps, and stood for a moment outside the door to Berit's room. *Her* room. She didn't hear any sounds within, so she busied herself by hauling armfuls of her books and journals up to the attic study. After agreeing to rent the rooms to Berit, she had installed some inexpensive bookshelves and a large table for a desk in the tiny room, and she filled them haphazardly with her own belongings. Once she was finished—and sweaty enough to need another shower—she got on the phone and called every contractor in the phone book until she found one that had both experience and reasonable prices. She'd been tempted to install the ramp herself, but she imagined Berit falling off the side or gaining too much momentum if her slope was wrong, and she decided a professional was the better option. For liability reasons, of course, although the thought of Berit getting hurt worse made her queasy.

By the time a sleepy-looking yet fully dressed and showered Berit came out of the bedroom, Tace was scrambling some eggs for their breakfast. She had no choice other than to feed Berit since she hadn't had a chance to shop yet, but Tace worried about the precedent she was setting. She was treating Berit like a guest instead of her tenant. Fine for now, just not for the long term. She had been fretting about their skewed relationship while she cooked, but the sight of Berit made her forget all her reservations, at least for the moment.

"Something smells good," Berit said. She rubbed her eyes like a tired child and stopped next to the island. "What a beautiful kitchen."

Tace looked around the room she had designed herself. Anything to keep from staring at Berit and wanting to kiss away the signs of fatigue still haunting her face. Tace had refinished the cabinets and painted them a bright, clean white. She'd had the counters installed. Not expensive granite, but a pretty gray-and-cream laminate. The butcher-block island had been a costly purchase, but worth every penny.

"Thank you," she said, answering both of Berit's comments. She carried a tub of butter and some huckleberry jam to the table. "It's just eggs and toast. I hope that's okay."

"Perfect." Berit wheeled over to the table, and Tace brought the breakfast on large plates. "I'd been living on trail mix and powdered eggs in Peru. People complain about hospital food, but it tasted heavenly to me after eating canned beans every night."

Tace sat in the chair opposite Berit and dished up some eggs. She'd been considering making some excuse and either skipping breakfast or taking her plate upstairs. What the hell would she have in common with Berit? How could she possibly carry on a conversation with her? The quick description of her South American adventure sounded exciting to Tace, though, and she decided to stay. Except on her hikes, she'd never been out of range of a McDonald's drive-through, and the thought of eating canned food while camping near an archaeology site was intriguing.

"Peru? Was that where you got hurt?"

Berit sprinkled a hefty dose of pepper on her eggs. "Yes. Mark and I were running toward a shaft leading down to the tombs because we needed to stop some students from filling in—" She paused. "Let me start from the beginning. We were in the lowlands of Peru, in the rainforest…"

Berit talked while she spread jam on her toast, stopping now and again to take quick bites of her food. Tace's breakfast sat untouched while she listened to the story. In her mind, she filled in the sounds of chirping insects and shrieking birds, the discomfort of slogging through mud and rain, the thrill of unlocking the puzzle of the dead woman's position, the urgency of the sprint toward the endangered tomb. The story was a fascinating one, but it was Berit's pacing and humor that made Tace feel part of the events.

"Did they get the baby's skeleton out in time?" she asked when Berit finished her explanation of her fractured and now fused spine.

"Yes. It's tiny and beautifully preserved. Quite a find." Berit scooped up the last of her eggs and put them on a bit of toast. She popped the bite in her mouth. "Jim, the intern I had just started training, sent me some great photos. I'll show them to you as soon as my stuff arrives."

Tace sat back in her chair. "Amazing. You must be a popular teacher. I'll bet your students could listen to you tell stories for hours."

Berit frowned. "I haven't actually taught before. I've had some interns on digs and I was a TA for a few classes in grad school, but never anything like I'll be doing here. I suppose I'll just be following the textbooks, not talking about myself."

Tace wondered what was behind Berit's frown. She seemed almost unsure of herself and her ability to teach. Tace couldn't understand why, and she decided she must be reading Berit wrong. She'd enjoyed the tale Berit had just told and had felt, for a moment, part of her huge world. Now that she was done, Tace saw the chasm between them was even deeper and wider than she'd expected. What stories could she share that would ever interest Berit? *The other day at Drake's a customer wanted a pair of Levi's, but we didn't have the right size. I tracked some down in the Kennewick store, and they're being shipped here as we speak!*

Right.

She wouldn't hold Berit's interest, but she'd help her get some much-needed sleep. Tace stood up and gathered Berit's empty plate and her own full one.

"You cooked, so I'll do dishes," Berit said as she followed Tace to the sink.

Tace scraped her food into the garbage. She wasn't sure how she'd be able to set up the kitchen so Berit could reach the sink or counters. "I don't mind doing them."

Berit set her brake and grabbed the countertop, pulling herself to her feet. Tace hadn't been at eye level with her since their short walk up the stairs last night. Now, the memory of Berit's body pressed close to hers made her hot. Berit stepped closer and Tace wondered if she'd need to splash herself with cold water.

"I'm supposed to be on my feet and walking short distances every day," she said, "to get my muscles back in shape. I might as well be doing something useful while I'm upright."

Tace nodded and backed away from the sink as much to give Berit her independence as to put some distance between them. She put the jam and butter into the fridge.

"I have some errands to run this morning," she said. "Do you need me to get anything for you?"

Berit looked at her and bit her lip. "I don't expect you to be my personal assistant or chef. Once I'm familiar with the area, I'll do everything on my own."

Even though Tace was aware of the gulf between her and Berit, and all too aware of her attraction's attempts to span that gulf, she had to laugh at Berit's momentary transparency. "In other words, you have some things you need me to do. Do you want to make a list?"

Berit grinned. "I suppose I should look through the texts for my classes. If you wouldn't mind stopping by the college bookstore, they're supposed to have a packet of them ready for me. I'll need to get groceries since I don't expect to eat all your food, and there's a reception for new students at the president's house this afternoon, but I can call a cab to take me there."

Tace sighed. She didn't want to be pulled into the college's sphere, but she could get in and out of the bookstore unscathed. Hopefully. She had to keep her focus on the big picture here. Berit needed her, but soon she'd be able to live her own life. She could easily get to and from the campus from Tace's house, and Tace needed the money from her rent. For a few days, maybe a couple of weeks, Tace would help her out.

"I'll get the books for you this morning and we can shop for groceries later tonight or tomorrow. Help yourself to whatever you want in the meantime. I'll drive you to the reception. The campus is only a few blocks away if you feel up to getting home on your own, or you can call me to pick you up."

"Are you sure? I hate to—"

"Be an inconvenience. I know, you told me last night. Let me help you get acclimated until school starts, and soon you'll be doing everything on your own."

"Okay. Thank you." Berit pulled a folded check out of her pants pocket. "Here's my first month's rent."

Tace glanced at the amount and handed it back to Berit. "This is more than we'd discussed."

"What we discussed was for the smaller rooms upstairs, not your own bedroom and study. When I'm ready to climb up there, I'll start paying the lower rent. It'll give me an incentive to get better."

Tace wanted to argue more. She didn't need the extra money, this upheaval in her life wasn't a big deal, and she didn't mind carting Berit and her books back and forth from Whitman. None of that was true, though, and Tace didn't want to admit how she really felt. Berit had already turned back to the sink, so Tace shoved the check in her jeans with a sigh of relief and climbed the stairs to the attic.

❖

Tace parked near the Reid Campus Center and followed signs to the downstairs bookstore. She'd driven past the building often enough and had even considered going inside to look at the books but had never actually done so. She expected to look out of place—worse, to *feel* out of place—but except for an occasional smile or hello from a passing person, she seemed to be unremarkable in the crowd. She entered the store and came face-to-face with Berit.

Or, rather, with a life-sized photo of her face. It looked like a model's head shot, with her face tilted slightly away and her eyes looking up toward the camera. Stunning. Tace read the sign announcing Berit as a world-famous archaeologist and author who was gracing the college with her illustrious presence. Stacks of her books were piled on the table, and a group of students were eagerly picking through them. Tace picked up one with a photo of an intricate bronze medallion and read the back cover. There was the head shot of Berit again, plus a picture of her in rolled up khaki shorts and a white tank, with her foot on the runner of a Jeep and a clay statuette in her hands. The book was about her adventures while on a dig in Lebanon and some stupendous discovery she'd made about the Phoenicians. Tace shook her head. Maybe if she announced that she had the actual, live Berit Katsaros in her house she could charge for sightseeing tours. Or she could collect Berit's used clothing and auction it off to her adoring fans.

Tace walked away from the display without putting Berit's book back. She'd loved hearing the story about Peru this morning and she thought this one sounded even more interesting. Berit would lose interest in her boring landlord after she'd made friends and was more mobile on her own. Tace could at least read about her.

Tace approached the counter in the textbook section with more confidence. "Hi. I need to pick up a packet of books for Dr. Katsaros."

"Awesome," the young woman said. "I'll be right back."

She went through a swinging door and came out only moments later, with a box full of books. "Do you want to make sure everything is there?" she asked.

"Um, sure," Tace said. She had no idea what she was supposed to find in the box, but she pulled the books out one after the other. She meant to just go through the motions of checking the contents, but she stopped and looked through each text. A Greek language book. A small, plainly covered paperback of one of Plato's dialogues in Greek. Tace opened to the first page and glanced at the unfamiliar shapes of the Greek letters. At first they seemed to be merely squiggles on the page, but after only a short scan, she began to see patterns and repeated words and phrases emerge. Socrates, Crito. A common word that might mean *and*? Tace was tempted to use the Greek textbook to decipher the puzzle, but the girl was watching her, so she moved on.

A basic archaeology text. Tace skimmed the index and found several references to Berit. A book of poems by Pindar, translated into English. Tace opened to a random page and read about a charioteer being honored after winning in the ancient Olympic Games. She got caught in the rhythm of the words, but the student helping her couldn't seem to contain her enthusiasm any longer.

"Are you a friend of Dr. Katsaros? I'm so excited she's here, but I couldn't get any of her classes. I'm a transfer student, so I got last choice during registration. Her archaeology intro filled up right away, of course, but I was going to take Greek just to hear her teach. No luck. Her books are fantastic. Have you read them? Maybe you could get her to sign one for me?"

"I don't know her well, but I'll tell her you want one autographed. Maybe she can stop by." Tace said. She repacked the box except for the one about Pindar. "Do you have another copy of this one?"

"Sure, right over here." She showed Tace where the Classics section was and handed her the paperback.

Tace paid for her own two books and carried the box out to the car, relieved to get away from the president of the Berit fan club. She'd known Berit was smart and educated since she was teaching at the college, and this morning's story had proven her to be somewhat of an Indiana Jones, but she hadn't realized Berit was some sort of intellectual superstar. For the time being, she'd probably be having meals with Berit and driving her around. What would they talk about? Tace didn't have a clue how she could add to any conversation. Maybe Berit could bring along some books on tape when they were in the car.

Berit had said she'd be able to handle the contractor when he came to install the ramp, so instead of going straight home after tackling the college bookstore, Tace stopped by the brewery. She walked over to the woodpile without needing to climb through weeds since this had been the first area she'd cleared after sending Joan on her way. She put a bowl of fresh cat food near the pile. She heard the kitty yowling at her from under a shrub, but he wouldn't come out to eat until she was a few yards away. Progress. The brewer—she'd learned his name was Joseph—waved at her from the doorway before disappearing into the shadows. Yet more progress.

Tace got the trimmer from a small toolshed she'd unearthed during her first cleaning expedition and started wreaking havoc on the mess behind the main warehouse. The feel of the plastic string zinging against the metal siding made her clench her teeth, but with every pass, she felt her body and mind relax. Somehow, the brewery had become her one safe haven, and she needed this respite after spending the morning in Berit's out-of-reach world. Work at Drake's was mind-numbing, and she didn't have the time or money to go out as often as she had before, so she had welcomed physically demanding chores at the brewery because they released stress. Now Berit had come into her home, bringing with her a list of chores and a need for assistance.

Before the brewery, Tace would never have considered having a college professor—especially one so time-consuming—live in her house no matter how much she needed the cash. For once, Tace had something to work for besides her family, something of her own. It happened to be a run-down, failing business, but it was hers. She'd put up with anything to give it a chance to succeed and at least break even in the sale. To give *herself* a chance to succeed at something. Anything.

She'd be much happier if Berit weren't so damned beautiful. Tace was used to being able to walk away from anyone connected to teaching or the college. Anyone who might make her feel inadequate. She couldn't walk away from Berit without leaving her house, and even then she'd have to return to drive Berit somewhere. Just a physical attraction would have been bad enough, but Berit was interesting and worldly as well. Things Tace definitely wasn't. Soon enough, she'd ask about Tace's job and education, and then she'd move on to find friends with more interests in common.

Tace swung the trimmer forcefully and jarred her entire body when she smacked into a hidden rock. She tossed it out of her way and continued. She was making headway on the yard, but she knew the brewery needed more than a pretty garden to have a chance. She'd been learning a little about the brewing process, when she could get Joseph to give her more than a monosyllabic answer to any question she asked. He seemed painfully shy, but also passionate about brewing, so Tace hoped she'd be able to get him to open up eventually. She now knew the difference between a mashing tun and a whirlpool and between top- and bottom-fermented beers. Every time she went into a store or bar, she checked out the beer selections. She needed a catchy name for the brewery and for its individual beers, and she had excitedly talked to Joseph about making specialty brews for each season. He had seemed a bit frightened by her enthusiasm, but hc was coming around. He'd been much more inclined to talk after she'd given him a paycheck—she presumed it was the first he'd seen in a long while.

Besides his salary and the cat's food, Tace had splurged on fees for a lawyer. He was young and fairly inexperienced—meaning cheap—and he'd returned to Walla Walla where he'd done his undergraduate work. Tace's ties to the college were getting too numerous for comfort, but Lawrence had been helpful and seemed delighted to be combining his love of beer with his legal career. He'd already helped by stopping her brilliant marketing plan of giving free kegs to the local frats. He'd turned pale and had lectured her for half an hour on liability issues. In the end, they'd agreed on deeply discounted kegs for local restaurants. Without a name, though, Tace couldn't get a following.

She turned off the trimmer and wiped her forehead with the sleeve of her shirt. She'd cleared most of this side of the building, and her arms were aching with the echoing vibrations from the trimmer. She'd worked off some of her simmering desire for Berit and a little of her boiling anxiety about having such a famous scholar in her house and at her dinner table. She needed to get home and take a shower before Berit needed her again.

CHAPTER SIX

Berit roamed through the first floor of Tace's house while she waited for her to return. The contractor had made quick work of the ramp, and Berit had rolled on and off the porch until her arms were sore. She'd lost some muscle tone during her recuperation after the surgery and she was anxious to get back to her pre-accident strength. She was eager to get back to everything pre-accident—her job, the excitement of discovery, and even the primitive lifestyle she often had to endure. She'd be happy to bring Tace's bed with her when she moved on, though. The sheets had been worn and washed to cotton-ball softness and, even better, they smelled like Tace. Lavender and pine. Sweet, yet with a bite.

Berit went into the study she'd use while she was downstairs. She might not be on a dig in some far-off location, but she couldn't stop her mind from searching for clues and recreating events. The den was clean, but there were swathes of fine dust on some of the shelves, as if Tace had wiped them down quickly after emptying them. The outline of books was still visible in some areas. Some pressed, dried leaves had fallen on the floor under a large pine table. A reader. A nature lover? She was impressed by how much Tace had gotten accomplished since her arrival last night. Berit had a ramp, an accessible room, and a clean study just waiting for the shipment of her books and other belongings to arrive. Tace must have cleaned out the room for Berit after she went to bed or before she got up. Berit had slept so soundly, Tace could have driven a pickup into the room to move her things, and she wouldn't have noticed.

The kitchen and patio next. The pantry shelves were well-stocked with spices, and bunches of fresh herbs grew in a sunny window box on the back porch. The fridge was practically bare, though, with eggs, milk, and a few containers of takeout. Tace seemed to like the chemistry of cooking and flavor, but to have little time for actually making meals. She had beer. Several dark, unmarked bottles. Berit was tempted to sample one of the mysterious liquids, but she didn't think Kim would appreciate her showing up at today's reception with beer breath. Berit closed the fridge and moved into the living room where she continued to unearth details of Tace's life.

Lots of magazines, all with subscription labels. Berit flipped through the eclectic pile. Biking, astronomy, and beer. The latter were well-worn and seemed to be favorites. Local periodicals and hiking guides. A shallow glass bowl by the front door with a name tag from Drake's. Stacy, not Tace.

Berit eased herself off the chair and onto the sofa. She felt restless. She usually could occupy herself for hours sifting through the lives of alive or long-dead people, but she was having trouble reducing Tace to a handful of objects. She wanted to talk to her, ask her questions about her name and her job. Find out how to combine the clues she had discovered into one textured, whole person. Berit wasn't used to feeling this way—usually she preferred a distance between her and her subjects of inquiry. Like a millennium or two.

She was going to go stir crazy here.

What would occupy her mind for the next academic year? Yes, she was fascinated by the hints of Tace's character she'd found and she wanted to know more. Tace was clearly a homegrown woman. Her tastes seemed to emphasize what she could experience right here—the stars she could see, the trails she could hike or bike, and the produce she could find. How long would Berit be interested in the local flavor? So far what she'd seen in Walla Walla hadn't been promising, Tace excepted. Her job would surely prove to be stupefying. Teaching first-year Greek students how to conjugate verbs and parse sentences? Crawling through Plato with the second years?

Berit sat up with a start when she heard a car pull in to the driveway. Tace. She shifted back into her chair and went out to greet her.

"Look," she called as she came down the ramp to meet Tace on the pathway. She wasn't sure why she was so glad to see Tace. She'd been alone all morning, but she usually relished her time by herself since she got far too little on digs. Maybe she had just gotten out of the habit of being on her own. That was an acceptable explanation for her response of being happier to see Tace than she wanted to admit. She was wearing dirty and grass-stained jeans, her cheeks were flushed, and her hair was slightly damp as if she'd been sweating. Berit couldn't keep from staring. What had she been doing? Moonlighting as a gardener? Tace had the look of an earth goddess. Connected to the land, strong and physical. Berit could imagine her out on a dig, dirty and perspiring and excited over some new find.

"Are you supposed to go that fast?" Tace asked with a concerned look. "You might need your brakes checked so you don't roll across the street before you can stop."

"Going down is the fun part," Berit said with a grin. "Getting back up on the porch is a killer. Are those my books?"

Tace was holding a box with a plastic Whitman bag on top. She pulled the bag off as if she wanted to hide it. "Yes, these are yours. You have quite the cult following on campus. I expect I'll have paparazzi hiding in my bushes once they find out you're staying here."

Berit was about to say that any new blood was probably welcome in this town, but she didn't want Tace to feel insulted by any disparaging comments about her home. Instead, she gave a self-deprecating laugh. "Once they fall asleep to one of my lectures they'll realize I'm just as dull as the other professors."

"You're anything but dull," Tace said, with a hint of something—sadness?—in her voice. Berit tried to read her expression, but Tace got behind her and helped push her up the ramp.

"What time is your reception?"

"It starts at two. I should get ready for it, I suppose."

Tace let go of the chair once she had crossed into the house. "I'll take a quick shower and then we can go. Let me put these in the study for you."

Berit went into the bedroom while Tace continued down the hall to the den with the box. She heard Tace going up the squeaky attic stairs as she rummaged through her bag and found a sheer ivory blouse made of crinkly, soft cotton that she'd bought in Thailand. A matching camisole underneath and a pair of brown cargo pants, and she was as dressed up as she could get. She never had to spend much time thinking about what to wear since she traveled with only a handful of outfits, all of which could survive being folded up in her duffel for weeks at a time without looking too wrinkled. She fastened a leather cord around her neck with a teal chrysocolla pendant hanging from it. A gift from her grandfather on her first trip to Greece with him, when she'd stood among the ruins of an old temple and found her true home.

Tace was waiting when she came into the living room, and Berit thought she saw a glimmer of appreciation on her face before she looked away.

"You look very nice," Tace said, grabbing her keys and heading toward the door. "Ready to go?"

Berit was anything but ready. She was dreading the afternoon. Chatting with students she didn't want to teach, being asked questions about the career she'd had to put on hold while she festered in this little college town. She wanted open air. Windblown dust and bone-melting heat. Hours spent crouched over a shard of pottery, sweeping away the dirt one layer at a time until she held a piece of history in her hand. Instead, she'd be spending the next nine months trapped in a classroom reciting Greek conjugations.

Berit inhaled the fresh scent of Tace's lavender shampoo when she leaned close to help her into the passenger seat. She had washed away all traces of her morning work and was wearing a crisp blue shirt and black jeans. Her just-shampooed hair was slightly tousled and sexy, and Berit had to clasp her fingers on her lap to keep from touching it. She'd always been a tactile person, needing to feel and hold things to really understand them. The ancient world had become real to her when she was able to grasp its artifacts. She wanted to understand Tace the same way—to run fingers over and through her until she was completely known. Berit looked out the window at the rows of Craftsman houses they passed. She'd never felt this way about another person, this need to understand. She'd only felt the urge to truly connect with lives lived long ago, safely in the past.

Tace turned off Boyer Avenue and parked in the shade of a huge chestnut tree, a few doors down from the college president's house. Students and faculty, singly and in small groups, were approaching from all directions and filing through the gate leading into the back garden. Berit sat and watched them while Tace got her wheelchair out of the Chrysler's cavernous trunk. She didn't move until Tace tapped on her window and startled her. She reluctantly opened the passenger door and eased her legs out of the car.

"You'll be fine," Tace said, apparently reading the misapprehension on Berit's face. She'd hoped she had hidden it well, but it must be showing. She needed to get control before she faced the crowd of three-hundred-plus freshmen and at least another hundred professors who would be at the reception.

"They obviously see it as an honor that you're here," Tace continued. "You'll be the star of the party."

Berit sat in her chair and got as comfortable as she could. She had a sinking feeling Tace was correct, and she would get more attention today than she wanted. She was new and she'd written a few books that admittedly made her life seem more glamorous than it was—the finds she'd chronicled were as exciting as they sounded, but the books had glossed over the hours and years of painstaking work unearthing and cataloging non-spectacular, but still important, relics.

Tace pushed her chair a few feet toward the house, as if giving Berit a running start, but she didn't make any move to continue the forward progress. Berit wasn't about to admit her agoraphobia to Tace—she never told anyone about it—but she knew she couldn't face so many people at one time, especially if they gathered around her. She felt the chest-tightening she'd experienced since childhood when faced with large groups of people in closed spaces. Hours spent in casinos, waiting just outside the line marking adults-only gambling areas from the sections where minors were allowed, while her mother played *just one more quarter, honey.*

"I'm not going," Berit said, pushing on her right wheel and turning back toward the car.

Tace crouched beside her and held her gaze with those direct, clear eyes. "No one here will care about your injury or this chair. You're gorgeous and famous, and they're going to adore you. Apparently there are long wait lists for students hoping to take your classes. The girl in the bookstore was devastated because she couldn't learn Greek from you. She said her life was ruined and she was going to drop out of college and become a hobo, riding the rails in despair."

Berit had to laugh as Tace's goofy story released some of her anxiety. She playfully pushed at Tace's shoulder, and Tace pretended to lose her balance and staggered back a few steps. Berit didn't care about her chair, although Tace seemed to think it was the reason she was hesitating.

"I'll go in there with two conditions," Berit said. "One, I will only stay an hour. And two, you have to come with me."

"No way." Tace's expression lost all sign of humor.

"Come on," Berit said. "You know I'm still having trouble maneuvering. What if I run over someone's feet, like I did last night?"

"So I'd be there as your, what, valet?"

"Of course not," Berit said. She was torn between her own need to have someone familiar by her side while she suffered through the hour among too many people and her desire to understand what was behind Tace's reluctance. She could understand if Tace thought the reception would be boring, or if she didn't want to be roped into taking care of Berit, but there seemed to be something more going on. Tace's expression had completely shut down, and her arms were crossed tightly over her chest. Berit had never been as good at reading people as she was at deciphering relics, but she couldn't help but see Tace's discomfort.

"I just want you there as a friend," Berit explained. "Someone familiar. I hate large groups of people. I've spent most of my life on digs in remote areas, with only a few other archaeologists around. But I don't want to make you miserable, too. I'll be okay."

Tace looked at the people entering the garden and she visibly and audibly sighed. "One hour. You can have your tea with the president, and then I'm leaving."

Berit's relief didn't last long. Tace helped her get through the gate and down a gravel path to the lush grass of the president's backyard, but as soon as she was spotted, a wave of people descended on her. She was soon the center of a circle of admirers, even more uncomfortable than she'd expected because she was forced to look up at everyone, and Tace was jostled away from her. Someone handed her a cup and saucer and another person gave her a plate full of food she hadn't picked out herself. She balanced the tea on one thigh and tried to remain polite while she answered questions about her books and responded to the numerous gushing comments about her classes from enthusiastic students.

"Yes, I'm looking forward to reading Pindar with you, too," she lied. She wasn't. To her, the daily implements of normal human life told more about the past than words. She traveled the world, never staying in one place for long, to discover how other people—long ago—had set up their homes and strengthened their roots. She loved to study the connection between people and the place where they existed. She didn't want to settle and forge such connections herself. She had to pretend she wanted to be here to teach, but she was itching to be well enough to leave.

"I'm excited about the Greek class, too. I'm sure you'll enjoy studying the language." Berit repeated words she had spoken just five minutes ago, but she was searching the throngs of people for Tace. She finally spotted her, standing in a corner of the lawn near a huge rhododendron and talking to a youngish male professor. He was animated and making sweeping gestures while he spoke, but Tace seemed to have shut down even more than she had been by the car. Her arms were crossed again, and her expression neutral, almost masklike. She was as still as he was volatile. Berit gripped her wheels to go to her rescue, to chase the guy away and tease Tace into laughter and expressiveness again.

"You still have the knack."

Berit stopped and turned at the familiar voice and reached up to return Kim's hug. Her arms barely fit around her pregnant friend's waist. "The knack for what? You look superb, by the way. When are you due?"

"During winter break. That's *my* plan, at least." Kim pushed her wire-rimmed glasses higher on the bridge of her nose and then rubbed her belly. "God knows what this little guy has in mind. And I meant your ability to attract the prettiest woman in town. You've been here, what, one day? Or did you bring her to Washington with you?"

"Stacy is my landlord," Berit said. She didn't deny Kim's assessment of Tace's beauty, but she couldn't claim to have attracted her. Tace seemed to tolerate her and to need her as a tenant, but little more. "I found her by chance, not by any chick-magnetizing skill. She's been helping me get around while I get familiar with the town and with this thing." Berit patted the arms of her chair.

"Well, you should probably save her from Theodore." Kim drew his name out with a snobby-sounding accent. "He's most likely regaling her with stories about his glory days at Cambridge or trying to engage her in a heated philosophic debate about Kierkegaard's theories on personal choice. She'll need a caffeine transfusion to stay awake."

Berit frowned. She didn't think either lecture topic sounded like one Tace would find pleasant. She turned around again, but Tace wasn't where she had been just a moment ago.

"…and I've submitted your name. I know you weren't planning on staying long-term, but I think you might fall in love with teaching and want to stay. Whitman has a lot to offer someone with your prestige."

Berit looked at Kim, trying to catch up with the words she'd missed while looking for Tace. "What? I'm only here until my back gets better. No way am I staying any longer than that."

Kim patted her shoulder. "I know. You told me. But at least consider staying here after the year is out. You can't keep up this globetrotting lifestyle forever." She gestured at Berit's chair. "It's dangerous on those remote digs, and it has to be exhausting. Someday you'll need to settle down, so why not here?"

Suddenly the garden seemed to close in around Berit, paralyzing her in place. Kim's settled, reasonable, pregnant presence. A group of students pointing toward them and whispering before they started across the lawn toward her, probably to say how excited they were to take her boring Greek 101 class. And Tace, out of sight and possibly on her way back to her car without Berit, after being grilled by Theodore the Annoying Philosopher. None of this was what Berit wanted, and she felt trapped not just by her injury and her awkward wheelchair, but by the expectations of all these people. She was good at archaeology, not at personal relationships. She'd spent her career following her strengths, and now her weaknesses were about to be exposed.

"I have no desire to stay in this pathetic town any longer than I have to," she whispered in what sounded more like a hiss than she meant it to. "I've already been here one day too long. You've made the choice to be here, Kim, and I'm glad you're happy with this life, but it has nothing to offer me. As soon as I can handle a shovel again, I'll be heading to my next dig. I need to travel and see the world, not just teach students about it. I'm not the kind of person who can stay in one place forever, especially not a place like Walla Walla."

Her energetic emphasis on some of the words made her little speech sound rude and disparaging. She hadn't been trying to insult Kim or her choices, but she had to make it clear she wasn't staying at the college or at this damned reception. She was about to apologize, find Tace, and make her less-than-graceful exit when Kim shifted her attention. She had been listening to Berit's outburst with an understanding and indulgent smile—Berit knew Kim was familiar enough with her passionate and often rash outbursts, although she had no excuse for being rude—but then Kim looked over Berit's shoulder.

"You must be Stacy," she said. "Nice to meet you. I see you survived your encounter with Theodore."

Berit backed up a few paces as Tace came forward and shook Kim's hand. "I suppose I did," she said with a smile that looked strained to Berit. "Nice to meet you, too. Berit, I have to get home."

Berit tried to make eye contact, but Tace wouldn't look directly at her. How much of Berit's speech had she heard? Most likely enough to be insulted by the comments about Walla Walla and anyone who might choose to live here. "I'm getting tired," she said. "I can come with you."

"You haven't even talked to the president yet," Kim reminded her. "She's a fan of your writing and has been looking forward to meeting you in person. Don't worry about Berit, Stacy. I wanted to ask her over for dinner, anyway, so I'll drive her home after."

Tace nodded and left with just a quick good-bye in Berit's direction. The crowds shifted for Tace as she hurried away, and then they closed in around Berit once more. She didn't have a chance of catching up to Tace before she got in her car. She sighed and forced a tight smile on her face as the approaching students gathered around her chair. Kim backed away with a wink, apparently unaffected by Berit's little scene.

"Are you Dr. Katsaros?" one of the freshmen asked. "I wanted to take one of your classes, but they're all full. Do you have a wait list?"

Berit had no idea. She had an office, a schedule, and a box full of textbooks, but she hadn't looked at any of them yet. She told the student to check with her during office hours next week—whatever they might be—and moved on to the next unanswerable question about her classes. She felt as deflated now as she'd been edgy before. Kim had managed to ensure she'd stay for the entire reception, followed by dinner with her husband and young daughter. A fitting punishment for her insults. She'd have to wait until tonight to apologize to Tace.

CHAPTER SEVEN

Tace came downstairs the next morning and found Berit in the kitchen, propped against the stove and pouring an egg mixture into a sauté pan. She hesitated for a moment, tempted to go back upstairs and hide, but Berit turned and saw her.

"Good morning," Berit said. "I wanted to make you breakfast to apologize for yesterday, but I still haven't been to the store. You don't have much in the fridge, so I hope you don't mind *omelette aux fines herbes*."

"It smells good," Tace said. She hadn't eaten dinner last night, and the scent of basil and tarragon was too tempting to refuse, even with a pretentious-sounding name. She got plates out of the cupboard and set them on the table. "You don't have to apologize for anything."

Berit folded the omelet with an expert flip of the pan. "I said mean things about your town. I was just cranky. I hadn't planned on coming here to teach until I got hurt, and Kim was pressuring me to take a more permanent job here. I lashed out, and I'm sorry."

"Apology accepted," Tace said, mostly to get past the conversation about yesterday. She hadn't been hurt or angered by Berit's words because she believed them herself. Who would want to spend their life in Walla Walla if they had other options? She had already been feeling inadequate and like a child again after her conversation with the philosophy professor, and she'd needed to get out of the collegiate atmosphere and back to the safety of her own home. She had moved more of her clothes into the attic rooms and had stayed up there to avoid talking to Berit. She'd heard her come home and had shut her bedroom door in a cowardly way when Berit had called to her from the bottom of the staircase. Ridiculous, but she'd needed to be alone. Still, she hadn't been able to—nor had she wanted to—escape Berit completely. She had sat on her bed long into the night, reading Berit's book about digging in Lebanon.

Berit put the first omelet in the oven to stay warm and poured more of the egg mixture into the pan. "Was Theodore awful? Kim said he has a reputation for grilling people and trying to pick academic fights."

"I wouldn't say *awful*," Tace said. She'd pick something much worse. "He asked about my education and seemed horrified by my lack of a college degree."

She tried to pass it off as a joke, but the experience had been humiliating. She'd been forced back in time—not to high school when being a townie had been stigma enough, but to the years after high school. Then she'd not only been aware of the social rift between her and the elite collegians, but she'd had to accept that she'd never be able to change her own fate. Tace had never even bothered to fill out college applications. She had been working since she was old enough to hold a job, and she'd added more hours as soon as she graduated from high school. She'd managed to keep her grades respectable, but she'd nearly come up short with credits. A few of her teachers had been kind enough to help, and they'd encouraged her to at least apply for scholarships, but Tace had turned her dreams and hopes toward Chris. She couldn't remember having many of her own.

"A degree isn't the only way to measure success," Berit said.

She was being kind, but Tace waited for the expected shift in their relationship. She'd experienced it often enough, the few times she'd met professors or other educated women in the local bars and had tried to have more of a conversation than *your place or mine*. Once she admitted to only having a high school diploma— barely—she'd seen the changes in their expressions. Berit would be the same. She'd feel sorry for Tace. Maybe suggest she enroll in some night classes or get a degree online. No one ever thought she was good enough as she was, least of all herself.

Berit got an oven mitt and retrieved the omelet from the warm oven. She clicked off the stove. "It's interesting. The institution of higher education is a very recent development, as far as human history goes. Throughout most of our development as a species, knowledge has been obtained by experience, through the community or tribal legends, or through apprenticeships. Not through a structured schooling program. I've uncovered amazing art and artifacts created by people with no degrees. And I've seen a lot of crap created by people with a string of them."

Tace took the platter of food from Berit and carried it to the table while Berit lowered herself into her wheelchair and joined her. Berit's voice and demeanor hadn't changed at all, at least not in any way noticeable to Tace—and she was looking for the familiar signs. Berit actually did seem interested in the topic in a detached, nonjudgmental way. Still, her argument had a serious flaw.

"You can say how great these finds are, but you needed your advanced degree for your career in the first place. Without it, you wouldn't even be an archaeologist."

Berit laughed. "Good point. My career used to be in the realm of laypeople who either were fascinated by history or who craved its treasures. Now it belongs to academia, too. But anyone can be involved in archaeology, or any of the field sciences like paleontology, if they really have the desire. You don't need any degree to volunteer on a dig, and plenty of them welcome any warm body who can wield a trowel and a brush. You could excavate pottery or dinosaurs or old temples, if you really had the desire to do so."

Tace turned away and picked up the coffeepot. She'd always felt her limitations magnified when someone found out about her lack of education. Berit had managed to make her feel limitless, for just a moment. The thought of having choices, of being responsible for making them and not just accepting a life without them, was oddly uncomfortable to her, and she was about to change the subject when Berit spoke again.

"Theodore aside, I shouldn't have asked you to come with me," Berit said, apparently still needing to talk about yesterday. "I hate being in crowds. I was raised in Las Vegas and I spent too much time in casinos."

"When you were young?" Tace paused as she was filling their mugs with coffee and frowned at Berit. What kind of a childhood was that? "I didn't think kids were allowed in them."

"My mom worked in a casino. Not a fancy touristy one, but way, way off the Strip. First as a cocktail waitress and later as a dealer. When school was out and we didn't have money for a sitter, she'd bring me to work and I'd either wander around the parts where minors could be, or I'd hide in a corner and read."

Berit hesitated, and Tace waited for her to continue. She seemed to want to tell the story, to explain why she'd needed Tace to stay at the reception yesterday. The woman Tace had read about in Berit's book seemed far too daring and self-reliant to need anyone.

"Mom has a gambling…well, she calls it a hobby. I call it an addiction. When I was little, it was just plain scary."

"I had a similar experience, without the casinos," Tace said, thinking about her own mom, with her penchant for betting on anything that could run, fight, or play ball. She'd also had hobbies like taking drugs and sleeping around. She'd called herself a free spirit and walked out of their lives, leaving ten-year-old Tace to take over her responsibilities. Over the years, Tace had wasted hundreds of wishes, hoping her mother would come back. But even if she had, she'd probably never have changed, and Tace could hear in Berit's voice and see in her eyes how difficult it had been to grow up with someone with her mom's weaknesses. "What did your dad do?"

"He tore down casinos for a living," Berit said with a shake of her head. "I used to think it was a noble profession, that if he destroyed enough of them, my mom would stop chasing cherries on the slot machines and suddenly be normal, whatever normal is. But he gave most of his paychecks to her, telling me she was going to make us rich someday. A sick cycle, but he loved her and he loved his job." Berit paused while she put a dollop of sour cream on top of her omelet, where it melted over the hot eggs. She continued in a quieter voice. "He took me to see a demolition once. It was a beautiful old art deco style casino, with these graceful arches and pretty colors, and then there was a huge explosion and it was just gone. Destroyed, in seconds. I cried for hours, and once I found out they just rebuilt new, fancier casinos where the old ones had been, I never went to see him work again."

Berit shook her head as if trying to dispel the memories as thoroughly as dynamite did a building. "I should stop talking and let you eat while it's still warm," she said.

Tace had only shared two meals with Berit, but during each she had been captivated—in very different ways—by her stories. Berit's nomadic lifestyle probably made the act of sitting at a table like some sort of pseudo-family so uncommon for her that now she felt almost compelled to talk more about herself than Tace expected she ever did. She didn't want to pry further into Berit's past, so she took a bite of her omelet.

"Oh my God, this is great," she said, scooping up another bite with her fork. A slender ring around the edge was crisp and buttery, but the rest was fluffy and melted in her mouth. The combination of herbs was surprising and subtle. "Do I taste lavender? I didn't realize I had any in the house."

"I…I've had lavender on my mind lately. I smell it on your sheets."

Tace looked up in surprise, her fork halfway to her mouth, but Berit was busily chopping her omelet into tiny pieces. The thought of Berit's own citrusy scent mixing with hers was more delectable than the food.

"I thought the floral notes would mix well with the basil. I added a little tarragon and just a few drops of fireweed honey, too, to add a little sweetness. I'd never heard of it before."

"I knew there was another flavor I couldn't identify. I think fireweed honey is local to the Northwest and Alaska. It's my favorite."

Tace ate the rest of her omelet in silence while her mind combined the flavors in different ways. "The IPA," she said. "These herbs would be perfect for a seasonal ale."

"I saw the beer in your fridge. Do you homebrew?"

"I sort of own a brewery," Tace said. She hadn't told anyone about her new place except for Allie and the people who'd been involved in the paperwork process.

"You're kidding. Why haven't you mentioned it before? I thought you worked at Drake's."

"I don't remember mentioning *that* before, either."

Berit shrugged. "I snooped around and found your name tag. It's what I do for a living. Don't make that face, most of your stuff is upstairs now, so I'll have to wait until I can walk better before I really start digging around."

Tace smiled. "Well, the brewery is only temporary, until I can get the business running and sell it for at least what I paid."

"Why'd you buy it if you didn't want it?" Berit asked as she piled their empty plates together and put them on her lap. She took them over to the sink and lifted them over the rim.

"My brother. Gambling debts." Tace made a dismissive gesture and Berit nodded.

"In other words, stop digging in that particular trench. What's the brewery called? The beer in the fridge doesn't have any labels, so I thought it might be some sort of evil experiment. I was going to try one before yesterday's reception. I think we both could have used a beer or two before that party. And after."

"I agree." Tace got a bottle out of the fridge and set it on the island. She gathered some of the ingredients still on the counter from Berit's breakfast. Her mind was spinning with the new flavor, as if she could actually taste it on her tongue, and she wanted to share the experience. Get some sort of confirmation about her hunch. "I don't have a name or logo for the place yet. I need something soon, though, or I won't be able to market it. A few taverns in town have agreed to try a keg, and I need to give new customers a way to find us and order more."

Berit laughed. "If you don't pick something, you'll end up with different names depending on the bar. One will call it No Name Beer. In another place it'll be the Third Tap from the Left."

"The last one is catchy," Tace said with a grin. She chopped a small leaf of fresh basil with a few petals of dried lavender and added a drop of the honey. She put the mixture on a spoon and handed it to Berit before uncapping the beer and pouring two small glasses. "Here, try this. Put the herbs in your mouth and take a drink of beer, like you're filtering it through the lavender and basil."

Tace took a small taste of the herbs with a swallow of beer and let the flavors meld in her mouth. "A little less honey," she said.

"And a touch more basil," Berit added. "The lavender overwhelms it."

Tace agreed. She changed the ratio and gave Berit another spoon.

"Perfect," they said at the same time after tasting the concoction.

Berit laughed. "It's a great ale on its own, but the lavender brings out the hoppy taste even more than usual in an IPA."

"And the basil gives an almost minty bite. Thank you," Tace said, putting their spoons and glasses in the sink. "Your omelet gave me the idea for this."

Berit shook her head. "I put a few herbs from your garden and pantry into some eggs. You were the one who picked out the ideal ones to complement the beer. You might have a real gift for this."

Tace shook her head with a derisive laugh. "I got lucky. Maybe other people will like it, too, and I'll be able to sell the place before I have to sink all my money into it."

She filled the sink with sudsy water and started washing the breakfast dishes. Berit's comment made her feel a flicker of hope, but she snuffed it out as quickly as she could. She'd learned not to give those little flames a chance to burn too long or they'd threaten to consume her when they were doused by reality.

"I have to get to work in an hour, but I can take you grocery shopping after my shift. I'll go to the brewery later this evening."

"Don't worry about me today. Kim is coming to take me to the college. I have to find my office and take care of some paperwork before classes start. I guess I'll look through those textbooks, too, while I'm there. On the way home last night, I saw a grocery store just a couple blocks away. I'll have her drop me there when I'm done, and then I can make it back here by myself."

Tace submerged her hands in the hot water and felt disappointment when she should have been relieved. Berit had other friends and was becoming independent more quickly than Tace had anticipated. Soon she would be busy with classes and students, and even these occasional meals together would end. Berit wouldn't need her for long, and neither would the failing brewery. Tace had been happy enough with her life—or at least resigned to it—before these two new obligations had been thrust upon her. Now the idea of going back to nothing but her work at the store and occasional moments of relief in the wilderness or in a bar made her feel a sense of loss. She imagined herself going to the Blue and seeing Berit there with another woman, drinking beer from a tap that had Tace's former brewery's label on it.

She wiped a plate clean with a blue sponge and wiped away the picture of Berit as well. "If you don't need me, I guess I'll ride out to the brewery instead of driving. It's on one of my favorite bike trails."

"A bike-trail brewery. That should help bring more customers out your way."

She left the kitchen, and Tace let one of the beer glasses slip from her soapy fingers. It plopped into the water and settled, unbroken, on the bottom of the sink.

Bike Trail Brewery.

Tace could see a label in her mind, could think of names for the different beers. One step closer to making it a real business.

And one step closer to selling it.

CHAPTER EIGHT

Berit gathered her notes for Intro to Archaeology and tapped them into a neat pile. She put them into her messenger bag along with the text and a folder full of syllabi. She did the same with her Greek language materials. She slung the bag over the handle of her wheelchair and checked her office to make sure she had everything she needed for her back-to-back morning classes. The room was fairly bare, so she wasn't likely to have overlooked anything. The desk, table, and two chairs had been there when she arrived. She'd added little more than a couple of reference books she might need during the semester, and the few books and papers she'd collected for each class.

She double-checked the schedule she had taped to her door. Archaeology and Greek back-to-back, Monday, Wednesday, and Friday starting at nine. Pindar on Monday, Wednesday, and Friday afternoons. Intermediate Greek Tuesday and Thursday afternoons for two hours. Should be a breeze. Shouldn't it?

Berit's chair rolled easily on the low-pile carpet lining Olin Hall's corridor. She was early, but she wanted to go over her course material one more time before the students arrived. She'd been certain she wouldn't need to do much prep work for these classes since the subjects were familiar and the classes had been easy for her when she took them as an undergrad. Plus, she'd spent more than ten years in the field as a top-level archaeologist. She'd managed to convince herself that the year would be simple. She could teach these classes in her sleep. Over the past week leading up to the first day of classes, she had devoted more hours to dwelling on her pitiful exile to this excruciatingly quaint college town and to thinking about her too-desirable landlord than to making lesson plans.

Now, though, faced with the prospect of actually teaching the information to a class full of students—*her* students—she was starting to worry. She'd written each syllabus in less than ten minutes last month when she'd decided to take the job, sketchily outlining the semester based on an online table of contents she'd found for each textbook. She'd foolishly believed what Kim and the college dean had said—they were lucky to have someone of her caliber at their college. She'd even felt a little ego boost when Tace had told her how entertaining she was and how much her students would adore her. She'd expected the college to be as grateful for her presence as she was reluctant to offer it.

If she'd learned anything at all in the field, she should have learned not to fall prey to her ego. The harsh conditions and still-rudimentary nature of her job—even in advanced technological times—meant discoveries were as often made by rookies and amateurs as by seasoned pros. Good fortune, good weather, the right political climate, the right friends in high places. Berit opened the door to her classroom and dropped her messenger bag on top of the bare Formica table. She had a feeling today's lesson for the professor would be humility. Hopefully the students would learn a little something about the classical world at the same time.

Berit opened her archaeology book and started to read the first chapter. None of the information was new to her, but she hadn't given any thought to the structure of her lecture or her objectives for the day. She found a pen and was about to create an outline of her ideas when her class started to arrive. She watched the tiered rows fill with students, all wearing the same eager expressions. She hated to disappoint so many kids all at once, but her failure as a teacher seemed inevitable. She moved in front of her desk.

"Welcome to Introduction to Archaeology. I'm Berit Katsaros and I'll be—"

She paused when two guys came into the room. She was about to mention how much she disapproved of tardiness when she glanced at the clock and saw there were still five minutes before her class was supposed to start. She felt her chest flush with an embarrassment she hadn't felt since she'd been her students' age. She silently recited Shelley's "Ozymandias" while she waited for nine o'clock.

"Welcome again," she said. "I guess I was a little too eager to start. For those of you who missed my pre-class introduction, I'm Berit Katsaros."

The students laughed and Berit felt her tension ease a little. She'd taught plenty of interns and she loved sharing her knowledge with them. This wasn't much different. True, they were in a classroom, without the tools of her trade around them, and she'd only had one or two interns at a time while working on digs. Otherwise, the process was the same, wasn't it?

Berit took out the form she'd received from the registrar and called roll. She went as slowly as she could, making sure she pronounced every name correctly and trying to attach mnemonic tags to each student so she'd have a better chance of remembering them by sight. She handed out the syllabus and read through it, reciting the words she'd written about tests and quizzes and papers. At the time, she hadn't given much thought to them—they were standard parts of every college class. But she'd be the one creating and grading those quizzes and she'd be spending hours reading through the papers. The reality of her job hadn't sunk in until right now. She paused for a moment before reading the week-by-week reading assignments for the class. She'd been thinking of herself as merely a place-filler. She didn't want to be here and wasn't planning to make this a permanent career change, but this class meant a lot to these kids. She looked at them, some already familiar to her by name. They'd be investing a lot of time and money—or their parents' money—into this class and their education here. She owed them more than a last-minute, cobbled-together lecture.

And they deserved more than a professor who wasn't engaged in the class. She dropped her paper, and a student in the front row hurried to pick it up and return it to her. She thanked him and continued reading aloud about the final exam. For the first time, she was identifying herself as a professor. She didn't want the job, didn't want to be hurt and unable to follow her dreams, but she'd accepted the role. Professor Berit Katsaros.

Temporary, not-very-enthused Professor Berit Katsaros, more like it. She finished all the introductory materials and glanced hopefully at the clock. Five after nine. Was the damned thing running slow?

"Has anyone read the first chapter in our text?" Every student raised a hand. Drat. Berit had been hoping she could just move from section to section in the first chapter, reading small bits from each as she familiarized her students—and herself—with the material. She looked at the topic she'd put next to today's date. *What is Archaeology?* Okay. She could usually talk about her job for hours, if anyone cared to listen. She'd spent her first evening with Tace telling her about Peru, and over the past week she'd told her about other digs as well. But Tace was different. She had been what Berit's grandfather had always encouraged her to be—an active listener. Consuming the information and making it her own by connecting it to other ideas in her head. Asking questions that made Berit think about what she was saying in new ways.

Not to mention the sexy way Tace would sort of squint in concentration when she was truly interested in what she was hearing, bringing her dark brows toward each other so her exotic eyes became even more mysterious and captivating. Causing Berit to falter and lose her way in a story…

She cleared her throat and began to talk. Only forty-five more minutes to fill.

"Today we're talking about the definition of archaeology. Archaeologists study the physical things left behind by people in the past. We don't study dinosaurs, so if any of you were hoping to learn how to tell the difference between a pterodactyl and a stegosaurus, you're in the wrong class." She paused, as if waiting for a group of students to pack up and leave. "No one? Good. All of you just passed the first test."

Not the most original joke, but the class laughed again, and Berit relaxed another fraction. She could do this.

"Most people picture archaeologists on their knees in the dirt, excavating ancient houses and tombs, but the job requires more than an ability to dig. In foreign countries, we're often acting as diplomats and we need to be tactful and respectful. We also have to catalog and report on our finds, so an ability to write well is important. And if a dig is on private property, we'll need to research and find the landowner for permission. Oh, and researching the culture and history of the area before we dig is important, too, so we understand the objects we find."

Stop reciting job requirements—you sound like a poster advertising a field-school opportunity.

Berit switched to a different approach. "As an archaeologist, you can specialize in different ways. Some people study certain time periods, or specific countries or ethnic groups. But there's often overlap, or even a shortage of jobs, so you'd be unlikely to devote your entire career to a highly specialized field. I'm a classical archaeologist, and I'm mainly interested in Ancient Greece, but I've also spent time in areas outside the Mediterranean. I was on a dig in Peru, for example, when I was injured this summer. The shelf between ground level and the excavated tombs below us was compromised by rain and collapsed. So an archaeologist needs to have some knowledge of structural engineering to understand how to maintain a safe multilayered site. Or *should* have that knowledge, because someone obviously didn't in Peru."

Berit stopped again. What was the topic? She seemed to be covering a range of subjects at once, and not going into depth in any of them. They'd probably learned more from the first paragraph of the book than they were getting from her. She needed another subject, one that she was passionate enough about to devote the next—what time was it?—forty minutes to it.

"Why don't we go over some of the tools used in the field. This is a fascinating area because even in our high-tech world, the basic mechanical tools of archaeology haven't changed much. Take trowels, for example. They come in a variety of shapes and sizes, and everyone will have their personal preference, depending on many factors, both environmental and physical."

Berit realized she should have saved this particular lecture for a day when she had either slides or actual tools to show the class. She finished describing the difference between a leaf and a square trowel and somehow, before she could stop herself, segued into a discussion of the different types of soil and sand on digs and how each affected the way she worked. She had to keep saying words until it was time to dismiss the students, though, and she said a whole lot of them before 9:50 finally came.

Berit watched as her archaeology class left and the students in first-year Greek filtered into the room. She wanted to go back to her office and hide in shame while she diligently prepared Wednesday's lecture, but she had another class to teach. She noticed with a sinking feeling how many students were taking both classes. There'd probably be a stampede of students asking for tuition refunds in the administration building this afternoon.

Berit's Greek class was marginally better than her first one. She'd thought archaeology would be easy—it had consumed her life since she was thirteen, for heaven's sake—but collecting her knowledge and experience and then conveying them in a systematic way was more challenging than she'd expected. At least in the Greek language class, she had a ready-made program in the textbook, complete with drills that took up quite a bit of time. She wrote the alphabet horizontally on the white board, where it was within her reach, and she explained rules for pronunciation and accent as slowly as she could. The fifty-minute class crawled by, but she had enough material to fill it without needing to rein in a wandering lecture.

Berit skipped lunch and spent the two-hour break cramming for her next class like she was an undergrad who'd spent too much time partying instead of studying. She brought a stack of notecards covered with facts about Pindar and his poetry, as well as questions to ask the students about his first Olympian ode. She had enough to fill the hour and a half, but she had to peek at her cards several times, and she felt the conversation about the poem remained surface-level at best. There was nothing spectacular gleaned from the beautiful words, and nothing inspiring in the work she'd done that entire day.

Berit was relieved when she shut the door to her office at the end of her day. She had a bagful of homework, and she'd probably be pulling all-nighters to prepare for the next two days' classes. She was heading down Boyer Avenue toward home when she saw the familiar powder blue of Tace's car approaching. She held out her thumb like a hitchhiker and felt a curious lift in her spirits when Tace pulled to the side of the road and got out with a smile on her face.

"I'm glad I came this way from work. I thought I might see you out here. How was your first day?" Tace asked as she collapsed Berit's chair and put it in the trunk. She laughed. "That reminds me of greeting Chris and Kyle when they got home from school. Chris always loved her teachers and classes, but Kyle usually had already been sent to the principal's office before the first day ended. I hope that didn't happen to you."

"Well, not yet, but the dean might put me in detention because I suck at teaching. It seems you have another problem child on your hands."

"I'll bet every professor at every college on every first day of school feels the same way," Tace said. She held her arm out for Berit to use as she got in the car.

"I think that was the exact right thing to say," Berit said. She put her hand on Tace's forearm and eased into the seat slowly, not so much to protect her back but to prolong the contact with Tace's muscles as they contracted to keep her steady and protected. Berit leaned back in the passenger seat with a happy sigh. She was exhausted already, just from a few hours of classes, and she hadn't been looking forward to even the short few blocks between her and a hot bath. She tried to tell herself she was glad to see Tace for the lift home, but she knew it was something more. She'd been feeling unsure of herself after the fiasco of her teaching debut, and she wasn't accustomed to the feeling. Even more unusual—and more unsettling—was her reaction to Tace's presence. She made Berit lighter somehow. Safe and reassured. Berit had expected to be a spectacular teacher without doing any work. She'd been very wrong, but Tace was probably correct. Berit surely wasn't the only new professor to sense a disheartening distance between their imagined and actual performances in class.

"I'll need to work harder than I thought, though. I want to encourage the students' interest, not put them to sleep. Halfway through my archaeology class, they stopped taking notes and just watched me with the pitying looks only kids that age can give you."

Tace shook her head with a rueful smile. "I know those looks well," she said.

Berit figured Tace had been on the receiving end and not the giver. She talked about her siblings like a mother, but had she ever had the chance to be a child and not a parent? She was about to ask, but before she could find a way to phrase the question, Tace continued.

"I'll bet tomorrow will be easier, because now you know what to expect. And every day will just make you more familiar with the job."

"Ugh. Familiarity means boring. The thought of repeating these same classes every day for one semester makes me feel like I'm suffocating. I can't imagine doing this for a whole career. A lifetime of first-year Greek? Ugh, again."

Tace pulled into her driveway and turned off the engine. She looked at Berit with her brow furrowed in the adorable way she had. Berit tightened her hold on the straps of her bag—she always felt about a millimeter of willpower away from touching Tace. But Tace was part of this small world, and Berit was clawing at her cage and trying to get back to her nomadic way of life. Tace had the potential to tether her here, and she couldn't let that happen. No touching. Well, maybe a little…

"What are you thinking?" she asked instead.

"I'm confused," Tace said. "I thought your area of expertise was Ancient Greece. And you mentioned your grandfather and trips to Greece being a big reason you went into the field of archaeology."

Berit thought of her grandfather, with his sun-weathered features and gray mustache. His calm affection helped center her even now, as it always did when she thought of him. His memory was as steadfast and ageless as a temple's column. "Yes, of course. He was the only reliable person in my life when I was young. Without him, I don't know what would have happened to me. When he took me to Greece and introduced me to my own culture, I found something there. Roots, I suppose. Stability."

"And when you learned the language, was it as boring as you seem to think teaching it will be?"

"Not at all. It was like speaking to the past. I loved everything about it from the sounds of the words to the shades of meaning behind them. It helped that I had a really great—"

"Professor?" Tace prompted.

"I was going to say I had a really great dictionary," Berit said with a haughty look. Her pretense didn't last, though, and she laughed at the way Tace had caught her contradicting herself. She had forgotten the connection between her love of the past and the people like her grandfather and professors who had encouraged and inspired her.

"Fine, you got me. I had a really great professor. He was all over the place while he was teaching, jumping on tables and moving around the room like he couldn't contain his passion for what we were discussing. I appreciate what he did to inspire me, but I can't teach the same way. I can barely stand."

Tace shook her head. "Come on. Was it his actual movement that made him so motivating, or was it his enthusiasm? Because you don't have to stand upright or leap around in order to share your excitement and passion with your students."

"I'll try to remember your words of wisdom while I'm preparing my thrilling lecture on first-declension nouns," Berit said with a dismissive snort. She opened the door and stood carefully, knowing Tace's words wouldn't be forgotten. She admired people who were driven and excited about teaching, and she was grateful for the ones who had helped her along the way. Could she *be* one of them? Did she want to be? She doubted it.

CHAPTER NINE

Tace changed out of her work clothes and drove to the brewery. She sat on the neatly mown lawn with her back against the woodpile while the cat ate a bowl of food only a few feet away from her.

She closed her eyes and let the sounds of birdsong and the kitten's hungry chomping soothe away the stress of her morning in the store. She felt less tired than usual, less anxious about her busy schedule and the nonstop list of things to do at the brewery. Her time with Berit, especially during their short drive together on Berit's first day of class, had done more to untie the knots inside her stomach than anything or anyone else managed to do.

"Who'd ever believe that I'd be giving advice to an uncertain college professor?" she asked the cat. "Especially one as talented and successful as Berit. The world has gone insane."

At least her tiny corner of it had. A little over a month ago, she'd been in the same comfortable rut she'd lived in since high school. Her life and work hadn't been meaningless to her. Helping her siblings to a wider array of choices and possibilities than she had meant something. But her life and work hadn't been interesting or fulfilling, either.

Now she owned a brewery and she was actually getting involved in the process of creating an artisan microbrew. She'd been working with Joseph on perfecting the summer IPA, and she'd also made the decision to add a hefeweizen to their regular brewing repertoire. They lived in the heart of wheat fields, and Tace had grown up in and around them. They were as much part of her personal landscape as Walla Walla's streets. Of course, most of her friends had hung out in the fields on weekend nights, drinking or making out in the shadows. Not her. She'd driven a combine every spring and summer, starting at age thirteen, as soon as she'd been able to convince the farmers to hire an underage kid. A brewery in this town without a wheat beer didn't make sense to her. For someone who'd rarely had anything besides mass-produced, bland beer to drink, she somehow had ideas to spare once she let them start to flow.

Shaking up her world even more was Berit, even though Tace didn't see much of her these days. They hadn't been avoiding each other, but they'd both been busy with work. Tace had two careers to juggle, and Berit had spent hours at the college preparing for classes and attending faculty functions and the convocation. They'd passed each other in the kitchen every once in a while and had chatted over a cup of coffee or piece of toast, but conversations had remained light. Tace was content with that. She'd been intimidated by Berit's reputation, career, and education. Spending time with her in small doses, without pressure to carry on an interesting and deep discussion, was making her more comfortable. She was starting to see Berit as a normal person now, not as someone too far out of her sphere to talk to.

Well, not exactly a *normal* person. Tace had met plenty of women, and none of them had been capable of controlling her pulse rate just by walking into the room. The sight of Berit's sharply intelligent eyes or the pink curve of her lips made Tace's heart beat as fast as if she'd been scaling a mountain. She was as out of reach to Tace as Mount Everest, though, and would soon be just as far away. Tace couldn't let herself forget that, and anytime she was tempted to get closer to Berit, she just had to look at her book's dust jacket to remember that Berit belonged in some foreign land, having fascinating adventures.

The cat finished his food and remained near her, his tail whipping back and forth as he watched a bee hover around some wildflowers growing through the rotting logs. Tace moved a little closer and rested her hand just inches from him. She wasn't meant to be with someone like Berit, and Berit would never settle for someone like Tace, but their companionable and casual relationship was good for Tace. Berit had helped her with the seasonal ale, and last week Tace had actually been able to help Berit lose the worried look after her first day of classes. Tace didn't believe for one minute that Berit's classes had been anything less than spectacular, but Berit had definitely been upset. After a short car ride with Tace, she'd seemed to feel much better.

Joseph came over with a notebook tucked under his arm and a glass of beer in each hand, like he'd had when she first met him. He handed her a glass of pale gold liquid and sat down. They'd taken to having informal business meetings out here by the woodpile whenever Tace came to the brewery. If she came in the morning, before work, he brought lemonade. When she came after work, he brought her a beer. She tried to work as many morning shifts at Drake's as she could.

She took a sip and nodded in appreciation. "You've nailed it," she said. The lavender notes in their first attempt at a seasonal beer were bold and risky, but they were tempered by the earthy lemon-mint tones of the basil. A splash of local fireweed honey enhanced the natural sweetness, usually barely discernible, of the base IPA. An explosion of hoppy bitterness held back the cloyingly perfumed flavor they'd tasted on the first few tries. "I hope you remember the ratios, because this is excellent."

Joseph tapped his notebook and gave her the shy, pleased smile he got whenever she praised his brewing abilities. She had been tempted to hide her admiration for his skills and avoid any effusive compliments because he'd eventually have to wonder why the hell he was wasting his talents in a deserted warehouse when he could find a job anywhere he wanted. She couldn't be less than honest with him, though, and she wouldn't keep him from moving on if he had the desire to go. She took another drink of her beer and sighed, leaning back against the rough logs. She'd even write him a damned good letter of recommendation. He'd earned it just with this one ale.

"Unfortunately, you've perfected our summer seasonal, but it's almost autumn. We should start working on a holiday beer now. I suppose pumpkin is the usual choice."

"Pumpkin's been done to death," Joseph said. "Cloves, too."

"Sage? Sweet potatoes?" Tace tossed out some ideas from remembered holiday meals. She had tried to make Thanksgiving and Christmas special for her family, but her main memories were of long hours waiting on customers and toiling over the meals. Once Chris had moved out, Tace had given up on special holiday meals and usually got takeout for herself instead.

"Celery? Cinnamon?" Joseph added.

They bandied flavors back and forth for a few minutes, and nothing sounded right. They were still behind in the seasonals, but Tace was trying not to feel pressured into creating a beer that wasn't exactly what they wanted. The leaves on the trees around them were just beginning to show hints of yellow on the edges. The sun was nearing the horizon earlier every day, and they'd just discovered the recipe for their ideal summer ale. Maybe by December they'd have an autumn beer. She had to keep her focus on the long-term prize. She was making plans and developing strategies for the next owner to implement, plans that would add value to the physical worth of the brewery. Whoever bought the brewery from her would benefit from the sales of these beers—a year of them already perfected and ready to go. She was working toward someone else's success, to make someone else's dreams come true. The way she'd lived her entire life.

"We'll keep thinking about it. There's no hurry," she said, wanting to change the subject. She wouldn't be here next autumn to actually market and distribute the beer. She was happy about that, of course. She'd be relieved to get this shabby brewery off her hands and have the money she needed to repay some of her loans. "I wanted to talk to you about adding a wheat beer to our regular stock. We're in the heart of wheat country here, and it makes sense to showcase some local produce."

Joseph got the dreamy look he wore when he started brewing in his head. He opened his notebook and wrote a few notes, crossing one out and adding another while he muttered to himself. "We'll need the right yeast, and maybe some German malt. Sixty-five percent wheat grain...no, sixty-two. Just a touch of hops. Mount Hood? Do you want a hefeweizen or kristal? Um, unfiltered or filtered?"

Tace took a moment to realize he had asked her a question and wasn't still talking to himself. She was about to say she had no idea—she hadn't tasted a wheat beer until she did some research online last week and went to the store to get a bottled one to try. It had been okay. Mild and clear. She thought about the fragments she'd just heard Joseph saying and pieced them together in her mind. A mild, fruity hop, yeast-forward flavor. She remembered the smell of threshing wheat when she'd driven combines as a summer job. The air around her had been thick with dust and chaff, and the smell had been bittersweet.

"Unfiltered, definitely," she said. What a great way to round out the brewery's offerings. Joseph already had great bright ales, both an amber and an IPA. Tace didn't like the heavier porter and stout as much, but she was slowly getting the confidence to believe she could start messing with those recipes until she was happier with them. The light but thick hefeweizen would be just right. Of course, the beer could be nectar from the gods, but without people to actually buy and drink it, it might as well be sewer water.

Joseph finished taking notes and turned to a different page in his notebook. "I have some drawings," he said, not meeting her eyes, "for the tap pulls. Even labels, maybe, if we bottle the beer."

Just last week—sitting in this same casual triangle of brewer, brewery owner, and the slender cat who remained stretched out and asleep near his food bowl—Tace had tentatively brought up the name Bike Trail Brewery. What had seemed like a good idea in her head, when she was still excited from sharing breakfast and the impromptu tasting with Berit, sounded presumptuous somehow when she spoke it out loud. Who was she to even consider running this brewery, let alone naming and marketing it? She had sketched out the picture she had in mind for the label, all the while thinking she should take Realtor Joan's advice and raze the property, but Joseph had perked up. He'd contributed some thoughts, and soon they'd been creating a logo in their imaginations. That had been the first unofficial meeting of the brewery staff. Tace had considered making them more businesslike, and had even searched for information about writing agendas and chairing meetings, but she'd soon given up. She wanted to give the brewery every chance to succeed—because she *had* to sell it for close to the amount she'd paid Kyle—but she couldn't do it by becoming someone she wasn't. She inched a little closer to the cat, and he didn't do more than flick his tail. The woodpile meetings worked for her, and she wasn't going to change them.

"Let's see what you have," she said to Joseph. He hesitated, then handed her the notebook. The page had a charcoal outline of rolling wheat fields and a cloud-dotted sky. A meandering asphalt road cut through the field, and an old-fashioned wooden signpost pointed to the right, with the words *Bike Trail Brewery* written in blocky print. The sketch had been washed with colors—yellows and ambers and blues.

"Did you draw this?" Tace asked in disbelief. He'd taken a thought existing only in her head and had brought it to life.

"You described it. I just drew it."

"I didn't know you were an artist," Tace said. She was thinking ahead, planning the way they could alter the label for each of the regular beers as well as the seasonals. She was seeing it on posters and advertisements and T-shirts and baseball caps. Etched on glasses.

"I was an art major at Whitman."

Tace looked up in surprise, her fantasies vanishing as she was brought back to the present. *Whitman.* She'd spent her life avoiding the college and the people associated with it. Now she had Berit, Joseph, Lawrence, and Allie...she was making more ties to the school than if she'd been a student there. "How did you end up working here?"

Joseph shrugged. "Couple of my frat buddies decided to stay here after school and start this place, and I offered to be the brewmaster. I think we were drunk at the time, but I ended up liking the job. They figured they could make a fortune since microbrews are so popular in the Northwest. This is a wine town, though, and they couldn't get the place going."

Of course he'd been hired at one point. Tace had never given much thought to how he got here—he'd just been a fixture around the place since day one. What'd she think? That he'd been delivered one day in a bag of hops? "Are they the ones who owned it before I got it?"

"Nope. There've been four owners in between."

"Four," Tace repeated, dumbfounded. Four, plus the original owners and herself. Six altogether. "Did any of them make money here?"

"Nope."

Of course. College graduates hadn't been able to make this a viable business. They'd probably had degrees in economics. Maybe some of the owners had MBAs. Bankruptcy—the great equalizer. One thing Tace had learned from her conversations with Berit, and now with Joseph, was that a fancy college degree didn't make one immune to either self-doubt or failure. The knowledge wasn't particularly comforting given her precarious situation here, but it was interesting.

"You're different, though," Joseph said, as if reading her thoughts.

"How?" *Less* likely to succeed? More likely to be the one to completely and irrevocably ruin the business?

"You have good ideas."

Simple as that. Tace didn't know how to answer, but she felt a twinge of something unfamiliar. Pride? The same way she'd felt when Berit seemed to appreciate her company. Her emotions where Berit was concerned carried more complexity, more arousal, and, if possible, even more doubt. In both cases, though, Tace was in unfamiliar territory. Dangling from a precipice, with no idea what waited below if she fell. Or above, if she somehow, against all conceivable odds, managed to climb.

She'd better get back to business, either way. She took out her phone and flicked through some photos she'd taken on her hikes and showed them to Joseph.

"Could you put a different mountain in the background for each of the seasonal labels? Mountains surrounding this area, that you could see if you were out on a bike trail. Here are a couple of pictures I took of peaks in the Blues. Maybe Blue Summer Ale? Umatilla Autumn Amber?"

"Seven Devils Spring Stout." Joseph held her phone in his left hand and started sketching in the notebook with his right.

"Wallowa Winter Wheat," Tace said with a clap of her hands. She might not have time now to meander through the mountains on her days off from the store, but she could use her experiences here, with the brewery.

Berit came into her mind again—not that she left Tace's thoughts very often. What had she said about people through the ages? They learned through experience, apprenticeship, and self-seeking. Tace was needing all three in this new job, temporary as it was. At least she wouldn't lose the knowledge she was gaining, even when she sold the place.

"Tell me about this German malt you need for the hefeweizen," she said. Berit had just paid next month's rent and Tace was about to spend it. Her money was a blessing and would help Tace with this foolhardy venture. But more important, Berit was helping in less definable ways. She'd given Tace things to think about, different ways to see her life and experiences. Berit would leave after a few more months, but she'd made an impact on Tace that would last much longer. And the memory of her, the fantasy of her, would stay with Tace for a lifetime.

CHAPTER TEN

"You're home," Berit stated the obvious with a big grin when she saw Tace sitting at the kitchen table on a Thursday morning and reading the paper.

"*You're* home," Tace said with an answering smile. "Are you playing hooky?"

"October break, thank God," Berit said. Only a month and a half into the semester, and she was ready to collapse. She'd been barely staying one step ahead of all her classes, planning lessons and writing exam and quiz questions in her office until dark and staying up until late grading papers and reading the texts she should have studied before she got here. "I have a long weekend."

"Do you want some pancakes? I have extras." Tace got up and got a platter stacked high with tiny golden disks out of the oven. "Chris would only eat them if they were small and thin, and I can't get out of the habit of making them that way. They're more like crepes than pancakes."

"They smell delicious," Berit said. She piled some on her plate and poured maple syrup over them. She took a bite and sighed, feeling part of herself relax for the first time in weeks. She'd decided to take these two days off and not read a single chapter or grade even a short quiz, and the relief of not having schoolwork made her cheerful. But the bonus of seeing Tace here in the house, looking settled and not rushing off to the store or the brewery made her ecstatic. The concern over her obvious reaction to Tace was mild and easily pushed away. Today, at least. She could worry about it Saturday, when she had to return to her routine of cramming and slogging through her lectures. "I haven't even seen you for over a week. Do you work this afternoon?"

"I have today off from Drake's and I made an executive decision that I don't have to go to the brewery. I finished clearing the yard and, well, I'm not really sure what to do next. I thought I might go to some local wineries today and see the way they run their tasting rooms. I don't suppose you'd want to come?"

Berit chewed her pancakes and watched Tace's expressions change while she talked. They hadn't spent much time together in the past month, and she couldn't claim to know Tace well, but she thought she saw self-doubt in her eyes. Even clearer was Tace's reluctance to admit her uncertainty about the brewery and how to run it.

"Spend a sunny afternoon drinking wine? I'm in. I suggest we try each winery in town to make sure you're getting plenty of research done."

Tace laughed. "There are over a hundred of them, but I'm game if you are. I'll be driving, so you're in charge of the drinking."

"Maybe you don't need to be as thorough as I first thought. When I was writing research papers, I found that three or four well-chosen citations were worth more than a hundred of them." Berit liked seeing Tace smile again and lose her worried frown. She understood what it was like to be in over her head at work. She herself could barely stay one page ahead of her four classes. The students were eager and full of questions, and Berit felt the stress of constantly being out of her depth. Perhaps she'd had the right idea about trying every winery in town. She needed to loosen up after six weeks of tension. A day of wine and laughter and Tace might be just the break she needed. She could forget about her injury and her exile in this Podunk town and about those midterms scheduled for two weeks from now that she hadn't yet written.

She had to get one chore out of the way, though. "Do you mind if we take some boxes by my office first? I have them packed and ready to go."

Tace put their dishes in the sink. "I suppose that's my cue to haul them out to my car."

"I was trying to be subtle," Berit said, following through with the joke even though she felt its sting. She'd always taken her strength and independence for granted, and she chafed under the necessity of asking for help every time she had to lift more than a teacup.

"You'll be back on your feet in no time," Tace said, as if able to read Berit's mind. Maybe it was because she was like her and would be as frustrated as Berit was if she were in the same situation. Tace understood. "It's short term. To make sure you heal."

Her understanding nature didn't keep her from complaining, though, as she carried the four heavy boxes and stowed them in the backseat, leaving the trunk empty for Berit's wheelchair. "I'm sure your office will look much nicer with all these anvils in it," she said when they were on the short drive to the college.

"Don't be so dramatic." Berit pushed at Tace's shoulder. She realized she'd been hoping for physical contact between them. Usually they were either at different levels when they talked—with Berit in her wheelchair and Tace standing—or they were seated across from each other at the kitchen table. She rarely was right next to Tace and she couldn't resist the urge to touch her, even if it was only a playful gesture. A natural reaction, she assured herself. Tace was the only person she knew here who wasn't connected to the college in some way, and Berit wanted to avoid Whitman as much as she could. Tace was a refreshing change—that was all. "I guess I'm supposed to put some things on the shelves next to my desk."

"I think they're called books." Tace parked in the lot behind Olin Hall.

"Very funny. I mean some of the artifacts I have in my room. I've been told my office is sort of spartan." Berit thought back to

Kim's visit last week. Berit had been feeling a momentary sense of accomplishment since one of her classes had gone better than expected. She'd enjoyed lecturing for once and hadn't spent the *entire* hour internally criticizing her delivery. She'd just talked, and the students had responded well. Then Kim had come into her office, looked around, and told Berit she needed to make some changes. But if she changed any more, she'd be barely recognizable to herself. "Kim—you met her at the reception—called it *empty*. She said she knows I want to be on the first plane heading out of town as soon as I'm better, but that I should keep up appearances and look like I really want to be here until then."

"And having your heaviest treasures on the shelves will accomplish that. You'd at least have to wait long enough for me to come pick you up before you left."

"Exactly. It's the kind of helpless permanence the college wants to see from me."

Tace helped Berit out of the car and looked at the three-story brick building. "Don't tell me. Your office is on the third floor."

Berit nodded. "At the end of the hall. You can put one of the boxes on my lap and we can do this in two trips."

"It'd cut off all circulation. I'll go check inside. There must be a handcart somewhere. Unless you happen to know those kids over there?"

"I think I know one of them." Berit pictured her classrooms in her mind, trying to place the young woman who was walking down the street with three friends, just beyond the low brick wall surrounding the campus. Diane? Diana? Berit had started the semester with the noble goal of getting to know all her students by name, but she'd long since had to give up on everything but staying up-to-date with her own reading and homework. She'd been focused more on herself than on her kids. She raised her voice. "Diana?"

"Hello, Dr. Katsaros." She waved and came through an opening in the wall. "Do you need help with something?"

"We're taking some boxes up to my office. Do you mind giving us a hand?"

"Of course not. Hey, guys, come grab a box."

Tace pushed Berit into the building and to the elevator with the four students following, each carrying a box. They all crammed onto the elevator and Berit—uncomfortably waist-level with everyone—was glad they only had a short ride. She was surprised Tace, who seemed to avoid all things collegiate, had suggested they ask Diana and company for help. Berit should be the one wanting to engage with her students, but she was silent while Tace introduced herself to the kids.

"I remember you from Drake's," Diana said as they got off the elevator and started down the hall. "You helped me pick out a dress for my sorority pledge dance last year. I was going to get something pastel, but you suggested royal blue."

"I did?" Tace asked. "How was the dance?"

"Awesome."

"She looked beautiful," one of the guys said, hoisting the heavy box under his left arm and putting his other around Diana's shoulders. "You helped her pick the perfect dress."

Berit unlocked her office door and the students put her boxes on the empty desk before saying good-bye and leaving the room. After their brief, energetic company, Berit and Tace seemed to fall into an awkward silence.

"I should have you pick out my clothes since you seem to have such awesome taste," Berit said, mimicking Diana's voice.

Tace gave a little laugh, but she shook her head. "I don't even remember her. My friend Allie says I'm too detached at work, but I thought it was my customers who were unfriendly. Especially the college kids. They always seemed to pay more attention to their phones than to me."

"Maybe you were wrong," Berit suggested. Tace seemed to think her lack of college education made her less interesting or less worthy of notice than someone either with or working toward a degree. She was very wrong about that. To Berit, Tace was fascinating and bright. Distractingly worthy of notice.

"Maybe I was," Tace said. She seemed about to say more, but just shook her head and glanced around the office. "When you said spartan, I thought you might be exaggerating and your office wouldn't be that bad. But it's worse than you described."

Berit pushed at the books on her desk, straightening the small stack. She had the texts for her classes here, along with a Greek grammar and a critique of Pindar's odes. On one shelf was a copy of the poems in Greek. Berit had meant to read them and offer the class one of her own translations to compare to the text, or at least give them some sort of enlightening insight about the original version. She hadn't found the time to do more than scan them in English. She didn't keep anything else in her office except for a sweater, since she carried her laptop, paper, and pens with her. She'd noticed Tace looking in the few open offices they'd passed on the way here. The professors' doors were covered with cartoons, flyers for job and study opportunities, and colorful schedules. The insides were full of books, overflowing inboxes, and mementos from travels. Walls were lined with maps and posters.

"I never saw the point of really settling in since I'll be—"

"Leaving as soon as you can," Tace finished for her. "We all know that you don't want to be here, Berit. You don't need to prove it to us every minute."

Berit thought she detected a note of sadness in Tace's voice, but Tace turned away and Berit chose to ignore what she'd heard. As much as Berit was attracted to her, Tace belonged here in Walla Walla. Berit had a secret hope that as her body started to get stronger, she might have a chance to explore Tace's, but no matter how their relationship evolved, it would end with Berit leaving and Tace staying. They both knew it.

"I don't belong here," Berit said. "Not just because I don't want to be here, but because I'm really a miserable teacher."

Tace looked up from the box she was unpacking. "I can't believe that. I know you thought your first day didn't go well, but surely you're more comfortable now."

Berit picked up one of the objects Tace had taken out of the box. It was a small clay bowl from a dig in Turkey. A household object with no scholarly significance, but Berit had rescued it from a trash pile. She had several more treasured items like it, everyday utensils and dishes people had used centuries ago. Objects for home and hearth. Berit loved them, but she had very few personal things like them, from her own time period and for her own use. She went over to a bare shelf and put the bowl on it. She'd paid for it to sit in storage and was glad to have it displayed where she'd be able to see it every day, but the thought of buying a modern mixing bowl for herself made her unable to breathe right. Too confining.

"I thought this job would be easy," Berit said. She picked up a clay figurine of a chthonic deity. The little earth goddess statue was a replica of one she and her grandfather had seen at a museum on their first trip to Greece, when she'd known without a doubt she'd become an archaeologist. She'd been good at her classes in school, good at learning about the languages and cultures of ancient peoples, very good at her job. She couldn't remember the last time she'd been so appallingly *bad* at something. "Embarrassing as it is to say, I thought I'd be able to do this job without any trouble. I guess I fell for my own hype. I figured I'd be everyone's favorite teacher, and they'd…"

Berit hated to acknowledge the next part of the thought, but Tace finished the sentence for her.

"They'd hate to see you leave? They'd beg you to stay?"

Berit rolled her eyes at Tace's dramatic rendering of the words, complete with an exaggerated supplicating gesture. She felt a rising tide of anger because Tace seemed to be taking her too lightly. "Tease all you want. This last month has been humiliating. I might not have taught my students anything, but I've learned a humbling lesson about my own vanity. And I still have seven more months to endure, watching their pitying expressions while I stammer through my lectures and…Why are you laughing? This isn't funny. They feel sorry for me."

"I'm not laughing at you. I just think it *is* funny because you keep saying how much you hate it here, but you actually care about teaching and your students. If you didn't, none of this would matter."

Berit put the tiny goddess on the shelf next to the bowl, careful not to harm either one even though she felt like smashing something. She'd thought Tace understood her, but she didn't get what Berit was saying at all. She didn't get how embarrassing it was for Berit to admit she was worthless in the classroom. How foolish and confused she felt for thinking she'd be such a brilliant teacher that no one would want her to leave, even though all she wanted to do was leave. Tace was being ridiculous. Berit was discomfited by her inability to teach, and angry at Tace's words, but both were just momentary emotions. Once she was out of here…"I have a reputation to maintain."

"Reputation? Please. You don't seem the type to care about that sort of thing. I've read your books and I've spent some time with you. You're more renegade than people-pleaser. Besides, you already know you're a success in your field. You have nothing to prove here. You don't need Whitman's validation. What you *do* need, although you hate to admit it, is to feel like you're doing well at a job you truly believe is worthwhile."

"I…of course I think teaching is a worthwhile career. For other people. I'd rather be…" Berit paused. Tace's words were seeping into her mind and somehow her perception of her position here at the school was shifting faster than she could follow. Something about this place was turning her into a bumbling fool. She hadn't been able to carry on a coherent conversation or lecture since coming here.

"I know you'd rather be on one of your digs, excavating some ancient burial site or whatever. But for the time being, you're here.

And like it or not, this temporary job has meaning for you. I've seen you working at the kitchen table for hours at a time, and I've noticed the light under your bedroom door at night. You're hiding it by feeling sorry for yourself, but really you're scared you might not live up to the true value you place on this job."

Berit was distracted momentarily from her irritation by the arousing thought of Tace outside her bedroom door at night. Would she ever knock and come in? Why did Berit even care, especially when she was feeling so annoyed with Tace right now? Berit tossed an empty cardboard box into the corner of her office and pulled a beautiful red-figure vase out of the next box. Even though she was mad and the vase was a replica, she was careful as she put it on display on her desk. The original had been her first significant find while she was still paying her dues in field school. Her instincts in the field had led her right to it. Her instincts in the classroom were nonexistent. "I'm not saying you're right. But if you are, then I'm doomed to a failure even worse than a little embarrassment if no one is inspired or educated in my classes."

"As long as you fight against being here, you're going to struggle in your classes." Tace shrugged, and Berit wanted to throw the vase at her. Why did Tace think she was so wise all of a sudden? And how could she be so right? "Just admit that you're doing work that matters to you. You'll still leave when planned, but you'll either take a great memory of sharing what you know with these kids, or you'll take a memory of being miserable for an entire year."

Berit pushed the box aside. She could finish unpacking her few belongings on Monday. She wanted to stop thinking about what Tace was saying, because she might be too late to give this year with Whitman's students the meaning it deserved. And she didn't want to face how she'd feel if she really dedicated herself to teaching only to find out she had absolutely no talent for it.

"You promised me wine," she said. "I didn't realize it came with a lecture."

Tace laughed. "Lecture over, I promise. Let's go."

CHAPTER ELEVEN

Tace drove back the way they'd come, passing her house and heading out of town. She'd considered going to some of the tasting rooms downtown, but she'd never be able to afford a store in the middle of Walla Walla. If people wanted to go on a tour or taste her beer, they'd have to come out to the brewery itself, so she wanted to see how these fancy wineries attracted such huge crowds to the outskirts of town.

"Hey, I didn't know there was a park so close to us," Berit said when they passed Pioneer Park.

"We haven't had any time for sightseeing." Tace probably should have offered to show Berit around, but they'd both been too busy to do much besides work over the past weeks. She forgot sometimes how limited Berit's activities were with her wheelchair. She went to the college or the store and back again. Tace would have to make more of an effort to get her beyond the few familiar blocks around the house and Whitman, to show her the beauty of this place. And as she got more mobile, Tace could take her into the Blues or to Pendleton or to...

And then what? Berit would fall in love with this area and want to stay forever? Tace sighed and accepted the inevitable. Berit would leave and Tace would stay. Once she sold the brewery and got back on her financial feet, she'd still have the mountains and hiking and solitude to help her through the boring workweeks. She'd show Berit around the town and the local area, but she didn't need Berit's presence imbued in the mountains where Tace sought peace, or she'd never find that peace again.

"I should have told you about it. In the spring when it's warmer, it'd be a nice place for you to study. There's an aviary and some easy paths along the river."

Tace loved to sit in the park and read, but she'd always avoided it when she saw kids from Whitman there. She'd skirt around them, in their sweatshirts with Greek sorority or fraternity letters and their backpacks full of textbooks, and find a quiet corner. She'd been shocked today when she'd felt comfortable having Diana and her friends helping haul Berit's boxes upstairs. She'd walked through Olin Hall—the first time she'd ever set foot in one of Whitman's buildings—with an honest-to-God famous scholar and her students. She'd helped decorate a professor's office, although putting out a few knickknacks hardly counted as decorating.

She'd even delivered her first and only lecture on a college campus. Tace smiled to herself. She'd been able to see through Berit's constant protests about how much she hated her teaching job. At first, Tace had been unsure if she was right about Berit's reasons for being so upset by her lack of success in teaching, but then she'd watched as Berit listened to her and seemed to be realizing the truth in what Tace was saying. Berit really did care about the students and what they were learning from her.

Why had Tace been able to understand what Berit was going through? She certainly didn't have any experience with professors or higher education. Tace moved her shoulders against the driver's seat as she felt an uncomfortable tightening in her shoulders. Maybe she'd understood Berit's situation because she was feeling some of the same emotions as she walked through those quiet, carpeted halls. Tace had spent most of her life avoiding the campus and disliking the students and anyone associated with them. Was there any basis to her dismissal of the entire Whitman population? Or was she, like Berit, avoiding the fact that she really did see meaning in education and wished she'd had the chance to go someplace like Whitman? Sour grapes. Tace ran a hand over the nape of her neck, massaging the tense muscles. She didn't mind telling Berit to face her true feelings, but she was uncomfortable doing the same thing herself.

She should have been mortified when Diana recognized her from the store—and she would have been, if this had happened only a few weeks ago—but she hadn't sensed any judgment from the students. Had it been there in the past, but wasn't present in this particular case? Or had she always been so prepared to encounter condescension and judgment that she saw it even where it didn't exist? Had the students changed, or had she? She *was* different now, or at least her situation was. She had ties to the college community through Berit and Joseph. She had a dream of her own, albeit a temporary and financial one, of turning her brewery into a profitable business.

"Look at the field over there." Berit broke Tace out of her ruminations and pointed out the passenger window at some rows of frilly plants. Waist high, the delicate green fronds had tinges of pastel shades of lilac, muted orange, and pinks. "How beautiful."

"Those are asparagus plants," Tace said.

Berit leaned toward the window as if trying to see better. "Do the asparagus stalks grow on the plants? I can't see any."

Tace laughed. "No. The spears are the stalks of the plants. If they aren't harvested and are allowed to go to seed, they look like these. During the spring and early summer, you'll see fields full of single pieces of asparagus sticking out of the ground, like someone stuck them in the dirt one by one. It's interesting to look at, but backbreaking if you have to harvest them."

"You sound like you're speaking from experience," Berit said. She leaned back in her seat again. "Do you grow them in your garden?"

Tace grimaced. "Not a chance. I love to eat asparagus, but I spent too many springs picking them for money. I'm still sore from all the bending."

"What other jobs have you had?"

Tace thought back and tried to remember all of them. "I picked asparagus in the spring and berries in the summer. I was driving combines in the wheat and pea fields before I was old enough to get my license. I had to beg the farmers to hire me even though I was underage, but the money was great."

"It sounds like a dangerous job for a young kid. Aren't those machines huge?"

"Yes, and the hills in the fields can be steep. The combines are designed to be stable no matter how unleveled the terrain, but sometimes you'd get the angle wrong and they'd tip. Mostly, though, it was boring driving around in circles all day."

Berit reached over and caught Tace's hand in hers. She turned it over and traced the lines on Tace's palm. Tace thought her heart would pound right out of her rib cage at the tentative touch. "You don't have calluses, so you must not do much farmwork anymore. My hands are rough from the tools I use in the field."

Tace rubbed her fingers over the calluses on Berit's hand, and then gripped it with her own. "Be careful, or Whitman will make you soft. You'll have hands like a baby after months holding nothing more than a pencil."

"Yet another reason to go," Berit said, but her voice held more question than statement, and she replaced Tace's hand on the steering wheel. "What else did you harvest?"

Tace glanced over, wondering what Berit, with her degrees and her international career, was thinking about Tace's farm-girl childhood. She was looking at Tace with an interested expression, probably studying her like a specimen of primitive human.

"I've picked apples and pears on small farms, and I worked in the cornfields for a few years. I used to help harvest Walla Walla sweet onions every summer, too. I'd smell like an onion for weeks after, but no one noticed because even the air around town has the same odor during the peak of the season." Tace paused and thought back to her youth. While most kids' lives had revolved around the school year, hers had been tied to the seasons for harvesting and planting. "I had to start working in junior high to help my dad support me, Chris, and Kyle, and agricultural jobs were the highest paying. More interesting than any other work a kid could get, too." More interesting than working at Drake's. "I liked being in tune with the rhythms of the world around me. I hadn't realized it until now, but I guess that's why I got the idea to create four seasonal beers for the brewery. I've always been connected to local, seasonal produce whether through cooking on a tight budget or finding good-paying jobs."

Berit looked out the window again. "I never had that kind of experience, of being connected to the land around me. We usually ate food my mom brought home from the casino's restaurant when I was a kid. And now I travel so much and I'm usually in such remote desert areas on digs that I eat more canned food than anything. Sometimes we'll get fresh fruits and vegetables for a treat, but it depends on the country we're in. I like trying the local cuisine whenever I get a chance, though. Mmm…"

Berit paused, and when Tace glanced at her she saw the kind of dreamy smile on her face that good memories tended to cause.

"I think the only time I really ate with the seasons was when I was in Greece with my grandfather," Berit continued. "We'd have fresh-caught seafood with nothing but lemon on it. Yogurt that had just been made, mixed with honey straight from the hive and figs we picked moments before. I've never tasted anything so wonderful and…hey, look! Did we drive to Italy while I was talking?"

Tace had been caught up in Berit's story and hadn't been paying attention to where she was going. She recognized what a revelation those trips to Greece must have been for a young girl who'd been raised amidst the artificiality of Las Vegas. A loving grandfather to introduce her to real food, the preserved and honored past, a connection to her own history and to the land where her ancestors had lived. Tace broke out of her reverie and saw what had captured Berit's attention. A few acres of leafy vines followed the arch of a small hill. A driveway lined with wild roses led to a large stone building. Tace parked in the lot next to a garden area with ornate wrought-iron furniture where a clematis wove around a trellis, making a canopy of dusky green leaves and vivid purple blooms. The garden must be a riot of color in the spring, and even now in early fall it was still gorgeous.

Tace got out of the car and looked around. She had been proud of the work she'd done around her brewery, reclaiming the land from the weeds and tall grass, but this place put hers to shame. How could she compete with this? She hadn't even gone inside or tasted the wine yet, and already she had been captured by a spirit of elegance and permanence. She'd expect to pay a fortune for a bottle of wine here, and she had no doubt it would be worth it—all because of the atmosphere of the place. People coming to her brewery would be convinced her beer should cost a dollar a bottle, if her own landscaping was doing the selling. She was beginning to think this tasting trip wasn't a good idea. She was already intimidated, and she hadn't yet stepped inside.

Berit seemed as thrilled by the winery as Tace was devastated. "I've read about Walla Walla being compared to Tuscany, but I thought it was a joke. This place really does look like vineyards I've seen in Italy."

Tace held the heavy wooden door open for her and they entered through it, out of the autumn warmth and into the air-conditioned coolness of the tasting room. The huge area had wine barrels and bunches of fake grapes everywhere. Photos of the wine-making process along with placards explaining them adorned the walls. Shelves were lined with things for sale—apparel, crackers and biscotti, bottles of wine. A large oak bar spanned the length of an entire wall, and about twenty tourists were standing in front of it, swishing and sipping from delicate, large-bowled wineglasses. Several elegantly dressed servers stood behind the bar and poured small amounts of wine at a time. Yeesh. Tace pictured herself and

Joseph standing behind a card table with a keg and filling plastic cups with beer. Not quite the same effect.

One of the servers noticed them and beckoned for Berit to come to one end of the bar so she was able to see behind it easily.

"I'm Angela. Welcome to Campton Estate Winery. Our tasting is twenty dollars for three samples and a complimentary wineglass. If you'd like to try our reserve wines, those are ten dollars per sample."

Tace wasn't sure how a twenty-dollar wineglass was supposed to be complimentary, but she handed Angela forty dollars. She was given a tiny sip of wine in a glass etched with the vineyard's name. She'd pictured the drawing Joseph had done on a beer glass, but now she had serious doubts about the dreams she'd had.

"This is our chardonnay," Angela said. She handed them each a piece of paper with tasting notes, and Tace let the cool teaspoon of wine warm on her tongue while she read the notes. Damn it, she really did taste the fruit-forward pear and apple flavors and the lingering finish of oak and sweet vanilla.

"Is this your first time at our vineyard?"

"Yes," Berit said. "This is delicious. I didn't realize what high-quality wines this region produces."

"We're quickly becoming a world-class wine region. Here's our cabernet."

Tace swirled the wine in her glass. She had come here for research, not just to taste. She'd never before identified herself—either internally or to anyone else—as a serious brewery owner, but she had to start sometime. "I recently bought the Bike Trail Brewery, and I'm interested in having a tasting room on-site. I know we'd never be able to compete with the business you do at a place like this, but I'd appreciate any suggestions you might have for me."

"Move to Seattle?" Angela said it with a playful, questioning intonation, and a smile, but Tace felt the patronizing truth behind her words. "Seriously, this area draws wine connoisseurs from around the globe. They come here for the total experience of being immersed in an Old World atmosphere and drinking fine, European-style wines with five-star cuisine. Microbrews are more successful in larger cities in the Northwest. Portland, perhaps. Although I suppose you might find some customers in the college crowds. You can cater keggers."

She laughed and rinsed their glasses. "Our most popular wine is our merlot. It pairs well with most dishes, but my favorite is prime rib served with wild huckleberry glaze."

Tace drank the wine but didn't really taste it. She was humiliated by Angela's dismissal of her chances, but she really wasn't saying anything Tace hadn't already told herself. She thought about the fancy dish Angela had described. Tace had grown up cooking hamburger steaks with ketchup, so what did she know about sophisticated food and wine pairings?

That's not fair. She stopped her self-destructive line of thought while Angela wrapped their precious glasses in tissue paper. She had cooked plenty of meals as classy as prime rib. She thought of Joseph's porter. If they tweaked the recipe and enhanced the mild toffee notes? Maybe added some juniper berries and coffee beans to the wort for a floral richness? She'd match it with Angela's prime rib without hesitation.

In her mind, at least. In reality, who would ever have a chance to try the combination she could almost picture on her tongue?

"Here you go," Angela said, handing Tace a gift bag with the Campton Estate label emblazoned on it. "Be sure to stop by our booth if you come to the balloon festival this weekend. We're selling raffle tickets for a chance to win a trip to Napa Valley."

"What a pretentious prig," Berit said when they were back in the car. She seemed cheerful, though, and unaffected by Angela's prediction of Tace's failure. "What's a balloon festival? Does someone walk around town making balloon animals for the kids?"

"Speaking of pretentious. You have an amusingly low opinion of our town." Tace was still feeling the shame from having her beer considered a lower class of beverage and her voice was sharper than she intended it to be. Berit hadn't been the one to insult her craft. And when had she started to consider it her *craft*? She was only a surrogate, until a rich but foolish buyer could be found. "Sorry, I didn't mean to snap. The festival is for hot-air balloons, and people come from all over the country to fly here. I forgot it was this weekend, since it used to be in the spring. I think they changed it because there's a better chance of good weather in October. I used to take Chris and Kyle every year."

"Sounds like fun," Berit said, with a sort of wistful sound. Tace had a feeling she was about to be wrangled into driving Berit to the park for the festival.

"Fun? Not really." Tace remembered the stress of bundling two complaining kids onto their bikes and down to the fairgrounds every year. Kyle would complain about the early morning, and Chris would cry at every food stand until Tace bought her something to eat. Not exactly Tace's idea of a good time. "It's an amazing sight, though. All those brightly colored balloons lifting off the ground and floating away. They seem so light and graceful. Weightless."

Tace had stood at rapt attention until the balloons were out of sight, while two kids pulled on her arms and begged to go. "You know, Kyle hated getting up early, so I never could get there in time to see the pilots laying out the balloons and filling them. Chris whined about being cold or hot or hungry, depending on the moment. I always told myself I was going through the effort for them, and once they were out of the house I stopped going, but I was really the one who loved being there. I'll take you if you want to go."

"I promise I'll get up as early as you want, and you won't hear a peep from me, no matter how cold or hot it is," Berit said with a grin, and Tace had the sudden desire to be holding her hand again.

"I'd love to go. Now, where's the next winery? We still need to research these tasting rooms for your brewery."

"Okay, but I'm done tasting. I'll just be the designated driver from now on." Maybe Tace could just sit in the car and wait for Berit. She didn't have any desire to bring up the brewery again. Angela's pronouncement had hurt, but Tace believed she was right. Beer had no place out here among the wineries. She could supply some kegs to local pubs and restaurants and hope to make a small profit over the cost of supplies and Joseph's salary, but she shouldn't dream beyond those boundaries. All she'd find on the other side would be disappointment.

She pulled onto a driveway leading to yet another picture-perfect winery. "Back to the delightful world of Tuscany," she said. And another step away from the reality of her life in Walla Walla.

CHAPTER TWELVE

Even after Berit had accompanied Tace to ten different wineries, she still hadn't come close to feeling buzzed from the samples she'd consumed. She'd had the equivalent of perhaps a glass and a half of alcohol, but between them, they'd spent enough money to have bought twenty full bottles of decent wine. She had collected a mismatched assortment of glasses and had eaten a meal's worth of crackers to cleanse her palate. Most important, she had managed to spend the afternoon *not* thinking about teaching classes.

On the disquieting side, her mind had been consumed by Tace. She was constantly surprised by her. Tace's observations about her hidden feelings for the job at Whitman were astute and probably correct—although Berit was avoiding any real contemplation of them until they had a few days to simmer inside her. The image of Tace riding a combine and working in fields was arousing and persistently in the front of her thoughts. Suntanned and strong, laboring in the elements just like Berit was used to doing on digs.

More than anything, though, Berit had been upset by the way Tace had been treated whenever she mentioned her brewery. Berit had tried to keep her spirits up and turn the insults into jokes about the people who had spoken them, but she saw Tace's demeanor gradually fade as the afternoon wore on. Berit had some suggestions that might help Tace. She had no idea how to broach the subject without making Tace feel belittled by her as she had been by the winery staffs and owners. Tace had bluntly called Berit on her attitude toward teaching today, but Berit wasn't sure if she felt comfortable doing the same in reverse. Were they good enough friends?

Friends? Berit watched the darkening fields as they drove past. She'd touched friends before. Hugs, handshakes, casual brushes of hands or arms. She hadn't ever felt the intensity of focus that she had experienced when she had done nothing more than hold Tace's hand and rub her palm. Every nerve ending in Berit had concentrated on the place where skin met skin. She'd let go of Tace and had felt as physically drained and emotionally electrified as if they'd had sex right there on the front seat of Tace's car.

Berit moved in her seat. There was plenty of room for sex in here. She sighed and looked out the window again, trying to find something to distract her awareness away from Tace, who sat so close to her.

"There's another one," Tace said. Her voice sounded weary, but she pointed at a sign for a winery that was just a mile up the road. "Do you want to stop?"

"Do you mean stop at the winery, or stop going to wineries? I hope it's the latter, because I can't stand another one of those tasting rooms. I've had enough Tuscan charm to last me a few years."

Tace laughed. "I'm glad you said that. I was beginning to wonder if we'd been to ten different wineries, or to the same one ten times."

"They're all beautiful," Berit said, cautiously approaching the subject she'd wanted to talk about for over an hour now. "The grounds are fabulous, and the wines are excellent. Over and over again. No matter what the people we've met have said to you, I can't believe there isn't room for a change of pace. A unique artisan brewery with local charm and local flavors, plus an approachable, inclusive atmosphere. You might be just the breath of fresh air this town needs, Tace. That could be your niche."

"I don't know. Am I looking for a niche, or do I just need to sell enough beer to make the business marketable? There are hundreds of wineries working together to make this town a destination for a specific group of tourists. I'd be all alone, trying to market a different product to people who aren't interested in it." Tace's voice trailed off. "Do you want to see one of the wheat fields where I worked?"

Berit was surprised both by the change in subject and by how much she wanted to see more of Tace's world. She nearly made an excuse about her back hurting after all the unaccustomed activity, just so she could get back to the house and lock herself away from Tace and these uncomfortable feelings. She was having to face the fact that teaching might be more important to her than she wanted it to be, and then run the risk of failing miserably at it. Could she handle a relationship with meaning, too? Both would end soon enough, but Berit had planned to leave this town whole and healed again, not heartbroken and ashamed.

The thought of being alone with Tace and prolonging her day off from studies won the internal debate she was having. "I'd like to see it. I won't have to ride in a combine to get there, will I?"

Tace laughed. "I think we'll save that experience for another day. We'll just be on the side of the road, near the edge of the field. You'll be safe."

Berit had her doubts about her emotional safety as she watched the sky darken outside the car window. Here, beyond the city limits, the night seemed to drop a curtain over the two of them. She felt the quiet and isolation even while the noise of the engine and the headlights fought against the darkness. Tace pulled off the empty highway and onto a gravel road. She drove behind some trees and parked.

The silence fell like a guillotine once the car was shut off. Berit felt the same juxtaposed sensations of weightiness and expansion she had felt when she'd wandered away from camp while on remote digs. Tace was about to get her wheelchair out, but Berit stopped her.

"Are we going far?"

"No. Just a few yards up this hill, and we should have a great view. Can you walk a little?"

Berit pulled herself to a standing position. She was feeling stronger in small increments, but she was being obediently careful—for once in her life—until she was checked by her doctors in Florida over winter break. She felt good on this soft and beautiful night, however, and she wanted a chance to stretch her legs. As she had expected, Tace came over and offered her arm to help Berit over the ruts and furrows of the bare field. An added bonus.

Berit wasn't sure what she had been expecting when Tace offered to show her a wheat field. Wheat, she supposed. Dirt. They were only yards away from the backwoods highway, but the little stand of trees separated them from any sign of pavement or civilization. They walked to the top of a gentle hill and Berit got the same disorienting sensation of being in a vacuum, while having the world open up before her at the same time.

Tace spread a blanket she'd gotten out of her trunk on the rough ground and helped Berit lower herself to a seated position. Berit eased back until she was lying down and staring at a carpet of stars above her. The silence filled her head until she thought it might explode from the pressure.

"What a magical place," she whispered.

"It is," Tace agreed in a similarly quiet voice. "Why are we whispering?"

"I feel like I'm in a cathedral," Berit said. She inched her hand along the ground between them until her fingers touched Tace's and intertwined with them. "What's the glow over there? Is it lights from the town?"

Tace laughed. "I hate to spoil the romantic mood, but it's the state penitentiary."

"Oh, my. Well, we can pretend it's candlelight. Prisons aside, this is a beautiful place to work."

"Picture it during the day when it's over one hundred degrees outside. Add lots of bugs, a smelly diesel-guzzling combine, and whirlwinds of dust." Tace shifted and her arm came into contact with Berit's.

Berit nearly gasped out loud at the touch of their bare arms. She needed to distract herself from the exquisite pain of finally being close to Tace and being unsure how to react. The pressure on her back from the dried clods of dirt reminded her of her injury. She still needed to nurse her spine back to health. Even without her back problems, she didn't want to start anything with Tace—unless, that is, Tace was willing to have a short-term relationship. She didn't seem the sort. She seemed grounded here, and she'd probably expect nothing less from a lover.

The sky and stars and seclusion out here made Berit want to forget about the past and the future and concentrate on now. If she did, though, the soil beneath her might turn to quicksand and trap her in this place. She pointed to the sky with her free hand.

"Do you know the constellations? I can see Cassiopeia and Ursa Major and Minor, but I've never learned the others."

Tace gestured toward the east, where the sky was nearly pitch blue-black and the stars shone in sharp relief. "There's Andromeda and Perseus. See the square shape near them, with lines there and there? That's Pegasus."

"The winged horse. He was my imaginary friend when I was a girl. I'd sit in a corner of the casino, waiting for my mom to finish work or to lose the last of her cash at poker, and I'd imagine he'd come get me and we'd fly back in time. The sounds of slot machines and people yelling, and the smell of cigarette smoke and gin all faded away while I was back in Ancient Greece with Pegasus." She sighed at the memory, then returned to the now. To Tace. "Did you ever have a make-believe friend?"

"No…well, not really. I don't think it counts as an imaginary friend, but I used to pretend my mom was with me. I'd ask her questions about the kids and how to do things around the house.

She's the reason I was forced into the role of mother before I was out of elementary school, but she also helped me get through tough times, in a way."

Berit felt her heart breaking for Tace and the childhood she missed. Berit understood because she hadn't had a real one, either. She hadn't had to handle the responsibilities Tace had borne, but Berit hadn't been nurtured. She'd been left to her own devices most of the time.

"You must have done well with them. Didn't you say your sister is in graduate school?"

"Chris is working toward her master's at OSU, in Corvallis, Oregon. She's studying English literature. She's a good kid. Very smart and serious about her studies. Kyle, on the other hand, isn't so serious. He's charming and funny—you can't help but love him even though he's sort of…flaky. He's been in and out of different colleges and jobs, and now I'm worried he's following Mom's tendency to float through life, gambling with his future, not just with money."

"He's the reason you got the brewery?"

"Yes. He won it in a poker game, of all things. He had the previous owner sign it over to me, and in exchange I gave Kyle the amount we thought would be the price I could get when I sold the place. Both of us were delusional about how much the brewery was worth."

"Then," Berit said. She turned her head and looked at Tace. She looked so beautiful in the pale light from the crescent moon. Her eyes seemed to reflect the stars, and Berit wanted to trace the contours of her profile with her fingertips. "Your brewery might not have been worth much when you took over as owner, but you've made improvements, haven't you?"

"Joseph and I have made a few changes for the better, I think," Tace said with cautious admission. "We've got tap pulls and a sign with our logo. I'm really happy with the hefeweizen—it's my favorite of the beers because of the flavor, not just because it's the first recipe I helped Joseph create." Her voice got stronger and more enthusiastic as she talked. "We've made a couple of our seasonals, but that's not the same as adding a regular to the repertoire. The porter is improving, too, and it's almost good enough to be sold. Oh, and the property is much more presentable now. It's nothing like these wineries, but it's tidy enough."

Berit pictured Tace coming in the house after a long day at the brewery. "I'll bet it looks great. You usually come home all sweaty and covered with grass clippings, so you're obviously working hard there."

Tace laughed. "Ugh. That doesn't sound appealing."

"Are you kidding? Sweat is very sexy."

Tace shifted and looked at Berit. "I never thought you'd notice."

"Well, I have."

Tace propped herself on one elbow, and Berit met her gaze with an open invitation. She wanted Tace to kiss her, here in this place where Tace was connected to the soil and to the stars, but she wasn't prepared for the way her body responded to the first tentative brush of Tace's lips against hers. She reached up and laid her hand on the back of Tace's neck, feeling the tense muscles there as Tace seemed to be holding herself in check. Their mouths moved together gently, but the sensations echoed through the deep stillness of the night.

Berit sighed and opened her lips in an answer to the questioning touch of Tace's tongue. Tace kept her weight balanced on one elbow and seemed determined not to put any pressure on Berit even though she craved the sensation of their bodies pressed tightly together. Berit had been fighting against pity and assistance since she'd been injured, but now she welcomed the way Tace was moving slowly and carefully with her. Berit wasn't afraid of being hurt physically, but she wasn't ready for the emotional vibration she felt between her and Tace.

Tace's fingers stroked Berit's hair and left temple while her tongue moved against Berit's. Berit was losing control of her feelings. She wanted more. She wanted all Tace had to offer. Berit arched toward Tace, trying to get closer, but she felt a twinge in her back and reflexively inhaled with a sharp gasp. She tried to relax again, but Tace was already moving away.

"I'm sorry. I shouldn't have—"

Berit put a hand on Tace's arm and stopped her apology. "I wanted you to kiss me," she said. She didn't know when she'd ever wanted anything as much, but she didn't say so. Her relationship with Tace was already putting a strain on her ability to remain detached and free. "My back didn't really hurt, I just felt the muscles tighten a little and I was worried I'd feel pain. But I'm okay."

"Still, I should have been more careful with you." Tace lay back again with a sigh.

"If you're any more careful with me, I'll be Bubble Wrapped and locked in a padded room." Berit kept her voice light and teasing, but she was struggling inside between frustration at having the kiss end and relief over the same thing. The arousal Tace had stirred to life in her was relentless and uncomfortable. She needed distance between them, but she was going to be close to Tace and relying on her until they got home again. Berit felt her chest constrict at the thought. She couldn't even walk away on her own, to give herself space. She was stuck on her back like an overturned turtle, and she'd need Tace's hand to help her up. She hated the feeling of helplessness, and her growing anger was fueled by her unfulfilled desire for Tace. She lashed out the only way she could, by returning to a topic she knew would cause Tace to pull back emotionally.

"I watched how you changed when you were talking to the people in the wineries today. Can I give you some advice?" Berit had started this line of conversation with the intent of finding distance, but she had really wanted to share her thoughts with Tace. She wanted to help her. Even worse, Berit somehow had come to care whether Tace found success or not.

"I'd rather you didn't," Tace said, her words clipped. She and Berit had still been holding hands, but Tace let go now.

Berit hadn't exactly heard a *no*. "A big part of my job is getting funding and support from people who don't want to give it to me. I sometimes need permission to excavate in countries that are more concerned about fighting with their neighbors than uncovering relics from the past. Or I need money from universities that would rather see it go to profitable ventures like a new football stadium or medical research lab."

"Are you trying to compare my brewery to your job and prove how much more important yours is?"

Berit wanted to sit up and emphasize her point with direct eye contact, but her core muscles were still weak, and she was stuck. She only had her words and sharp gestures with her hands if she wanted to convince Tace she wasn't being mean.

"Of course not. I'm only saying that both of us need to use diplomacy and determination because we're selling products the world can honestly live without. These wineries don't need you, but you need their help, just like I need something from the people I approach. I have to make them believe it matters if the university's press has first rights to publish a book no one but a handful of archaeology professionals and students will read. Or that finding a fire pit from twelve hundred BCE might give a country an advantage in a border war."

"*Does* it matter?"

Berit shrugged and felt the rasp of her shoulders against the uneven ground. "It matters to me. I honestly believe what I do in the field is important, and I have to show it when I'm asking for money. When you were adding basil and lavender to your IPA, or when you were talking just now about the changes you've made to the brewery, your voice and your face both prove how much you're enjoying this work. When you talked to the people at the winery, though, you were defeated before you even opened your mouth to speak. You were different, like you didn't believe anyone would—or should—give you the time of day, let alone advice and support."

"What if I really don't believe it?"

Berit heard the doubt creeping into Tace's voice, and she knew it was directed at Tace herself, not at the brewery. She pretended to deal with the business side of it, not about Tace's personal sense of self-worth. "Why can't you believe it? There are obviously more vital issues in the world today than whether I'll bring another red-figure vase to light, but I believe it's important to understand and honor our past. You're creating an artisanal, local product. Time and care go into making it, and people enjoy drinking it. That's no less meaningful than anything I do. I've seen and heard you. You care more about this brewery than you'll admit, and it's time you showed this town how you really feel about it."

Tace nudged her with an elbow. "Didn't I deliver this same lecture earlier today? I think you're plagiarizing." She sighed, and Berit wasn't sure if the resignation she heard was due to Tace's discouragement, or to her acceptance of Berit's words. Either way, Berit had effectively shut down the physical portion of the evening. Should she celebrate or cry? Maybe both.

Tace got to her knees and reached out to help Berit sit up. "It's been a long day, and I'm tired. Plus, we need to get you off the ground because it's getting cold. Time to go home."

Berit walked slowly back to the car with Tace's arm wrapped loosely around her waist. Berit was ready to go, but she had no idea where home was for her. A dirty tent pitched on the sand in another new country? The rooms from which she'd ousted Tace? Berit had no idea, but she was weary and a little sore. Tonight she'd settle for a comfortable bed, and let the question of home fade away while she slept.

CHAPTER THIRTEEN

Tace was jolted out of a restless sleep early Saturday morning by a crashing sound coming from the kitchen.

"Tace? Come down here!" Berit's voice called to her from the bottom of the stairs.

She was out of bed and running down the steep, narrow staircase before she was fully aware of what was happening. She pictured Berit lying in a heap on the kitchen floor, her wheelchair tipped on its side. Instead she found Berit fully dressed and smiling, holding the two saucepans she'd been banging together.

"What the hell are you doing?" Tace hadn't slept much since she and Berit had kissed. She'd lain awake, tossing and turning in a desperate attempt to ignore the desire she didn't want to feel for Berit, until she'd finally dozed off near dawn. She squinted out the kitchen window. The sky was gray and yellow just before sunrise. "What time is it?"

"You said you always wanted to watch the balloons getting filled and taking off," Berit said. "Hurry and get dressed or we'll miss it."

"I was hoping you'd forgotten about the festival," Tace said. Her words were partially true. She'd been distressed by Berit's bossiness in the wheat fields and would have preferred to avoid being in her company. Berit expected Tace to commit herself to this brewery, admit she cared about it, but doing so would only wound her in the long run. Tace supposed she deserved the lecture after delivering one of her own, when she had pushed Berit to break out of her comfort zone and fully accept the role of teacher, but Tace had only said those things to Berit because she could see how much doing a good job for her students meant to her. Had Berit really seen the same hidden hopes in Tace? If so, Tace had better get busy and crush her foolish aspirations before they destroyed her. She had gotten this far in life—and would get her siblings even further if possible—by focusing on what she *could* achieve. A nice home, as few bills as possible, and whatever help she could offer Chris and Kyle.

Still, the thought of going to the festival with Berit was too enticing to refuse. "I'll go, as long as you stop making such a racket."

"Deal," Berit said. She put the pans on the counter and held up her hands in surrender. "Quiet as a mouse. Just get ready to go!"

Tace jogged up the stairs again and got in the shower. She'd admittedly been a tiny bit resentful when she'd needed to give up her newly decorated and comfortable downstairs rooms and move into the cramped attic suite, but she'd since had a change of heart. Her books filled the shelves in what was supposed to be Berit's study, and her personal items made the other rooms look cozy. She spent most of her time in the bedroom she'd used when she was very small, either reading in bed or in a chair by the dormer window. Somehow, childhood dreams seemed able to exist up here, even though she'd learned to banish them from her mind when she'd moved downstairs.

Tace let the hot water run over her scalp and down her naked body. She'd been fighting Berit's advice because she was afraid to trust in a dream. When had one ever come true for her? But maybe a logical approach would let her have the best of both worlds. Financially, she had to get the business established. She needed to have a base of customers, and a viable plan for the next owner to turn a profit. But was there any harm in having fun along the way? Enjoying the creative process when she and Joseph crafted new recipes, sharing her excitement without expecting people to demean her, really believing in the product she was delivering. All while accepting the limited time she'd be part of this venture. She wasn't a brewer—she was playing with the position for a short time. Why not be part of it wholeheartedly, appreciating it even more because it was temporary?

Tace picked up a jade-green towel and dried herself quickly. She combed her hair and dressed in several layers to protect against the morning chill. Her body was tingling from the hot water and vigorous towel-drying, but she knew part of her heightened sensation was due to Berit. Tace could apply the same logic to their relationship. Berit had never hidden her wish to leave Walla Walla and all its inhabitants far behind her, but she'd also seemed to be as attracted to Tace as she was to her. She went downstairs with a lighter feeling inside than she'd felt for years. Why not explore the short-term benefits of Berit's company as well, as long as she remained fully aware of its transitory nature? Could she survive the inevitable? She wasn't sure. She was more confident in her ability to do so with the brewery than with Berit.

She drove them to the fairgrounds and parallel parked along a nearby residential street. Small groups of people were approaching from all directions through the early morning fog and merging into a larger crowd as they neared the liftoff site. Tace and Berit joined them, cutting through an alley between houses and crossing a weedy parking lot. Even from a distance, Tace could see the bright colors of nylon envelopes, some partially filled and beginning to rise in the air.

Tace got behind Berit's chair and helped her move through the dense, short grass of the field. Hundreds of balloons were carefully spread on the ground behind their baskets, in neat rows and separated by uniform distances. Tace loved the tidy and organized layout of the whimsical, fantastical balloons.

"Look, it's a hamburger," Berit said.

"A hamburger for breakfast? You sound like Chris." Tace looked around for the concession stand, but Berit pointed down the row and laughed.

"Not to eat, silly. The balloon is shaped like a burger."

They went over to the oddly shaped bag while it slowly drifted higher as the burner heated the air inside it. Tace watched the bun, lettuce, and cheese expand.

"You could make a beer bottle for next year's festival," Berit said. "I'll bet you wouldn't have any trouble selling the brewery if you had your very own hot-air balloon."

"I like it," Tace said. "I'll have to buy Joseph a sewing machine so he can get started right away."

The thought of shy, flannel-and-coverall-clad Joseph stitching together a beer balloon made her laugh. She started walking down the next row. "We can have him make one for you, too. Maybe shaped like the vase we brought to your office on Thursday."

"Ooh, that would be pretty," Berit said, looking back at her. "I can see Herakles and the Nemean Lion floating against a bright blue sky."

"Nice. Or how about Pegasus? You could ride in the basket and sail away."

Berit laughed. "Even better."

Tace was silent for a moment. No matter how much logic she used, the thought of Berit leaving still made her feel a gaping hole in the pit of her stomach. Berit had only been here a short time, but already she'd worked her way inside Tace. She'd be missed.

They watched the first wave of balloons sail away until they were tiny pinpricks of color in the sky. This was what Tace had wanted to see, the way she had wanted to see it, when she was little. Instead, she had been a child-mother, tending two kids who had wishes of their own.

They walked toward a row of booths selling everything from handmade jewelry to hot dogs. The dirt path in front of the vendors was smooth and even, so Tace walked alongside Berit.

"This has been a great morning," she said. The weight of her thoughts made her voice sound more solemn than she'd intended. "Thank you for waking me up and bringing me here, Berit."

"You're welcome, Tace," Berit said, imitating her serious tone. She switched back to her normal voice. "I've been meaning to ask, why Tace instead of Stacy?"

"I've always been Tace, I guess. At least since Chris was born. She couldn't say the *S* sound at first, so she said Tace. I've used it ever since."

Berit looked at her and frowned. "You've always been defined by your family, haven't you."

Tace felt the sting of her words. Berit might not have meant them to hurt, but they seemed to lessen her somehow. Shortening her name hadn't diminished her as a person. Giving up her own options and dreams had. "Like you've been defined by your globetrotting lifestyle?"

"Touché," Berit said. She looked away for a moment, and then back at Tace. "Sorry. I didn't mean to sound critical. When I was young, I'd have loved a brother or sister to keep me company. In some ways, I envy how close you are with your family."

Tace shrugged. "I'm sorry, too. I envy your freedom."

"It's not all accolades and fun. Hey, there's a table for a winery. Want to stop and chat, or keep going?"

Tace looked at the booth with its burgundy and beige banner. A woman in her sixties was standing behind it, handing out flyers to people as they walked by.

"Oh, what the hell," Tace said. "I could use a little ego boost."

"Lead with sarcasm. There's a good plan."

Tace shook her head and laughed. She was fully expecting the same snobby reception she'd gotten at the other wineries on Thursday, but she kept Berit's unsolicited advice in mind. Her brewery was producing a quality product. Much of it was due to Joseph's talent as a brewer, but she'd contributed some good ideas of her own, using her own palate and instincts. Without her pushing and planning, he'd still be lurking in the shadows, brewing ales no one but he would ever taste.

The woman greeted Tace with a cheery smile. "Hello, I'm Margaret Chetham of Chetham Hill Winery. Are you in town just for the balloon festival, or will you be doing some wine tasting, too?"

Tace took the flyer. The winery's name was surrounded by images of clusters of grapes. A photo showed a beautiful Tuscan-style stone tasting room.

"Actually, I live here in town," she said, mustering a smile to match Margaret's. She pointed to the map on the flyer. "I own the Bike Trail Brewery, just a few blocks from your winery. We make microbrews using local ingredients."

"Interesting. Have you been in business long?"

Tace wasn't sure whether it would be better to say yes and then have Margaret wonder why she hadn't heard of the place yet, or say no and sound inexperienced. She opted for the truth. "The brewery has been running for several years, with the same brewmaster, but I recently bought it. It hadn't been managed well, and I'm trying to make some positive changes."

"I just opened to tourists this year," Margaret said, lowering her voice as if she were admitting to something bad. "I've been developing my wines for a while, but it's scary to make the step to being public. The more established wineries can be intimidating. This has been my dream since I was in my twenties, and I finally retired from my job as a CFO and decided to give it a try. Never too late, I hope."

Tace smiled. "I'm sure you'll do well, especially since you have such passion for the work. I never planned to own a brewery. It's a challenge in a region known for its wines, but I feel I can fill a real need in this area."

"What can you supply that the wineries can't?"

Margaret's question didn't sound challenging or patronizing. Instead, she seemed interested in hearing Tace's point of view. Tace took a deep breath and plunged ahead.

"Options," she said. She thought back to Thursday. She'd spent most of the time during the tastings feeling sorry for herself because the winery owners weren't receptive to her. While Berit had tasted wines, Tace had watched the groups of tourists come and go. "I've visited tasting rooms and I've noticed that about twenty percent of the people coming to the wineries don't actually drink any wine. Some might be drivers, but the number is consistent even with groups from tour buses. These people might be tagging along with friends, and it would be a great PR opportunity to offer them a different choice. Something as simple as a couple of tapped kegs might give an entire family or group a better impression of your winery."

Margaret nodded slowly. "You're right on with the percentage. I have water available, and I sell bottles of soft drinks, but a local craft beer might be popular, especially with the number of people who come from Seattle and Portland. If a winery were to implement your idea, what beers would you recommend?"

Tace imagined the taste of the wine in her mouth, and then she worked through her beer options to sense how well they'd blend. "The amber ale," she said with a convinced nod. "It's got depth and a sweet aftertaste, with a nice floral hoppiness. It'd be great on its own, and it wouldn't clash with the wines if anyone wanted to try both. I'd also suggest a rotating keg with our seasonal beers. They showcase specialty ingredients from this region, and would be a great way to get people excited about the area even if they aren't into the wine culture. Our autumn selection is the amber ale infused with anise, orange, and local hazelnuts."

Tace paused. She wasn't sure what else to say. She wanted to sound confident, not pushy. Berit was close beside her, and Tace rested the tips of her fingers on the arm of Berit's chair. Berit shifted her elbow until they were barely touching. Tace felt a welcome sense of support and companionship from her.

"I like the idea. Are you bottling yet, or do you only sell kegs?"

Tace wanted to sell beer, not to make false promises about expansion or change. The next owner would be responsible for the brewery's growth. She was only planning to establish a base of customers and markets for the beer. "Kegs only, and we'll fill growlers at the brewery. Bottling is an expensive step."

Margaret nodded, took a card out of her wallet, and handed it to Tace. "I agree. I'm farming out my bottling to a larger winery right now, although I'm interested in doing it myself as soon as I can afford to invest in the equipment. If you decide you want to take the next step and bottle, perhaps we could combine our resources and work together."

"Maybe," Tace said, but she was thinking *no* inside. Invest in bottling equipment? She wasn't even sure what went on during the process. Was there a difference between Margaret's needs with her wines and Tace's with beer? None of her questions mattered since she couldn't afford to take the brewery to the next step herself.

"For starters, I'd like to try offering a small selection of your beer in my tasting room, and I'll see what kind of feedback I get from customers."

"That'd be great. I don't have a public tasting room yet, but you're welcome to stop by the brewery and sample our beers anytime you want."

Tace and Berit left the winery's table, and Tace tucked Margaret's card in her back pocket. As soon as they were around a corner, Tace stopped and faced Berit.

"Thank you. I think that conversation went well, and it's because of your advice. I hadn't realized how much my own low expectations were getting in the way."

Berit held her hands in front of her chest, with her palms facing Tace. "Wait a minute." She closed her eyes and sighed. "Let me savor this for a moment...Okay, here goes..." She opened her eyes again. "I told you so."

Tace laughed and started walking again. "Don't be too smug. I'll be saying the same thing at your going-away party, while all the students and faculty from Whitman are weeping in despair because you're leaving."

"Ha. They'll be throwing a ticker-tape parade as they escort me out of town, more like."

Tace shook her head with a smile. She felt elated after a small step forward for the brewery and for her own self-confidence, but her mention of Berit leaving left her with the same hollow feeling in her belly she'd noticed before. Hungry. She was hungry, that was all.

"There's a diner around the corner," she said. "You hurried me out of the house before I had a chance to eat breakfast. How about I buy you a plate of the best pumpkin waffles you've ever had?"

Berit smiled. "Sounds good. I've never had them before, so I have a feeling your words will be prophetic."

Tace was quiet as they left the fairgrounds. She had felt happy before, of course. Hiking through the natural beauty of the Northwest or watching Chris graduate from high school and college. External things. This was different, however, this something stirring inside her. It had to do with her. With her achievements and her own effort. She wasn't sure how much to let this budding dream grow. Enough to fill her life for a short while, but not enough to really hurt her when the dreams came toppling down.

Even as she celebrated the small victory for the brewery, she couldn't help but caution herself against feeling and expecting too much. She wouldn't override a lifetime of restraint and common sense because of a word of encouragement from a single wine merchant, but she could certainly enjoy the high from it this morning. Tace lifted her face toward the sun as the second wave of balloons lifted into the air. A rainbow of colors, gliding silently across the sky. Tace turned her attention back to Berit and helped her cross a deep groove in the field. Waffles and plenty of hot, strong coffee were calling Tace back down to earth, where she belonged.

CHAPTER FOURTEEN

After New Year's, Tace walked into the Blue and wrinkled her nose at the powerful odor of stale beer. She'd never noticed it before, even though she'd been sort of a regular here for years. She'd been spending hours with Joseph at the brewery where they sampled warm, flat worts, analyzed the flavor components, and made small adjustments to the recipes. Her nose was becoming increasingly sensitive to the nuances of their different products. She'd never taste or smell mass-produced, bland lagers the same way again.

She went to the bar and the manager came over as soon as he saw her. "Hey, Tace. You here to sell or to drink?"

"Hey, Dan. I'm meeting a friend tonight, so I'll have a glass of the seasonal. Although, if you have time later this week, I'd like to bring a sample of our new stout for you to try. I'm sure you'll want to stock it by Saint Patrick's Day because it makes a delicious black-and-tan with our IPA."

Tace watched him pour her beer using the tap pull with Joseph's drawing on it. A picture of the snowy north ridge of Sawtooth Peak—based on a photo she'd taken while on a hike the previous winter—was in the background of his bike-trail scene. *Wallowa Winter Wheat* was printed in red letters under the logo, and *Bike Trail Brewery* was written in a blocky font across the top. She'd been seeing the taps in more and more bars lately, and she never got tired of the thrill of accomplishment she felt when she saw one.

Dan handed her the beer and waved off her money. "Bring a keg of the stout when you come, not just a sample. If it's anything as good as your others, I'll want to have it here. Remember, the big bike race is in April. I want to be sure I don't run out of anything with Bike Trail on the label."

"Great. I'll come by on Thursday, and we can get your order in early."

Tace spotted Allie across the bar. She took a sip of her beer as she walked over to the table, letting the subtle notes of nutmeg and pear wash over her tongue. Spicy warmth and a hint of sunshine from the fruit. Not the typical winter seasonal she had seen from other breweries—especially since she'd used her hefeweizen as the base—but she wouldn't change a thing about it. It was ideal on a cold January day.

Allie got up and gave her a hug. "I haven't seen you in ages," she said. "I was going to complain about how busy you are these days, but then I got a taste of your IPA. So, keep up the hard work."

Tace grinned and sat down across from her. "Thank you. It's still our biggest seller. People around here love their hops. How has your work been? I miss trying your new recipes."

"I have a freezer full of casseroles for you," Allie said. "I'll bring them by this week. We've been experimenting with some Moroccan dishes, trying to adjust the recipes to make them easier to make quickly and in bulk."

Tace half participated in the conversation about tagines and Moroccan spices. The rest of her mind was coming up with ideas for the upcoming bike race. The brewery should be one of the sponsors—she made a mental note to contact the organizers of the event. Maybe she could have a booth there, with flyers from the different restaurants and pubs that served her beer. There'd be plenty of people coming from out of town to ride in the race, and she wanted them to drink her beer while they were here. Was it too late to have some T-shirts or baseball caps printed with the logo?

"I got an offer on the brewery," she said abruptly. She'd wanted both to keep the information to herself until she figured out whether to accept it or not and to have a chance to talk it out. Rather, she had wanted to talk to Berit about it, but she was floating around Florida and the East Coast during Whitman's month-long winter break. Tace had known Allie for years and trusted her opinion, but Berit was tied to the brewery in Tace's mind. She'd been part of the journey to develop the first seasonal ale, and Tace didn't think she'd have broken through her self-imposed barriers to marketing her product without Berit's input. Her advice had helped Tace secure a place for her beers at Margaret's winery, and now Chetham Hill offered the two ales and the rotating seasonal. They'd been a big hit, and Tace had been working on a plan to get more wineries to carry them as well when Joan had called with the name of an interested buyer.

"It's not a fortune, but I think it's a generous offer since the business isn't exactly solvent yet. It'd cover my second mortgage and most of what I've invested."

Allie raised her glass. "Congratulations! I know how hard you've been working at two jobs. What a relief to get your money out of the place. You'll have more time off and you can stop taking in boarders."

"Exactly," Tace said. She lifted her glass in answer to Allie's toast, but didn't take a drink. "A relief."

Why didn't it feel like one? She'd been busting her ass ever since she made a deal with Margaret and with two restaurants in quick succession last October. Joseph needed an assistant to help with the extra workload, and Tace had taken the job instead of hiring someone else. She told herself she only wanted to save money, but she knew the reasons were more complicated and scary than that. After her weekend with Berit in the wheat fields and at the balloon festival, she'd felt herself falling out of control. She was falling for Berit—especially after the kiss they'd shared. But being with Berit required Tace to make a choice about her future. She'd never had the luxury of making more than sketchy plans. Money, family, obligations—those had kept her grounded in the present. Occasional lovers had come and gone, but she'd been sort of passive about letting them in and out of her life. They *happened* to her. If Tace listened to her libido and pursued Berit, she'd be making the choice to either be in a relationship that was doomed to end with Berit's expiration date on her time in Walla Walla, or she'd be making the decision to follow Berit wherever she went next.

The latter was too frightening to contemplate. She'd taken on more responsibility at the brewery partly to avoid spending too much time with Berit until she figured out what she wanted. And Tace wasn't accustomed to running her life according to what she wanted.

"What do you do there, anyway?" Allie asked. "Just taste beer every day?"

Tace laughed. "Actually, we do sample the worts quite often, to make sure the finished product will be consistent and to see if we need to make changes to the formula based on the specific batch of hops or grain we've used. Quality control, just like you do with the food you serve."

"But with alcohol. I'm jealous."

"Tasting the same beers day after day gets old after a while."

"After how long?"

Tace shrugged. "I'll have to let you know. Sometime over ten years apparently, since Joseph hasn't reached that point yet. But I'm sure it's bound to happen to us."

Tace couldn't hide her grin. She looked forward to every backbreaking sack of malted barley she'd carried and every sip of ale or stout she'd tasted. Not because she was playing around and drinking beer on the job, but because she was increasingly proud of what they were creating. The beers were getting better and better, and the good ones were getting more and more consistent across batches. Tace had never felt such a tangible form of accomplishment. Besides needing a little space from Berit, she'd taken on the role of Joseph's assistant because she was getting more wrapped up in the beer-brewing process, wanting to learn every aspect from the ground up.

She was falling for the brewery, too.

"Well, once it's sold, you'll still be able to drink it whenever you want, but without the added trouble of doing the gardening and paying the bills. A simple bar tab will seem like nothing to you after this."

Tace laughed along with Allie, but she felt a frown tugging on the corners of her mouth as she did. She forced a lighthearted smile on her face and an easy tone in her voice for the next hour, and then she set her empty glass on the table.

"I should go," she said. "I have to be at the brewery early tomorrow and then I'm closing at Drake's."

Allie stood when she did and gave her another hug. "Soon we'll be back to normal. You'll just have the store, a job you leave at the end of your shift and don't need to worry about after-hours. We'll be able to spend more time together, at least until you pick up the prettiest woman at the bar, like you used to do."

Tace shook her head. "Seems like a lifetime ago," she said. "See you soon, Allie. You'll have to come see the brewery sometime. You can taste test with us."

Tace walked out of the bar expecting a cold winter wind. When she'd gone inside, the temperature had been in the twenties, and she'd had snow up to her ankles, but now the breeze was at least thirty degrees warmer. A chinook wind. Tace wasn't sure what caused the phenomenon, but chinooks had been part of her life forever. Sometimes they only lasted minutes, other times they blew for hours, melting snow and ice. She'd always woken Chris and Kyle for them if they happened during the night, and she'd take them to Pioneer Park to play with the other kids who magically appeared along with the wind.

Tace closed her eyes and let the warmth muffle her from the rest of the world. She'd always loved these times because they seemed magical in a life filled with mostly unmagical moments. Out of time, out of place. She felt as if she was in a snow globe, but instead of flakes, heat was swirling around her. She opened her eyes again. She wished Berit were here. Tace could picture her beautiful face as she experienced the shift in temperature and feel of the air. Her eyes would have been bright and fascinated, her lips slightly opened as she threw her head back and let the wind buffet her.

Tace started walking toward home. She pulled off her heavy jacket and wool sweater until she was down to the tank top she wore underneath. She contemplated throwing herself into the closest snow drift. She needed to cool off somehow. Her thoughts of Berit were increasingly arousing—she'd considered Berit sexy from the start, but her desire for Berit had grown exponentially as Tace learned more about her. Talking to her, sharing life with her, reading her books…Physical was always resistible, if necessary, but Tace was attracted to Berit in ways that went far beyond her body, ways not so easy to resist.

Tace veered off her usual path and cut across Whitman's campus. She sat on a bench on the edge of the quad and watched an impromptu nighttime game of football on the snowy field. Tace figured most of the students must be out here, wearing shorts and T-shirts after weeks bundled in winter gear. They were walking or sitting or having snowball fights in the temporary heat wave, while their laughter carried on the breeze.

She'd always avoided Whitman whenever possible, and would never have considered using the campus as a shortcut to her house. Lately, though, since Berit had been gone, Tace had taken to coming here now and then. She'd found stone benches where she could watch mallards swim lazily on a hot-spring fed pond, and boulders to sit on while she read under the bare branches of oaks and horse chestnuts. She didn't have much free time between the store and the brewery, but most of what she did have was spent on the campus. She felt silly using this as a way to feel closer to Berit, but she'd discovered some peaceful oases on the campus. She couldn't get away for days at a time to hike like she used to, and this small touch of nature helped her unwind when she needed a break.

She'd even become a regular in the bookstore. She had felt self-conscious and conspicuous when she first went in there to get Berit's texts, but no one had seemed to pay much attention to her—except, of course, as someone who knew Berit. Now, she was recognized by most of the staff, and she didn't care about being noticed anymore. She shook her head, surprised at the changes she'd experienced since last summer. The other day, one of the clerks had greeted her when she walked into the store and told her he had put aside a new geology book he thought she'd like. If someone had told her six months ago that she'd have college students recommending books for her...

But everything had shifted since Berit. Tace seemed to accept any excuse to walk by Olin Hall these days—never going in, of course, but remembering the day she'd helped Berit move some of her mementos there. She'd accused Berit of caring more than she wanted to admit about teaching, and she smiled to think how she'd been proven right. After that day, Berit had seemed to plunge deeper into her job. She'd devoted more time to her students, even becoming an advisor for an extracurricular club in the Classics department. Even if Tace hadn't been very busy herself, she'd rarely have seen Berit. She sometimes wondered if Berit was avoiding her, like she was Berit. They'd managed, between their two packed schedules, to dodge any opportunity to be alone and close like they'd been in the wheat fields. Tace didn't have any doubt that Berit had felt their connection as strongly as she had when they'd kissed. But Berit had plans beyond this town and anyone in it. And Tace didn't want to be left behind when Berit followed her dreams.

Tace shifted her feet in the slushy snow. It was beginning to melt in the unseasonable warmth, and the layer of slush would most likely turn to ice overnight as the temperature returned to normal. Driving would be hazardous on the slick roads, but Tace wouldn't stay home. She'd slip and slide her way into her brewery's valley. She might not make it back up the hill in time to get to Drake's, but she didn't care so much about that. She had her priorities.

Allie was right. Tace needed to sell the brewery and go back to only having one job. Allie had probably noticed the same gaunt and worn look Tace saw every time she looked in a mirror. Yes, she was right. Tace's retail job was easy to leave at the end of the day, while the brewery was constantly on Tace's mind. She'd never expected to be one of those people so consumed by their work that they joked they were married to it. Berit was one of them—she lived for her career, and felt lessened when she wasn't on a dig somewhere exotic. She didn't work regular hours and walk away from the office at the end of the day. Archaeology lived in her heart and mind all the time. The brewery was consuming Tace in the same way.

Tace scraped some snow off the arm of the bench and formed a snowball. She packed it tight and tossed it from hand to hand. She was about to throw it at a nearby bike rack when she stopped suddenly, captured by the way she'd compared herself to Berit.

Was this why she'd wanted to talk to Berit about the offer on the brewery? She'd even considered calling her and sharing the news over the phone. Tace could picture Berit's reaction to the chance to sell. She'd encouraged Tace to be more confident when approaching potential customers. To be proud of what she was crafting and not to hide her belief in the quality of her beers. Tace had taken her words to heart over the past few months, but she'd only thought of her actions in terms of selling more beer, promoting her brewery, making the business marketable. Not in terms of following a budding and unexpected dream of her very own.

Berit would encourage her to wait. To give the brewery and herself an opportunity to grow. Not to give up on something Berit knew Tace enjoyed. She'd have said the words Tace wanted to hear but hadn't dared whisper even in her mind.

Cut back on your hours at Drake's. Devote even more time to the brewery. Give it a chance to become your career because you love it, and not to be a sideline occupation just so you can sell it.

Passion. Tace had lived without passion for anything other than her family since the day her mother walked out. Suddenly, she was consumed by it. For Berit and for her business.

Tace got up and threw the snowball as hard as she could toward the top of an evergreen sequoia. She hit the tree about three-quarters of the way up and knocked snow off a large branch. Maybe she'd follow imaginary Berit's advice and take a chance on herself for once. Her efforts had already made the brewery more appealing to buyers. Maybe someday she could make it profitable. Or at least self-sustaining.

And her other passion? Her growing attraction to Berit? Conversely, the more she cared for Berit and the more she appreciated the way Berit supported her and helped her grow, the more she wanted to run away from her feelings. Because she was going to hurt like hell when Berit ran away from her and back to her nomadic life.

CHAPTER FIFTEEN

B erit rapped on the door with her ornate new cane and didn't stop until Tace flung it open with a peeved expression on her face. When she saw Berit on her porch—three days earlier than Berit had told her she'd be arriving—a smile slowly spread across Tace's face and directly into Berit's heart. She'd wanted to surprise Tace, to get an unrehearsed response from her, to find out if Tace had missed her as much as she'd been missed. Berit got the answer she'd been both hoping for and afraid of.

"You weren't supposed to be here until Thursday," Tace said. "I couldn't figure out why someone would be banging on my door so obnoxiously."

They stood on opposite sides of the doorway for few seconds, as if neither was sure whether to greet with a handshake or a hug. Berit made the choice for them and stepped across the threshold and grabbed Tace in a quick, but tight hug.

"I wanted to show you my new cane," Berit said. She held the smooth oak cane with an intricate brass collar out for Tace to inspect.

"Fancy," Tace said, fingering the delicate Greek key pattern on the collar. "Congratulations. You must be healing well."

"My doctors were impressed by how thoroughly I followed their instructions." Berit released her hold on her duffel bag when Tace tugged on it. She followed Tace into the house and sat on the faded floral sofa. "To be honest, so was I."

Tace sat across from Berit on a green recliner with the bag at her feet. "You had a lot of incentive to get healthy again. You'll be ready to get back to your real work once school's out, I suppose?"

"Yes," Berit said, without elaborating. She'd spent some of her break in Florida going through testing and starting her physical therapy. The rest of the time, she'd been in DC with an old university friend, researching digs and sifting through options for summer. She'd had Tace in mind the whole time. She'd missed her company, but she'd also allowed an occasional dream of a future where the two of them were connected. She wasn't ready to talk about her thoughts yet, and she doubted Tace was ready to hear them. She'd wait until the time was right. "I guess we can take out the ramp now, and I can let you have your rooms again."

"Why don't you stay downstairs for now, but at the price we originally set for rent. The climb to the attic is steep, and we're both settled in place." Tace paused for a moment. "I sort of like being upstairs. It's cozy, and I feel like a kid again sometimes. I guess I'm not quite ready to return to the grown-up bedroom."

Berit joined in Tace's laughter. She was relieved, since she'd been worried about going up and down the stairs every day. Her bravado and elegant cane masked a still-healing and often sore body. "Thank you," she said. "I get tired easily, and I have a feeling my muscles will be protesting once I get working with a physical therapist here. I'm nowhere near one hundred percent. Maybe thirty, on a good day."

"I'm sure you'll improve fast now that you're able to walk and move more freely. I'll have the contractor out to take down the ramp. Maybe I can donate it to someone in the area and have it installed for them."

Berit felt the warmth of attraction for Tace. Of course she would think of donating the ramp. She wasn't ostentatious with her kindness, or trying to seek approval. She helped in a quiet, matter-of-fact way when she saw a need, like she had with Berit all last semester.

"You still travel light," Tace said, standing and putting the bag's strap over her shoulder. "I thought you might have brought more books or relics back with you."

She carried the duffel into the bedroom and Berit followed. "I did buy some reference books for this coming semester and I got some prints framed for my office walls. You'll be relieved to hear I'm having them shipped directly to the campus instead of making you tote them around."

Tace put the bag on Berit's bed and stretched with her hands on her lower back. "Thank goodness. I'm still aching from my afternoon of being your pack mule."

They faced each other in the bedroom. Another awkward moment. Berit wanted to step closer, but she waited. "How was your Christmas?"

Tace shrugged, her face expressionless. "Like any other day. Kyle's still out of touch, and Chris stayed in Oregon with her housemates. Even Joseph went back to Everett to see his family. What about yours?"

Berit mimicked Tace's shrug. "I had my first serious PT session two days before Christmas, so I was out of commission for a few days after. I sat in my hotel room and studied for this term's classes over the holidays."

Tace walked out of the room and gently bumped Berit's shoulder as she passed. "I'm glad you're back. And it should be a great semester for you. You sound more prepared for teaching, and your office will actually appear to be occupied. Coffee?"

"Sure." Berit limped after Tace. Tace was right—her office would now contain the books she'd shipped, as well as stuffed file folders and information packets for the jobs she was considering. She'd agreed to be on the search committee to fill the vacancy she was leaving here at Whitman, and she had stacks of information on potential candidates. Kim had told her to fill her office and she was—but mostly with papers and forms designed to get her out of Whitman and get someone here in her stead.

She had some good leads on excavations, and she'd love to lead almost any of them as long as it meant she was out of here. One stood out from the rest, though. A dig in Baja, searching a promising site for cave paintings and rudimentary dwellings. Not in her field of expertise, and not in an exciting, dangerous area. She wasn't even certain why she was drawn to it, except that she could picture Tace there. She'd love it. The area was beautiful, judging from the photos Berit had seen. She could imagine Tace finding a cave full of paintings, or identifying birds and stars as she explored this new place. Berit let her mind roam. Weekends in Cabo, sipping margaritas. Nights under a velvet expanse of sky, sharing a tent and making love in the vast silence. She'd never wanted a companion on a dig before, preferring to spend her time off work in a solitary way, but she wanted Tace with her, and she'd broach the subject once Tace was free to go.

"How's the brewery?" she asked, continuing her train of thought out loud.

Tace handed her a mug of coffee. "Good," she said. "We're sponsoring a division in an upcoming bike race, and I've expanded into three other bars since you were here last." She hesitated and stirred her coffee with a nervous, clanking sound of spoon on ceramic. "I got an offer on it last week."

"You did?" Berit knew she must be wearing a goofy grin. "That's wonderful. Is it enough?"

Tace furrowed her brow, as if she was taken aback by Berit's enthusiasm. Berit didn't understand why—this was what Tace had been working toward.

"It's enough. I'd be back where I started, or close to it."

Aha. Berit saw Tace's expression shift when she said those words. Back where she started. Before she got involved with the brewery and caught in the joy of creating and making a name for herself.

"You don't want to sell," Berit said in a subdued voice.

Tace shook her head. "I love working there, whether I'm brainstorming a new seasonal or pulling weeds. It's fun, and I feel good about what I'm making. About myself. I can't explain what it's like when someone compliments one of my ales, or a restaurant owner wants to expand what he offers because the beer is selling so well."

"I think I understand," Berit said. She did. She'd felt the same way every time she'd dug up a shard of plain pottery or an astonishing intact vase. Accomplishment and pride. How often had Tace experienced them for herself, not just for something her sister did?

Tace looked deep in her coffee mug, not meeting Berit's eyes. "I guess I thought you'd be excited about me wanting to keep the brewery. I know selling is the sensible thing to do..."

Berit doubted Tace had had many cheerleaders in the past. Berit would have to be one now. She mentally ripped up the application she'd already filled out for the Baja dig. "Of course I'm excited for you. You've made amazing improvements in such a short time, and there's no telling what you can do if you really commit yourself. I meant what I said in the wheat fields—your whole face lights up when you talk about hops and yeast. You obviously have found your vocation, and what's better in life than truly loving your work?"

Berit felt her conviction slip when she mentioned the wheat fields. Where they had shared a kiss Berit still tasted every night when she was in bed alone. She and Tace were good together, but Berit had spent her adult life enjoying a passion for her chosen field. Tace deserved the same experience. Any selfish desire to encourage Tace to sell was smashed by the smile on Tace's face when she heard Berit's words.

Berit sighed. No going back now. "I've been hearing a lot about this brewery of yours, but I've never actually seen it. How about taking me there for a tour and a free glass of your famous beer?"

❖

After hearing Tace talk about the brewery's run-down condition and the amount of weeding she had to do, Berit was expecting a lean-to in the middle of a field of dandelions and thistles. Instead, she was surprised to see a brown and beige metal building surrounded by a neat snow-covered lawn dotted with trees. Their branches were bare now, but in the spring they'd be lush and green. The whole area had the feel of a mountain meadow, secluded from the road and casually arranged. Berit saw the perfect spot for some tables and chairs, where customers could sit in the shade and sample Tace's beers.

"Those are redbuds." Tace pointed to a row of trees lining the driveway. "In the spring they'll be covered with pink blossoms. And over there are horse chestnuts and the smaller ones are dogwoods."

"It's going to be beautiful," Berit said, leaning on her cane and looking around the charming space. A sudden howl caught her attention, and she turned to see a small black-and-white cat running toward Tace and meowing.

"This is Suds," Tace said, picking up the cat and scratching under its chin.

"Because of the white mustache? Cute." Berit moved closer and patted the kitten on the head, feeling the rumble of his purrs vibrate under her hand. She felt an even deeper vibration when her fingers brushed against Tace's. She let their contact linger for a moment before stepping away. Tace set the cat down and he ran ahead of them to the brewery, scooting through a metal-framed cat door.

Tace held the door for Berit, and she stepped into a room full of shiny metal tanks of different shapes and sizes. She was staring at them and wondering how on earth anyone could keep them so clean when a man suddenly appeared at her side. Berit jumped in surprise and she heard Tace laugh behind her.

"Berit, this is Joseph, Bike Trail's brewmaster. Joseph, my friend Berit. Are you brewing the IPA today?" she asked while Berit shook hands with him.

"Yep. I can tap a keg for you, if you want. We only have the stout tapped right now."

"We can have some of the stout after our tour," Tace said. "I thought we'd taste our way through the brewing process first."

Joseph nodded. "I'll be around if you need me."

"He scared the crap out of me, too, the first time I met him," Tace said after Joseph climbed a ladder and vanished behind some tanks. "He has ninja skills."

"I hear they come in handy when you're brewing beer. So, what were you saying about tasting our way through the brewery? I can't wait to start."

"Come on. We'll start in the malt room."

Berit took the arm Tace offered and they walked slowly toward another door. Inside were huge sacks of grain. Berit sniffed. "I think I smell caramel."

"You'll get aromas of caramel and chocolate and toffee, depending on how long they were roasted. Here, taste the difference between this pilsner malt and this 2-row. We combine them in our IPA."

Tace touched the different sacks while she talked. She dipped a stainless-steel scoop into one of the bags and held Berit's hand in hers as she poured a few grains into her palm. Tace had always seemed physically detached from the outside world to Berit. An observer, whether of nature, stars, or other people. Here at the brewery, however, she was more tactile, connecting with the space around her in a way Berit hadn't noticed before, except during their kiss in the wheat fields. Then, Tace had held her and had felt extremely present.

Berit kept her hand cradled in Tace's while she picked up some grain and nibbled on it.

"What do you taste?"

"A raw nutty flavor. This darker one is a little sweet, too, and almost smoky. It's the roasted malt?"

"Yes, the pilsner." Tace scooped a few even darker grains out of another sack. "Try this. It's chocolate malt."

Berit tried it and made a face. "It doesn't taste like a chocolate malt. I get a little hint of molasses and dark pecans, though."

Tace laughed and squeezed Berit's hand before she let go. "The name refers to the color and roasting level, not to any milkshake-y qualities it might have. Malt is grain that's been prepared for milling. Usually barley for beer, but sometimes other grains like wheat, which we use for our hefeweizen. The grain is soaked, sprouted, dried, and roasted, but I don't know much more about the process." Tace tossed the uneaten grains in a sealed trash can and motioned for Berit to lead the way out of the room. "We buy malt instead of prepping the grain ourselves, and I need to learn more about it before I can decide if we'll keep doing it this way."

Berit admired how easily Tace admitted what she didn't know. She'd obviously learned a lot about the brewery's operations—throwing around terms like *knocking out* and *pitching yeast* with the assurance of a pro—but she seemed eager to learn more. Berit was increasingly seeing herself in Tace. Berit had met the challenge of archaeology the same way, devouring all the knowledge she could get and never being satisfied with remaining stagnant and content with what she knew. Tace had the same passion for this artisanal craft. Berit missed the intensity of living with passion. She was more interested in teaching this semester, but she wasn't consumed by it. Part of her was held back.

Nothing of Tace was held back here at the brewery. Not only was she enthusiastic about the brewing, but she was also more at ease and physical with Berit. She seemed to take any excuse to make contact, frequently putting her hand on Berit's waist or hip or arm. Berit had no complaints. She had made the decision to support Tace wholeheartedly in her choice to devote herself to the brewery, and Tace had never been anything but understanding of Berit's desire to leave this town far behind. The mutual understanding of their futures seemed to open them to intimacy in the present.

"This is a mash tun. The malt is steeped, or mashed, and the sugar and water extract is what will feed the yeast during the fermentation process." Tace opened a valve on the massive steel tank and poured a small amount of cloudy liquid into one of the numerous tasting glasses that sat next to almost every tank.

Berit took the glass and swirled the liquid along the sides. She motioned toward the pile of glasses. "Looks like you do a lot of tasting here."

"At every step of the process," Tace said. "I'm starting to learn what the finished product will taste like when I sample it during the different stages."

Berit raised her glass in a mock salute and took a sip. She winced. "Wow, that's sweet."

"Is it?" Tace asked in a throaty voice. She leaned closer and softly brushed her tongue across Berit's lips. "Mmm, you're right. I guess I wasn't kidding when I said sugar water." She laughed when Berit shoved at her playfully.

"When does it actually taste like beer?" Berit asked.

"We're getting there." Tace put her hands on Berit's hips and aimed her at the next stop on their tour. She let her arm linger around Berit's waist, and Berit leaned into the contact. She was enjoying the cramped quarters between tanks because her body was in near-constant contact with Tace's. Reality was suspended in here, where Tace was exploring dreams she'd never known she had. Berit had a feeling Tace's ease and confidence might fade when she left this place.

"We can add hops two ways," Tace said. She pulled a dried hop bud out of a bag and put it in Berit's hand, closing Berit's fingers around it and pressing to crush the bud into flakes. "Smell."

"Definitely floral," Berit said. The combination of Tace's lavender scent and the hops made her remember their morning together when they'd come up with the IPA. So long ago, when they'd barely known each other, but even then Berit had seen the way creating beer interested Tace. And even then, Berit had been part of the process. She liked knowing she'd always be tied to Tace and her brewery. "Maybe a little fruity and bitter."

"Yes, exactly. And those flavors will come through more or less depending on when we add the hops. We can add them during boiling, and the result will be bitter, like the IPA. It'll mellow by the time we fill the kegs. And we do a lot of dry hopping here, putting little sachets of hops directly into the keg. Then you'll get more of the floral notes and less bitterness. Taste."

Tace used a syringe-type instrument to pull some beer from a tank and put it in a glass for Berit. She drank some, still expecting the sweetness she'd experienced earlier, and the sharpness of the hopped wort caught her off guard. "Ugh." She gestured at her mouth. "Want a taste?"

Tace grinned. "Definitely." She captured Berit's lips with more pressure this time, but Berit still felt Tace's caution. Berit wanted to be shoved against one of the steel tanks and kissed with all the passion she sensed in Tace. She wanted to make love on the catwalk above them until she had a diamond imprint on her back from the patterned metal walkway. But both she and Tace seemed too aware of fragility—in Berit's injury and their uncertain relationship. The small tastes of their desire were mind-blowingly arousing, and intimidating at the same time. They were here to sample, not to get drunk.

Berit shifted away and raised her hand to brush across Tace's cheek. She was flushed, but she hadn't had more than a lick of beer from Berit's lips.

"I have to say, this is my favorite way to taste through the process." Tace said. "Joseph and I usually just each have our own glass to sample."

Berit smiled. "Let's keep this method between us, shall we? Now, let's move to the next step. I'm eventually expecting a drinkable glass of beer."

CHAPTER SIXTEEN

G ood morning, Tace," Berit said. She stopped by the kitchen table where Tace was sitting and reading the paper, and kissed her cheek.

Berit rested her hand on Tace's shoulder and Tace gave it a squeeze. "Good morning to you, too."

Tace tried to get control of her reaction to the simple greeting while Berit walked to the counter and put bread in the toaster. She and Berit had eased away from romantic kissing after the tour of the brewery, when Tace had sampled every stage of the brewing process from Berit's lips. Tace had been caught up in her excitement over the decision to take a chance on her own business, and she'd felt natural kissing and touching Berit while in the sanctuary of the building. Once they'd left and returned to reality, Tace had been less confident about everything, especially her chances of making a future with the brewery and with Berit—she still held a stubborn glimmer of hope for the brewery, while she was resigned to loss in Berit's case. She wasn't sure of the reasons why Berit, too, had seemed content to shift into a more casual way of being together, but she was relieved when they'd both settled on occasional touches and brief kisses.

But even such laid-back contact left Tace with a constant pang of hunger for more. She watched Berit pour a mug of coffee and wanted to walk over and hold her tight. Kiss her until Berit dropped the mug and it shattered on the floor, just before her body shattered in orgasm...

"How far is Washington State University from here?" Berit asked.

Tace took a moment to recover from the shock of being wrenched out of her beautiful daydream to talk about WSU. "Pullman? It's just a little over two hours. Maybe longer since the roads are still icy."

"After spending so much time in eternally desert-hot countries, it's nice to live in a place that actually has distinct seasons," Berit said as she set her plate and mug on the table and sat down. "But why does winter have to be so long?"

Tace laughed at her put-out tone. "Don't worry. It'll be over soon, and you'll see how beautiful spring is around here. Why do you want to go to Pullman?"

"I need to get a book from their library for my Greek class."

Tace's science teacher in high school had wanted her to apply to his alma mater WSU, but Tace hadn't even given the idea any thought before she said no. She knew it was a good school for the sciences, with a strong veterinary medicine program, but she hadn't realized it offered a program in Berit's field as well. "Huh. I didn't know they had a Classics department. Is it a big one?"

Berit buttered her toast and avoided Tace's eyes. "Well, I don't think they even offer a degree in Classics anymore."

"Can't you have Whitman's library get the book on loan for you?"

"I could." Berit drew the word out for several syllables. "But I really need it for class on Monday."

"I thought you'd been preparing lectures in advance lately. I didn't realize you'd need reference books on such short notice." Tace felt as if she were talking to Kyle, trying to draw out a longer story, but only getting bits and pieces at a time. Berit was much more adorable when she seemed to be hiding something than Kyle, though, and Tace was enjoying her interrogation. Berit seemed to get more evasive and fidgety as Tace asked her questions.

"It's not really a reference book. There's a photo of a krater—a large vessel used for mixing wine and water—and I wanted to show it to my class. I can't find it online."

"And they need to see it because..." Tace prompted.

"Okay, I really don't *need* to show it to them, but I want to. It's for the class that's reading Euripides's *Herakles*."

"And Herakles is on this...what did you call it? A krater?" Tace was reading a copy of the play in translation, ostensibly so Berit could practice her lectures on Tace before she gave them in class. She'd enjoyed the discussions with Berit, though, and was getting as much out of the arrangement as Berit seemed to.

"No, it's the goddess of madness. In the original, Euripides uses Lyssa—signifying more of a rabid, animalistic madness—instead of Ate, with more human connotations of insanity. I just think it's interesting and might spark some good ideas for my next lecture."

"And you can't provide this spark with words. You need the picture of this goddess."

Berit shrugged. "I'd prefer to have the actual krater, but I doubt I can get my hands on it by Monday. I can, however, drive to Pullman before then. I work better with physical or visual prompts than with words."

"Is this as important to your teaching as the coasters are to my brewery?" Tace asked. She'd spent an entire afternoon searching for places to make coasters with her logo on them and designing shapes and layouts on paper with her nonexistent drawing skills. She had more important things to do at the brewery, at home, and at the store, and more fundamental steps to take for the business, but the coasters had been a day's obsession.

Berit shrugged. "About the same level of necessity, I suppose."

"It's the only day off I've had in weeks," Tace said, but she felt herself giving in to Berit's plan already. She'd resist at first, to assuage her guilt about avoiding work, but she understood how these small obsessions could mean a lot, especially when the larger and more vital aspects of the job could sometimes be too frightening to contemplate.

"Did I ask you to drive me?" Her expression, with its covert smile, showed she already knew Tace would take her, but she continued with the dance they had started. "I'll rent a car. Can you drive me to a car rental place?"

Tace sighed and gave up her pretense of being too busy to go. She'd just have spent the day sitting here, anyway. Besides, Berit still wasn't supposed to be doing much driving, especially in winter conditions when she might have to turn or brake quickly. If Berit needed to go on a quest to find a photo, then Tace would support her.

"I'll drive you to Pullman," she said. "We should get going soon, though, so we're not on the road back after dark. It'll be a sheet of ice out there."

"I'll be ready in five minutes," Berit said. She gave Tace a hard kiss on the lips as she walked by. "Thank you."

Tace would have agreed to drive Berit anywhere for another kiss like that one. She folded her newspaper and went to put on warmer clothes. She had to admit, though, she'd been easily convinced to procrastinate. She'd cut back on her time at the store, then had immediately accepted any extra hours available there. She had spent the last three weeks working more than she had when she was full-time. For someone normally steadfast to a fault, she was having a hard time following through with her commitment to the brewery. And to herself. The thought of getting out of town, even if it meant going to Pullman, where the university was really the only draw, was enticing.

Of course, being in a car for such a long time with Berit was appealing, no matter the destination. Tace drove through the snow-covered fields and tiny towns as they wound along Highway 12, and she marveled at how easy it was to talk to Berit. They bantered back and forth, or shared stories about Suds and Joseph or the students in Berit's classes. Tace had thought—when they first met last August—that she'd never be able to hold Berit's interest, but she had lost her misgivings about being with someone with so much more education than she had. She traced the beginning of her confidence back to Berit's first day of classes, when Tace had been able to provide comfort and compassion, but the feeling of compatibility had grown incrementally since then.

Of course, the added element of physical contact helped keep Tace both at ease with Berit, and almost electrically charged at the same time. They held hands when the driving was smooth, and when Tace needed both hands on the wheel in tricky spots, Berit rested her palm on Tace's neck and gently played her fingers through Tace's hair.

When Tace finally parked near WSU's campus in Pullman, she was ready to get a hotel room for her and Berit. The constant touching—no matter how nonsexual—and the easy conversation between them were somehow more intimate than any overtly sexual interchange Tace had ever had with another woman. She helped Berit out of the car and kept their arms linked because the sidewalks were slick in places. She wanted to drag her quickly to the library, get the book she needed, and find someplace where she could take Berit's clothes off. Instead, they walked slowly toward a wide brick staircase and stopped at the foot of it to check the map Berit had printed out at home.

"Have you been here before?" Berit asked, turning the map clockwise and frowning.

Tace looked over her shoulder, and then pointed at one of the squares on the map. "I think we're in front of this building. I've driven past here on my way to Spokane before, but I've never stopped. It was bad enough living in a college town. I'd never purposefully drive two hours just to visit another one."

Berit looked at her. "It sounds like it was bad for you, being a townie. Is that why you didn't want to go to college?"

Tace leaned against the railing of the staircase, putting a little distance between her and Berit. Part of her was always waiting to be judged and found lacking because she didn't have a degree. No matter how much fun she and Berit had together, and no matter how strong the attraction between them, Tace honestly wouldn't be surprised if Berit decided she didn't matter enough to remain friends. She wondered when she'd ever be able to trust in someone like Berit's feelings enough to be confident in a relationship with her.

"I didn't *not* want to go to college, and I didn't want to go either. It wasn't an option, that's all." Tace frowned. "My chemistry teacher wanted me to apply here, but I figured why bother trying if I got accepted but couldn't go? I couldn't have left before Chris and Kyle got through school, even if it hadn't been a matter of money."

She struggled to recall the specific times she'd been harassed when she was younger. "To be honest, I'm not sure if it was really as bad as I remember it being, living so close to Whitman. There were some jerks, definitely, who bullied any townie they could find, but I think my resentment about not having choices or chances might have colored my past experiences with the other, less mean ones." Tace paused, surprised by how easy it was to get some perspective when she didn't believe she was as limited as she had been back then. Even though she hadn't considered college an option, she remembered the interests she'd had. She was using most of them in unexpected ways now as she studied the brewing process. "I had fleeting moments of dreams for the future—maybe studying chemistry or geology, or going to a tech school for culinary arts. But I never took them seriously, and never, never let myself believe in them."

Berit leaned against her side, and Tace was warmed by the contact with her. "But now you have a chance to do something for yourself. You might not have taken the traditional route of college right after high school, but look at the experiences you've had. You were a mother, not just a sister, and you've worked in fascinating jobs. You've studied the natural world around you. And now you're using your talents and the skills you've acquired at the brewery."

Tace put her arm around Berit and rubbed her back. Moments before, touching Berit had aroused Tace. Now she felt comfort from their closeness. Berit was becoming so many things to her—a safe place, a good friend, a loyal supporter, a fantasy that kept her up at night. Tace had experienced them in separate women before, but never had one woman had the potential to be everything for her. Why couldn't she have discovered this kind of multidimensional relationship with another townie? Someone who could be in her life for the long run?

"You've made me rethink my general disgust for anything academic. No, don't laugh, I really mean this. I think I condemned Whitman and the people who were connected with the college because I knew I had no chance of going myself. I'd never be good enough because I didn't have enough money or time or freedom to get a degree. But I have more possibilities now." Tace released some of the tight hold she kept on her aspirations and let her imagination tentatively explore some potential steps forward. "I could study brewing, or do some business classes. Or not. Either way, I'm making the choices now. I guess some of the jealousy and anger I felt for kids with more opportunities is disappearing."

Berit leaned forward and kissed Tace on the lips. Just like that, comfort and friendship were pushed to the side by Tace's more determined physical desire. She resisted the urge to wrap her fingers in Berit's short hair and pull her into a deeper kiss.

"People should be judged by what they do and who they are, not by what degree they have," Berit said. She brushed her fingertips over Tace's mouth, and Tace could see a passion that matched her own in Berit's expression.

"I wanted that courtesy for myself, but I didn't always offer it to other people," Tace admitted. She'd considered college students and people with degrees to be elitist, without giving them a chance to prove they were otherwise. "Double standard."

"Well, I'm glad you let me get close, even though I have my degrees and am soon to win the title of Worst Professor of the Year from Whitman."

Tace laughed and tucked Berit's hand in her arm. She took the map from her and started walking toward the library. "Everything will change once you have this picture for your class on Monday. You'll be voted Most Inspiring."

"I'll settle for Traveled Farthest to Get a Reference Book She Didn't Really Need."

"The trophy will need to be huge to get all those letters on it," Tace joked.

She and Berit laughed and teased as they walked across the large university campus. Tace felt relieved to have admitted her shortcomings and her own biases against anyone connected to higher education. Getting past those old habits would take time—and her sense of self-worth wouldn't heal overnight—but Tace recognized the hurt behind her judgments now. She was feeling more comfortable allowing herself to consider options and choices in her future, ones that would heal the old wounds she'd kept hidden because she had to take care of other people before herself. Berit had helped. Not just because she seemed to accept and like Tace for who she was, but also because she had proven to Tace that even a well-respected and brilliant scholar had more to her than a degree. Berit was witty, self-deprecating, silly, and the most primal and sexual woman Tace had ever encountered. When she had first walked into Tace's life, she had only been a professor in Tace's eyes. Now she was so much more. And she was changing Tace's life in ways she'd never imagined.

CHAPTER SEVENTEEN

Berit stared out the window of the car as Tace drove through the steep streets of Pullman and back to the highway. She'd been on a high all day and was now feeling a letdown from which she couldn't break free. She'd had a great time with Tace, enjoying their frequent contact. Lately, ever since the brewery tour, they'd fallen into a comfortable rapport. Touching and kissing often, but not forcing the relationship to go further than first-date casualness. They'd shared meals and discussions at the kitchen table. Aside from the near-constant sense of sexual frustration, Berit had been feeling content.

She frowned at her reflection in the passenger-side window. Contentment was something Berit avoided at all costs. She'd never felt it as a child, when instability and chaos had been the best ways to describe her home life. She'd never trusted contentment as an adult because she knew it wouldn't last. It would eventually turn into disillusionment, disenchantment, boredom.

She had gotten a glimpse of her former life—the one she was aching to return to—when she had been digging around for a good photo of the incarnation of madness. She'd felt the excitement of unearthing a rare find, the joy of sharing it with Tace and soon with her students. But she had only found a photo of the result of someone else's labor. She was too far removed from the actual discovery to make it her own. The elation of finally holding the book in her hands was a poor simulacrum of what she experienced after excavating something magnificent or mundane on a dig. The light and optimistic feelings she'd had on the drive here and during her talk with Tace on the brick staircase had disappeared in a blink once she'd filled out the inter-library-loan form, and she was left deflated.

"The suicide rate must be astronomical around here, with all this nothingness to look at day after day." Berit knew she sounded cranky, but she couldn't help it. Wheat fields stretched for miles on either side of the car, exacerbating her foul mood and reminding her of her exile in this foreign landscape.

Tace seemed unfazed by Berit's irritability. "Where you see nothingness, I see sustenance. Rich soil hiding under the snow, with the potential for growth. In the spring, the fields will be covered with shoots, all different shades of green. During harvest, the breeze will make the fields ripple like melted gold, like a hefeweizen pouring into a glass."

Berit snorted, trying not to laugh, but sounding instead like she was disparaging Tace's remarks. "Beer poetry. Nice."

"You've been in a pissy mood since we got your book. Care to tell me what's wrong?"

Berit sighed, regretting her tone. "I'm just feeling the letdown. I'm sorry. I wish I had been uncovering the krater myself instead of just tracking down a photo of it. I wish I were—"

"Anywhere but here," Tace finished for her. "Seriously, Berit, you should wear it on a sign around your neck, then you won't feel compelled to say it every five minutes."

"You don't know what I was about to say," Berit said, her voice rising. Of course, Tace had been correct to the letter, but Berit didn't want to admit it. She didn't want to face how surly she was being. "You finished my sentence without really knowing what I was thinking."

"Oh, okay. Were you going to say I wish I were able to live here forever? I wish I were a wheat farmer?"

"No. You were right with the first one," Berit said, her emotions changing too quickly to follow. At least the anger was something she could hold on to, something she could use to energize herself. Once it went away, she was left with a confusing sadness. "I don't know what's wrong. I think I'm homesick for a patched-together tent in the middle of nowhere. I need to be on my knees digging a trench while the desert around me seems determined to keep refilling it with sand. I don't know who I am here."

Tace didn't look at her, but she reached over and took Berit's hand, lacing their fingers together. "Only four more months," she said. "You're over halfway through your sentence."

"With no time off for good behavior," Berit said, still hearing an edge to her voice. Tace's touch and words calmed her, but Berit didn't want calm right now. She wanted passion and freedom—freedom from this place.

Tace laughed. "Good behavior? Really? You should get time added on for sulky behavior, not time off."

Berit punched her playfully on the arm, some of her foul mood easing. She'd never had anyone with whom she could be so messily and honestly herself like she could with Tace.

"Do you mind a short detour?" Tace asked. "It won't add much time to our trip, and I want to show you something."

"Another wheat field?"

"No. Something different. You wanted a change, didn't you?"

"Yes, please."

Tace turned off the main highway and onto the smaller Highway 261. They drove in silence for a few miles while Berit sorted through her mixed-up feelings. Tace had let her explode a little bit, and the release had helped Berit figure out the core of her shift from excitement to an annoyed ennui.

"I was hoping this photo would stimulate something in me," she admitted in a quiet voice. "You were right last fall, when you said teaching matters to me. But since then I've really been trying to do better and I'm still a failure at it. I want out of here because

I'm good in the field. I want to feel accomplished and capable again."

"What's been going wrong in your classes? We've talked about the books you're using in them, and I've learned a lot and have had fun reading with you. How do you know your students aren't feeling the same?"

Berit shrugged. "I know. I don't get the same sense of focus that I get when you and I talk. They look out the windows or pretend to take notes when they're really writing other things. I was exactly the same when I had boring professors. I was hoping this picture might prove to be the catalyst for some great lecture, but now, when I look at it, I don't feel inspired at all."

Tace looked over at her, and Berit saw a slight frown change the angle of her elegant eyebrows. "You don't lecture me."

"Of course not. Why would I?"

"Well, whenever you mention teaching, you say you're planning a lecture or giving a lecture. But we have discussions. You ask me questions about what I'm reading, you don't just talk at me about it."

"A dialogue," Berit said. A sudden memory of a café in Athens, where she sat across from her grandfather and drank iced coffees while the white hot sun baked the patio umbrella over their heads, came into her mind. He'd ask her what she thought about the pieces they'd seen in a museum or at an ancient ruin. He never told her how to experience the world to which he was exposing her.

"Right. You're not there to entertain or bore the students. You're there to ignite a passion in them. How can you if you aren't engaging them in the material?"

Berit thought of the book sitting on the backseat. She'd hoped it would give her an hour's worth of words to say to her class, but it wouldn't. She could describe it and show the picture in less than a minute. But what it represented…researching, digging for information, decoding texts and visual images simultaneously. Trying to understand the ancient past given the few clues they had in the present. Deciding what could be—and what shouldn't be—inferred about the people whose lives they merely glimpsed.

Berit raised Tace's hand and kissed the back of it. Suddenly, she had ideas swarming through her mind for Monday's class, but she didn't feel the usual need to write them down on notecards or to outline her thoughts for a lecture. She had questions to ask the students, and opinions of her own to give. They'd interpret the text together.

"Here we are," Tace said, breaking Berit out of her reverie.

Berit got out of the car and looked around. Not exactly wheat fields, but the snow-covered sages and stubby trees gave a similar sense of monotony to the land as far as she could see. She heard a soft roar in the background—cars on a nearby highway?—but otherwise there was little to see or hear out here.

"Nice place," she said, not even trying to hide the sarcasm in her voice.

Tace got her cane out of the backseat and handed it to her. "Come on. It's right over here."

"What is?" Berit asked as she walked several paces behind Tace. "Monotony Mountain? Humdrum Hill?"

Tace shook her head and came back to Berit's side. She put her right arm through Berit's and took the cane with her left hand. "Close your eyes, smarty-pants. It's just a short walk."

Berit did as she was told and kept her eyes tightly shut while she walked forward under Tace's guidance. She was just marveling at how much trust she was willing to put in Tace, and wondering why the highway roar was getting louder, when Tace told her to open her eyes.

Berit walked the last few yards on her own, and the world seemed to open up right before her feet. A huge basalt cavern appeared below her as if out of nowhere, with a waterfall crashing over the side. It had been hidden from view in the bare landscape, and only when she was close did Berit feel the full effect of power and spray.

"Wow," she said. Simple, but true.

"Palouse Falls, about a two hundred foot drop. Look at the basalt walls. You can practically read the formative geology of this area in the layers, even when they're covered with ice. Volcanic eruptions, over and over, creating the land we're standing on right now. See how the basalt cooled in columns?" Tace moved behind her, without touching, and pointed over her shoulder. Berit experienced the closeness of her, the promise of her touch, like a warm shiver moving across her skin. "And look at that layer, where the rock looks crumbly. It's called flow-top breccia. The top crust of the lava flow would cool and harden, then get tumbled back into the molten stuff below."

"It's amazing," Berit said. Layers of rock, like layers from different time periods on a dig. To her, the surrounding rock had only been important because of the human materials it encased and preserved, or for use in dating a site. Determine its age, and then remove it. But here, she was able to just appreciate the physical world for what it was, not what it kept from view. The grandeur of the falls helped pull her out of the self-focused, self-pitying state she unaccustomedly found herself in more often than not these days.

Tace wrapped her arms around Berit's waist and held her close. "You're used to looking for hidden treasure, buried under layers of dirt. Part of what I love about this corner of the world is how overt the beauty is. History is thrust into the open. Visible, and part of daily life. You don't have to put down roots here, but you can at least appreciate the natural beauty of my home."

Berit turned in Tace's arms and cupped her face with both hands. "Have no doubt, Tace, that I appreciate the beauty I've found here." She kissed her gently, then with an increasing passion. "The falls are gorgeous, but they're nothing compared to you."

Tace sighed, and the sensation moved through Berit's arms and her belly where she was pressed against Tace. Berit kissed her again, moving beyond the pecks on the cheek and the tentative samples they'd been sharing. She'd been learning about Tace's layers and origins, too, over the months she'd been here. She'd discovered parts of Tace that were strong and solid, like the basalt columns, and the other parts where Tace was fragile and had broken bits. Every part of her was growing more and more precious to Berit.

Berit felt Tace's fingers twist in her hair. For too long, their kisses and touches had held hints of tension and too-tight control. Now, Tace's lips softened against hers, and Berit unwound like a snapped cable when their tongues gently slid around each other. Berit felt an almost violent sense of letting go when she and Tace moved together in their kiss, with their bodies snugly close and their hands pressing lips even closer. Her life had been about herself—through necessity as a child and out of habit as an adult. How she lived, how she loved, and now how she taught. Tace had forced her to look at teaching as a collaboration with her students, and now Tace was showing her how to kiss the same way.

And then all thoughts of teaching and classes faded away, and there was only Tace left, touching something inside Berit that she'd always kept hidden and protected. Berit could only let Tace be this close for a short time, could only give up her independence for this brief recuperative stay in Walla Walla, but the decision was made for her by the questioning movement of Tace's hand along the curve of her waist. While she was here, she'd give herself to this unfamiliar sense of partnership with everything she had. And when she left? Berit brushed her fingertips along the curve of Tace's breast and felt her respond with a sharp inhale and a deep sigh. Maybe, when she left, she'd fight to keep Tace with her…

Tace broke away and glanced across the parking lot when another car pulled in. She tugged on Berit's hand and led them back the way they'd come.

Once they were in the car, Tace turned to her and took her hand again. "I know you'll be leaving in June, and you know I'm tied to this place, as much now as I was when I had the kids to care for. But I want more with you, no matter how little time we have left. I want all of you."

"You're sure?" Berit asked. She'd made her choice a moment ago, but she wouldn't move forward unless she was certain Tace understood and accepted exactly what she was offering. But what had seemed logical and certain in her head became muddled when she tried to talk about it. "I want you, too, but I don't want to push. I even hoped…"

Tace used her index finger on Berit's chin to make Berit look at her. "What? You hoped what?"

"I found a job opening on the Baja Peninsula when I was looking for work over winter break," Berit said in a rush. She wanted to be with Tace, and she had to share what had been on her mind before she shared her body. This new intimacy she felt with Tace deserved no less. "It looked like a place you'd enjoy. I guess I thought if you sold the brewery…but I know how much it means to you, and I'm glad you decided to keep it. I'd never get in the way of your dreams just because mine will take me away."

Berit was rambling, but she wanted Tace to understand both sides of her conundrum. She wanted them to have the possibility of a future together, but she didn't want to interfere when Tace had just found a dream and career for herself.

Tace shook her head with a humorless laugh and looked out the window. "That's another difference between us," she said.

"What is?" Berit asked when Tace remained silent.

Tace turned back to her with a tinge of sadness in the curve of her mouth. "You hoped I might go with you," she said, her palm resting on Berit's cheek, "but I never once thought you might stay here with me."

Berit put her hand over Tace's but she didn't speak because she'd never considered that option, either.

CHAPTER EIGHTEEN

Tace followed Berit into her bedroom once they got home. The car ride had been tense and silent—not because they were angry, although Tace had lingering and muddled emotions from their various conversations during the day—but because they had made the decision together to wring as much out of their time together as possible, and Tace, at least, couldn't wait to start.

Tace understood Berit's passionate nature even though it seemed so different from her own calm and unwavering personality. She didn't have the highs and lows Berit did, and she figured even Berit didn't usually vacillate as much as she had since coming to Walla Walla. Berit had been struggling with pain, with an injury that kept her from doing anything with as much freedom as she was accustomed to having. Her career—her vocation—had been put on hold while she worked at a job she found meaningful, but not easy or natural. Some mood swings and some hurt masquerading as anger or frustration were perfectly normal.

Tace had gone through changes, too, since last August. She was taking a chance on herself, on a new job, and now on a short-term, but oh-so-promising affair with Berit. She'd been quiet on the drive because she'd been concentrating on holding herself together. One slip in her control and she'd have pulled the car over to the side of the highway and pounced on Berit right there. She'd made it home, but now she felt a hesitation even as she kept her hands on Berit's back while they walked, needing the contact between them.

Second thoughts? No, not a chance. She had wanted Berit from the start, and she'd finally made the choice to accept what Berit had to offer. She walked into Berit's bedroom, her old bedroom, and felt like a guest in there, among Berit's randomly strewn clothes and piles of books. The mix of knowing and not knowing was getting to her. She'd learned about Berit's past, about her emotions, and about her endearing swings between self-criticism and self-confidence, depending on whether she was in the field or not. But as deeply as she knew Berit, her body was still a mystery to be deciphered.

Tace faced Berit once they were close to the bed and rested her hands on Berit's hips. A kiss, gentle and brief at first, like the ones they'd shared lately. A nuzzle along Berit's collarbone, making Berit drop her head back with a sigh. A gentle move of her hips across Berit's, with the rough catch of denim and buttons to emphasize the promise of yielding softness underneath.

Tace's relationships had never been so laden with intimacy as this one. She'd meet women, they'd be attracted to one another, and they'd have sex. Rarely did the relationship last longer than a weekend, and never had Tace felt as invested as she was now. She undid the buttons on Berit's shirt one at a time, not knowing what she'd find underneath. She'd been living with her for over half a year, and she'd never seen her less than fully dressed. They'd supported each other through problems at work and had opened up to each other about private doubts and vulnerabilities but had never gone beyond a kiss.

Tace inhaled deeply as she traced the curve of Berit's breasts. Perfect, of course. She'd never doubted Berit's body would be as beautiful on the outside as Tace knew her heart was on the inside. Her mouth replaced fingertips, and through the intermediary of her tongue she felt Berit's breaths become shallower and more rapid. Tace held her steady with an arm around her waist and her lips closed firmly over Berit's nipple.

A sharp gasp from Berit, and the sweet pain of hands tangled tightly in her hair. Tace felt as if her knees would buckle at any moment, and—without releasing her sucking and nibbling hold on Berit's breast—she unbuttoned Berit's jeans and shoved them over her hips. She finally let Berit go and watched her shimmy out of the jeans and sit on the bed. Tace stepped forward, and Berit spread her thighs, welcoming Tace between them. She stood in front of Berit and just touched her—her hair, her eyelids, the curve of her cheekbone, the arch of her neck.

"You'll tell me if you hurt at all?"

Berit bit her lip and gave a half nod.

Tace laughed, enjoying Berit's playful smile and her own response to the combination of humor and seriousness they both seemed to feel. "I'm not convinced. You have to promise."

"What if I don't want you to stop?"

Tace shook her head and leaned down to kiss Berit, thrusting her tongue deep in Berit's mouth before she pulled away again. "If you say ouch I'll ease off and be gentler. I won't stop completely unless you tell me."

"Deal." Berit said. She put her hand on the back of Tace's neck and pulled her down for another soul-crushing kiss. When they pulled apart, Tace saw Berit's hands trembling as much as her own insides were. Berit scooted back on the bed and was about to lie down, but Tace stopped her.

"Lie on your stomach. I want to see where you were hurt."

Berit did as she asked, and Tace sat next to her hip and pressed tightly against her side. She forgot to look for Berit's scars for a moment, mesmerized instead by the beautiful lines of her back. She moved her hand over Berit from her neck, down her spine, and into the curve of her lower back. She traced every vertebra with barely any pressure, but still she felt the three small incision marks before she saw them. A fine web of thin white scars covered Berit's lower rib cage on her right side.

"Fracture and dislocation of the two thoracic vertebrae," Berit said, her voice muffled because she was resting her forehead on her crossed arms. "The surgeon was worried about the extent of trauma to my spinal cord, and that's why I had to be so careful at first. We weren't sure how well the area would heal, or if there'd be permanent damage. I also cracked a couple of lower ribs in the fall, and had a tiny puncture in my lung."

Tace cringed at the thought of what might have been. She'd only had vague descriptions of the extent of Berit's wounds and, in this case, would have preferred ignorance to the more detailed explanation of the reason Berit had come to Walla Walla. She braced a hand on either side of Berit's waist and leaned over to kiss the small scars before moving her lips beyond them, deep in the valley of Berit's lower back. Berit had been speaking matter-of-factly about her injury, but now she gave a soft moan and pushed her hips toward Tace.

Tace didn't need more invitation than Berit's barely audible sounds and slight movements. She slid a hand over Berit's ass and between her legs, cupping her with enough pressure to feel wetness spread across her palm. She kept teasing Berit's spine with her lips and tongue, while her fingers spread through Berit's curls and finally moved deep inside her. Berit gasped again, pushing herself against Tace's probing fingers, and Tace matched her rhythm with increasingly insistent movement. The scent of Berit's arousal—so close and mouth-watering—made Tace want to flip her over and make her come with her tongue and teeth. But her head was resting on the reminder of Berit's injuries, and Tace wouldn't risk hurting her for anything. Instead, she inched her free hand under Berit's belly and found her dripping and hard clit. Berit ground down on her fingers and came while calling Tace's name.

Tace kept her hands still, with slight pressure, while Berit shuddered against her and sighed with the aftershocks of her climax. Tace's forehead was on Berit's lower back, fused there by a sheen of sweat, and her own breath came in short bursts. She'd never felt another woman's responses like this, as if her own body had been touched. The openness between them—after months of familiarity and given the brutal honesty of Berit's imminent and inevitable departure—had destroyed all Tace's boundaries. She'd been with Berit in a way she could feel, but couldn't describe.

Berit eased onto her back and held her arms out for Tace. Tace started to move into them, but Berit suddenly pushed her away.

"You're still fully clothed! Take care of that first, and then come here."

Tace laughed and got up, quickly shedding her jeans and shirt and tossing them on the floor. She gently bounced onto the bed next to Berit and gave her a kiss.

"I would have taken them off sooner, but someone seemed impatient to be touched."

"Well, someone has been waiting for months to get you into bed. Give someone a break."

Tace smiled against Berit's lips as the teasing turned with lightning quickness into arousal again. Berit made her head spin and her body do flips inside. Tace was used to living on an even keel, but Berit had turned her whole world on end.

Berit propped herself on one elbow and pushed Tace's shoulders down until she was flat on the bed. "I've never felt so connected, during sex or any other time, like I do with you," Berit said. "I don't know how you reach places I always kept private, but I'm glad you do. You fill me with…well, with emotions."

Tace wondered what Berit had been about to say. It was too soon for the word *love*, and it shouldn't be spoken between them anyway, not with only a few short months before Berit left. Her confused thoughts were silenced when Berit kissed her again, and Tace opened her mouth in response to Berit's exploring tongue. The kiss continued, ebbing and flowing with a clash of tongues and gentle brushes of teeth, until Tace couldn't keep still any longer. Her hips moved and her knees bent and straightened, her feet sliding across the comforter, as she fought to contain her arousal and keep control.

Movement. Their relationship was all about movement. Tace wriggled on the bed while Berit delved into every nook and cranny she had, excavating Tace's secrets and worshiping them like priceless relics. Change and motion.

Tace had always fought against change, and she felt herself fighting even now, trying to maintain control while Berit's fingers caressed her side with a tickling light touch. The switch between tender caress and out-of-control passion was wearing down her defenses. Berit's lips took over where her hands left off, and she sucked on Tace's neck, on her breasts, on her lower belly and inner thigh. Berit had been the one to help Tace move out of her rut and into this unexpected and wonderful world of passion, both with Berit and with her newfound career. She had taught Tace to move forward, not to stay in place.

Moving forward and away. Berit would be going soon, but not now. Tace cried out when Berit settled between her legs and rolled her tongue over the tendons high on her inner thighs. She'd been too aroused while touching Berit. She wouldn't survive a direct onslaught from Berit's mouth without completely shattering, body and soul.

But somehow she remained in one piece, writhing under Berit's seeking tongue but not being destroyed by it. Climbing higher until the air was too thin to breathe. Crashing down and into Berit's embrace when she climaxed with a heart-wrenching spasm.

Berit put a hand on the end table and stood up, careful not to disturb Tace or to twist her back. She stretched gently. She felt good, even after the unaccustomed activity. Or because of it. She went into the kitchen for a glass of water and came back to the bedroom to drink it, leaning on the doorjamb and watching Tace doze. The room seemed so tranquil and quiet with the even rise and fall of Tace's rib cage from Berit's casual position in the doorway, but the events of the past two hours had been anything but calm. Berit's pulse still raced at the thought of Tace touching her, again and again. Even now, she wanted to wake her for more.

Berit thrived by staying as far away from stability and predictability as she could. She'd never had those luxuries as a child, and she didn't trust them to last as an adult. Her grandfather had given her a glimpse of family and permanence, but he had died, leaving her to suffer through the final years of high school until she was finally able to get away from the chaos of home. Tace was everything her family hadn't been, but Berit had chosen her path and she wouldn't change course for anyone or anything.

She sure as hell was tempted, though. She eased onto the bed, trying not to jostle Tace awake, but Tace shifted and reached for her with still-closed eyes. Berit willingly moved into Tace's embrace.

Tace had been right today when she said Berit wouldn't stay here. She couldn't. She admired teachers and professors—even more so now that she'd experienced first-hand how difficult the job could be—but she wasn't meant to be one. She hated the job. Or, rather, she hated the sense of failure she felt on the job. She was better suited to roughing it on a far-off dig, not sitting in a classroom translating basic Greek sentences. *I came to the island. You came to the island. She/he/it came to the island.* Snore.

Tace flexed her back, bringing her hips in snug contact with Berit's, and she felt desire stirring in her exhausted body. She had four months to be with Tace. Four months of sex and companionship and laughter—whenever they could spare time from demanding and stressful schedules. Would she be tired of Tace by then? Ready and impatient to move away from her and get back to her old way of life? Berit kissed a hollow spot on Tace's neck and sighed against her skin when Tace moaned softly in her sleep. She doubted she'd deplete her interest in Tace's gorgeous body and captivating personality even if she had four years, four decades, four centuries with her. Four months to sate her desire and know every facet of her? Not likely, but she'd damn sure give it a try.

Chapter Nineteen

Tace went to the rack of khakis and pulled out several pair in different styles. On a hunch, she grabbed a couple of floral tops in a lightweight fabric perfect for spring. She tapped on the door to the changing room.

"This size should be a better fit for you," she said to the woman who opened the half-door, "and I brought these shirts in case you wanted to try them. They just came in last week and look good with the khakis. I can take those others if you're finished with them."

She left with an armload of pants and neatly put them back on their hangers and in the correct spot on the rack. She stopped by the register to ring up a customer's purchase, and then returned to the window display she was designing. The sky outside the window was blue and the sun was streaming across the mannequins as she rearranged them, but the beautiful early spring day wasn't filling her with depressed longing like similar ones had last year.

Tace returned to the register again when her customer got there with two pairs of pants and both tops Tace had suggested. Tace chatted easily with her, even though part of her mind was distracted by her amazement at how much she'd changed here at work lately. She'd always been comfortable talking to strangers or acquaintances, but something had held her back when she was at the store. She'd remained icily distant and on guard, never knowing if the people she met were from the college or not. Now she didn't care. She could talk to the students, to professors with Berit's caliber of education, or to fellow townies without faltering or feeling inferior. She was the same person—just as intelligent and with the same lack of formal education as before—but she was unrecognizable in other ways.

Tace glanced at her watch when the customer left and hurried to finish the display before she was off for the day. She'd actually followed through on her plan to reduce her hours at the store for real, and the resulting easing of her tight schedule did wonders for her attitude. For the first time, she was in charge of her time and the way she lived her life. She'd felt out of control before, being pushed and prodded along like a cow in a chute, without any choice in the direction she was to take. Now, the brewery was operating in the red, but not as deeply as before. Maybe someday she'd bring in enough money to work there full-time, but not yet. She'd have to work hard to make up for her lack of hours eventually. Once Berit's rent check was no longer coming in, Tace would probably need to work here full-time again.

Tace leaned on the shoulder of a mannequin and stared out the window. She usually loved seeing signs of spring in her town, but now they reminded her of Berit's approaching departure. They'd had four weeks of bliss, making love anywhere and everywhere that came to mind. In the backyard during another chinook wind. Out in the wheat fields on a cool evening, wrapped in wool blankets to ward off the chill. In Berit's bedroom most nights, after their work was done and they had snuggled under the covers and shared their news of the day. Tace had felt funny accepting rent from Berit once their relationship slid headlong into the intensely personal, but Berit refused to stop paying. She changed what she used to write in the memo section of her checks from *rent* to *my share of the house*. Tace would miss those notes in Berit's familiar scrawl more than the extra dollars in her account.

Tace put the last touches on her window display and went into the back room to clock out and change into more casual clothes for her afternoon at the brewery. She'd stay there late tonight since Berit would be at her committee meeting all evening, considering candidates for her replacement next fall. She'd been vague about those meetings, just making offhand comments about one applicant's boring delivery and another's pretentious and possibly faked accent. Tace figured she was joking because Berit must be eager to find someone to step into her role.

Tace shook her head as she walked out the door and into the weak but promising spring sunshine. She was comfortable enough in just a T-shirt with her jacket over her arm—a nice change from the usual thick layers she wore on colder days. She got in her car and drove the now-familiar route to her brewery. She noticed the early, slender stalks of asparagus in a dark-soiled field and made a note to bring Berit out this way when she had a chance. She wanted her to see the interesting plants before she left.

Too many of her thoughts about things to do with Berit ended with the phrase *before she left*.

Tace drove under the redbud trees. They were already showing some color and would be in full bloom in a couple of weeks. The yard was looking good—she'd been back on duty as gardener since the ground had thawed and everything had started to grow. She had pretty container plants scattered around the building, and several wrought-iron tables and chairs on the lawn. She hadn't set up times for beer tastings yet, and she was still unsure how to take her brewery to the next level in customer sales. Bottling was tempting, to expand her market, but the investment was out of reach right now. She was sponsoring the upcoming bike race, and—

Her daydreams and plans were cut short when she saw Kyle's Camaro parked near the front door, exactly where it had been the day he told her she owned the brewery. She felt the same sinking feeling when she saw his car as she had the last time. Her gut had been right then, and probably was again.

She walked into the building and saw Kyle sitting on a chair near the door. He had his feet propped on an empty keg and Suds was curled on his lap. The little traitor.

"Hey, sis! I'd get up, but this fellow seems comfortable."

"Hi, Kyle." Tace walked over and gave him a kiss on the cheek. She slapped his feet off the keg and perched on the empty chair next to him. "What are you doing here?"

"I came to see you, naturally. I stopped by the Blue on my way to the house, and Dan told me you were actually making a go of this place. I tried the IPA there—excellent, I must say—and came here to check it out. Your freaky brewer gave me the willies and this glass of amber."

Tace glanced up toward the fermentation tanks and saw Joseph watching from above. He gave her a wave and disappeared. He'd probably been keeping an eye on Kyle for her—she knew he was happy with the way she was running the brewery, and he was probably afraid things would change for him yet again. She was a little worried about it, too.

"This place was such a freaking mess when I saw it last." He took a drink of his beer and seemed to rethink what he'd just said. "I mean, I saw the potential here, of course, or I wouldn't have bought it for you. But you've really made it look good."

"It was a lot of hard work," Tace said. "And you didn't buy it for me. I paid you a lot more than what the brewery was worth and I didn't have a choice except to clean it up and get it running again."

Not exactly true. She'd had the option to cut her losses and sell, but she'd chosen to stay. She was uncomfortable with Kyle's presence here, in her haven. Her decision to devote herself to running the brewery was still fragile and risky. She needed it, though, if she was going to survive losing Berit.

"Dan said he'd heard some people were asking if the brewery was for sale, so I stopped by the Realtor on my way here. She said there've been several offers on our place, a couple for even more than you paid me."

"*Our* place?" Tace repeated in a shocked voice. He'd been busy during the short time he'd been in town. She'd known about the more recent and more tempting offers since Joan called her weekly to ask her to sell, always praising her effusively for the work she'd done. *You've done a super job! But someone with more experience can take the brewery to the next level, and you'll have a nice little nest egg if you sell now while the market's hot.* And Joan would have a tidy commission. Not a chance.

"My name is on the deed, Kyle. I did the work in the yard, I've helped create the beers, and I've paid Joseph's salary."

He sat up in the chair, and Suds jumped off his lap and came over to wind around Tace's legs.

"Look, I'm in a bind. I have a chance to chip in with a friend and buy a seafood shack on the beach near Malibu. It's a sure thing, with a strong base of customers and a killer location." He spread his hands in the same gesture she'd seen since childhood. "The way I see it, we sell the brewery and split the profits. It's only fair that I get something out of this, since I was the one who got it for you in the first place. Besides, what are you going to do now? You've mown the lawn and sold some kegs of beer. Do you really know enough about business or brewing to go any further?"

"If you need money, sell your car," Tace suggested, but she felt a twinge of hesitation. Sell the brewery and make some money. She'd be free then, to go with Berit to Baja or wherever she went next. The idea tempted her so much she felt as if a hand were squeezing her throat. Her weakness where Berit was concerned made her vulnerable to the doubts Kyle helped resurface in her mind. And there was always the issue of Chris's tuition…

"You know I can't sell my Camaro. Depreciation. And it might need some body work." He swallowed the rest of the beer and looked around as if hoping Joseph would materialize next to him with a refill. "I'm trying to find myself, Tace. I really think this restaurant will be my future. The guy who's selling it is retiring to the Caribbean because he made so much money there, and all we have to do is follow his recipes. I'm bound to make a fortune. It's not like this place, where you're starting practically from scratch with no customers and no money. Look, I already told your Realtor to set up an appointment—"

"You what?" Tace was angry, both at him for stepping in and taking over her business, and at herself for letting her fears take root in his unfair words. She was doing fine here, wasn't she? She'd keep the business afloat even after Berit's rent money stopped. Maybe she'd have to take in another boarder or two, although the thought of having anyone besides Berit in the house made her want to cry. She'd definitely need to go back to full-time at the store, where she'd barely make enough to cover Joseph's pay. She sighed. Her excitement about the brewery had been real, but maybe not realistic.

"Call Joan and cancel whatever plans you made," Tace said. "I need to get some work done here. Do you want to stay and help?"

"I'm exhausted, so I think I'll go home and crash for a while. Maybe tomorrow I'll do some PR work for us. I can schmooze the local bar owners and get more of them to carry our beer." Kyle stood up and stretched before bending over to give her a quick kiss on the cheek.

"I have a boarder now, a professor from Whitman," Tace said, standing up and stopping him before he left. "She's in the downstairs rooms, so take your stuff upstairs and be polite if you see her."

"A boarder? Is she pretty? How old?"

"Get out, Kyle."

❖

Tace worked off some of her frustration and negative energy with the trimmer, cutting wide and uneven swaths across the lawn. She was confused by her reaction to Kyle. She had never been able to resist him, probably because he'd been so young when she'd needed to step in as his parent. She'd wanted to make the younger kids happy, to protect them from the pain she felt when their mom left. They'd been fairly resilient and quickly learned to turn to her instead of crying for a long-gone mother. She hadn't been able to turn to anyone, and she'd focused instead on trying to be the nurturing, loving, and present mother she'd wished she had. They'd been spoiled—not with objects or money, but with affection and leniency. Chris's natural abilities in school and the love of reading Tace had instilled in her kept her on a good path. But Kyle had soon figured out how to get Tace to bend to his will.

She wasn't a child anymore, though. She was an adult who was just learning how to thrive and set goals for herself beyond the next hike she wanted to take. What was her duty to the wayward Kyle? Breaking old habits wasn't easy.

Tace finally left the brewery and made her slow and reluctant way home. She wanted to be there before Berit got home and found Kyle in the kitchen emptying the fridge. Berit was the major complication here. Tace would have been better able to resist Kyle if he hadn't been unknowingly providing her with a way to leave town and go with Berit on an exciting adventure—something far out of her sphere of experience. She could rent out the house or sell it. Combine that with the money from the brewery sale and have enough to be self-supporting for a short while. Follow Berit to her next job…

And then what? Once her money ran out, Tace would be in a foreign country with nothing of her own. Berit had said she'd had hopes of Tace coming with her, but did she want Tace, the semisuccessful entrepreneur, or unemployed and broke Tace?

More than that, was that who she wanted to be? She'd be bored and disappointed with herself. She'd be trailing in the shadow of someone else's career, and once Berit was finished with the job, Tace would be back here with no hopes and dreams for the future.

Tace parked in the driveway and shut off her gloomy thoughts along with the car engine. Berit obviously liked her, brewery or not. Tace just wasn't sure what she'd think of herself if she let this opportunity for a career slip away. But even worse was the thought of letting Berit slip away.

She walked in the kitchen and found Kyle at the kitchen table eating a huge sandwich and reading Berit's book. He must have found it upstairs when he put his things in her room. Her room? She hadn't slept up there since their trip to Pullman.

He tapped the back cover, Berit's photo. "She's your boarder? I saw her name on the rent check over there." He nodded toward the counter. "I didn't know she was a famous author and archaeologist, too. She must be loaded. You should really be charging her more rent, or maybe ask her to invest in our brewery."

Tace walked over and snatched the book out of his hands. She didn't correct his use of a personal pronoun this time because she was too focused on his new scheme. "You will *not* discuss money with Dr. Katsaros or ask her to invest in anything. If you do, you'll be out of the house, got it?"

He laughed. "You can't kick me out of my own house."

"It's not yours. I pay the mortgage and the taxes. If you bother Berit…Dr. Katsaros, you'll find out just how serious I am about—"

Tace stopped talking when she heard the front door open. She started toward the living room with Kyle close on her heels when Berit called out to her.

"Hey, sweetheart, I brought Thai food home. I thought we could eat it in—" She noticed Kyle. "Oh, hello. I didn't realize we…you had company."

Tace hurried over to take the bags from Berit. She met Berit's eyes and shook her head with a frown, mouthing the word *sorry*. "Berit, this is my brother Kyle. Kyle, this is Dr. Katsaros."

They nodded at each other across the living room, neither making a move to step forward and shake hands. The energy in the room gave Tace the impression the two of them had taken an instant dislike to each other. She felt like a referee in the middle of a boxing ring while the opponents sized each other up.

"What brings you to town, Kyle?" Berit asked. "I heard the last time you were here you dumped the brewery on Tace. What did you bring her this time?"

"Dumped it on her? I left her in charge of the family business while I took care of some personal matters," Kyle said. "We've just been making plans to sell it, and she can buy whatever she wants with the profit."

Berit turned to her with her mouth slightly open and her eyebrows raised in obvious surprise. "You're selling the brewery? After all the work you've put into it?"

"Kyle's just talking," Tace hastened to assure her, although she was still confused by the day's events. She'd been offered an out, a way to move out of Walla Walla for once in her life. She'd made the choice to keep the brewery despite the offers. Working there and making her beer with Joseph gave her a sense of fulfillment she'd never had before. But Berit had offered her something even more profound, and Tace got sadder as she simultaneously was getting closer to Berit and getting closer to her departure date. "We haven't decided anything."

Berit looked from one to the other with an unreadable expression. "I'm going to shower and change. Can we talk after?"

"I'll be right in," Tace said. She pushed past Kyle and went into the kitchen for plates.

"You're sleeping with your boarder?" Kyle asked with a laugh. "Priceless. You really should hit her up for more money if—"

"Don't you dare finish that sentence," Tace said, pointing a fork at Kyle. "Eat your sandwich and then go upstairs to bed. We'll talk tomorrow."

"Okay, okay. I'll shut up. Right after I say one more thing. Have you thought about using the money from the sale to get some sort of degree? If you're going to be dating a professor, you should at least have gone to college."

Tace ignored him and gathered up the plates and food. She went into the bedroom and precisely arranged everything on the end table. Kyle's parting words had cut somewhere deep inside her—the tenuous dream of a future she could be proud of had been slowly putting down roots and unfurling leaves and buds, but Kyle's parting words severed it and left her to bleed. He'd always treated college like a joke, and she'd never confided in him about her own insecurities, so he hadn't meant anything more than a weak attempt at humor with his comment. He'd managed to strike at her most vulnerable part, though, and the thought of having money for an education left her stunned by its potency.

She sat on the bed and listened to the sound of Berit splashing in the shower beyond the open bathroom door. For the first time since they'd begun sleeping together, Tace wasn't tempted to go in and join her. She had too much on her mind. Too many decisions to make after a lifetime of having them made for her.

CHAPTER TWENTY

B erit let herself in the house the next afternoon and found Kyle lying on the couch watching television. He muted the sound and stood up when she entered. She'd had her hackles raised since she first met him because she wanted to protect Tace and her newfound dream. Tace didn't need her brother dropping another unwanted business or scheme on her doorstep. Berit shouldn't interfere in Tace's family matters—she had no right to do so—but she couldn't stop herself from rising to Tace's defense.

"Tace said to apologize to you as soon as you got home," he said, with a disarming grin. Berit still mistrusted his motives, but she had to smile at the sorry-not-sorry expression he wore while he gave his obviously prepared speech. "I'm sorry I was rude to you and that I referred to the brewery as ours when it really belongs to Tace."

Berit wasn't ready to relent, no matter how charming he was. "I'm just looking out for her. You have no idea how much work she's put into the brewery, trying to get out of the hole of debt you put her in. She's damned good at what she does, too, and she deserves a chance to be happy on her own, not just to devote her life to supporting you and your sister."

"Jeez, why do I feel like I suddenly have two mothers when I don't even have one?" Kyle asked with a skewed attempt at a smile. "I care about Tace, too, you know. I just asked her for some help. She's always been willing to help."

Berit sighed. She'd felt compassion for Tace because her mother left and she had to be in charge, but Kyle had been abandoned, too. Tace had responded by becoming hyperresponsible. Kyle had swung the other way, but both were responding to being hurt.

"Maybe, just this once, you can think of her instead of yourself."

"Yeah, she said pretty much the same thing, so you can chill. She's not giving me the cash to buy my restaurant in Malibu, even if she does sell the brewery. Big mistake, since I'd have made easy money there. She did offer me a job at the brewery, though."

Berit crossed her arms over her chest. She was concerned to hear Tace was even considering selling, but she knew what it would mean to her if Kyle started acting more responsible and worked at the brewery with her. She wouldn't dare give up on her own chances with the business, if it meant helping her brother as well as herself. "Are you going to take it?"

He shrugged. "I don't know. She talked about hauling sacks of malt and moving kegs around. Sounds like slave labor in exchange for rent. Can you imagine? Having to pay rent in my own house."

"Whose name is on the mortgage?"

Kyle rolled his eyes. "You sound just like her. Are you her girlfriend or her clone?"

Neither. Berit had never defined her relationship with Tace. Was it an affair, brief but intense? Were they lovers? Fuck-buddies? Berit cringed at the sound of the last one, but unfortunately it best defined their relationship. They were friends, they were having sex, and they had an expiration date on their time together. Girlfriend implied something more committed. None of them captured the depth of feeling she had for Tace.

"I'm not her clone, but I imagine she also said something along the lines of this being a good opportunity for you to shape up and get some real work experience."

"Add something about character building, and you got it right."

"You should give it a try. Stick around and help her this time instead of leaving her alone."

"Oh, and you're planning to stick around, too? Or are you abandoning her once the school year ends?"

Berit was silent. He was right. She was angry with him for walking out on Tace, but she was going to do the same thing. Her case was different, though. She'd never hidden her desire to get out of here from Tace.

"Thought so," Kyle said. He sat on the couch again and watched the silent images flash across the screen. "I might go away now and then, but Stacy is my family. I'll never leave her for good."

"Where is she?" Berit had a sudden urge to find her. Tace had stood her ground with Kyle and Berit had a feeling the effort wasn't easy for her. Would she follow through with what she'd said to him? Berit hoped so, for both siblings' sakes and futures. What about her own future, and the guilt and sadness she'd feel once she left? Nothing a promising dig wouldn't cure. She hoped.

Kyle turned the volume on again and raised his voice to speak over it. "She's probably at the park. That's where she always used to go when she got frustrated with me when we were kids."

Berit left the house without another word and walked the short distance to Pioneer Park, her cane beating a quick rhythm as she hurried along the sidewalk. She hadn't found time to visit the park yet, even though she and Tace had talked about doing so several times lately. They usually ended up in bed together instead. Berit felt a flush of heat at the thought of her afternoons and evenings with Tace. She pulled off the sweater she was wearing over a T-shirt and let the cool spring breeze wash over her hot skin.

Berit entered on one of the paved walkways leading into the park. The grass was lushly green and mown short and even. Dogwoods lined the paths, with white and pink blossoms creating a thick, lacy canopy. Small hillocks provided shady places to sit or lie back and read a book, and a children's play area—with climbing toys made of wood and brightly colored banners—was filled with screaming and running toddlers. Berit veered away from the families and saw a large net spanning a corner of the park. The aviary. She'd bet money Tace was nearby.

She found her sitting on the grass with an open book on her lap, staring at the small songbirds as they flitted back and forth in the contained area. Berit put her hand on a tree trunk and watched Tace for several seconds. They hadn't spoken much since Kyle's arrival, but she'd felt incongruously closer to her even so. Last night, she'd come out of the shower ready for a fight, ready to give an impassioned plea for Tace to resist her brother's demands and keep her brewery. But she'd seen Tace's face when she walked into the bedroom, and she'd recognized the expression. Just like she'd give a fellow archaeologist space to work through a gnawing problem or question, she gave Tace the same courtesy. They'd eaten pad Thai and cuddled in bed, talking about trivialities. Berit had made jokes about suffering through more of the candidates' videos, and Tace had told her the asparagus was beginning to emerge. Berit had held her through the night, feeling the almost physical vibration of Tace's thoughts whirring through her mind.

Somehow, recognizing what Tace needed and providing it for her—even though Berit hadn't given advice or solved her problems—had strengthened her sense of intimacy with Tace. Berit tapped her cane against the tree while she considered the implications of her growing feelings. She needed to be pulling away now, slowly but steadily, so when she left they'd both be prepared. Ramping up their connection and then severing it abruptly would be too hard.

Berit finally walked over to Tace and sat on the grass. The dappled shade of a tall oak made Tace look like someone in a Seurat painting. Her face was inscrutable in the mottled light, but her smile when she saw Berit was unmistakably welcoming.

"You found me," Tace said. She reached over and squeezed Berit's leg, her hand lingering on Berit's thigh for a long moment. Berit caught it in her own before Tace could pull away.

"Your brother said you'd be here. Apparently you sought refuge here often when he was a difficult teenager."

"It was my second home," Tace said with a half smile. "Did he apologize to you?"

Berit laughed. Tace and Kyle were adults now, but the mother-son dynamic was still strong. "Yes. I have a feeling he repeated verbatim the apology you told him to give. He said you offered him a job at the brewery."

Tace nodded. "Anything else?"

"Well," Berit hesitated. Was Tace ready to talk to her? She decided to broach the subject and find out. She'd back off if Tace seemed unwilling to discuss it. "He said you're really thinking about selling the brewery, even though you won't use the money to fund his crab shack or whatever it is."

Tace shook her head. "Yeah, I resisted supporting his new scheme even though it sounds like such a wonderful investment opportunity."

"Then why sell? I thought you were excited about the business."

Tace sighed, and Berit gripped her hand tightly, offering support in the only way she could. Listen and be there for Tace. For now.

"He brought up some valid points, even in the midst of the goofy ones. Do I really have the knowledge and skill needed to make a living there? And there's no doubt the money would be useful in other ways. I could travel or go back to school."

"Both would be good, if you really want to do them. But you could also travel and take classes using the money you make once the brewery is established. I have no doubt you'll be able to learn what you need as you go. You've picked up so much in such a short time." Berit paused. She was arguing against herself, against the choice she'd prefer Tace to make, but she couldn't stop. She could either support her own dreams or Tace's, and she had to choose Tace. "Look at what's changed since you've invested yourself in the place for about eight months. What could you accomplish in two years? Five years? At the rate you're going, you could be selling bottles of your beer nationwide by then."

"But Kyle made me remember my priority needs to be my family. I have obligations, not to buy him what is probably a smelly and decrepit fish joint, but to help Chris get through school. Then she'll have all the chances I didn't have."

Berit frowned. She was about to tread into Tace's family business, and she wondered if Tace would push her out or let her in. Oh, well. She'd been thinking they needed to pull back emotionally. This might break them completely apart. "Tace, you don't owe Chris a debt-free education. There's nothing bad about getting out of grad school with some student loans. Maybe Chris will appreciate what she's working toward even more if she's helping to finance it." Berit switched her focus from the younger Lomonds to the one who really mattered to her—Tace. "You gave her and Kyle everything they wanted, no matter how hard you had to work to get it for them. You sacrificed yourself and your dreams to make theirs come true. When you were kids, you were doing your best to survive and take care of them, and I admire how fast you grew up and took responsibility. But they're adults now."

Berit remembered the day she finally paid off her student loans after years of dirty fieldwork. She'd earned the right to celebrate that night. Her grandfather hadn't been able to leave her much money when he passed—he'd spent most of what he had on their trips to Greece—but the gifts he'd given her were beyond price. Passion and a heritage. Connections to him and the past that money couldn't buy. Tace hadn't been given those things, but she could find them now, with a little push from Berit. "You know what the brewery has meant to you, what it's meant to see your hard work pay off and to feel the pride in doing something worthwhile. Don't you owe them *that* legacy? And don't you owe yourself that opportunity?"

Tace was silent. She didn't look at Berit but instead kept watching the birds.

Berit was about to say she was sorry. To agree Tace was right to pay for whatever her siblings asked. She'd say anything to make sure she hadn't alienated Tace, even though that had been a small part of her intention. Mostly, she wanted Tace to take a chance on herself, because she was more than worth it.

"I haven't done Kyle any favors, have I?" Tace spoke quietly, then sighed and squeezed Berit's hand. "Don't look so worried. You haven't overstepped any bounds. For as long as you are here, you're part of my life. You're actually the only voice speaking out for me, since I don't seem inclined to do it myself."

Berit felt an uncomfortable blossoming of feelings inside. Some were positive—she was proud of Tace for being open to reevaluation and self-scrutiny and she was honored to be counted as someone whose opinion and support mattered to her. But she was nearly overwhelmed by the less joyful emotions. Sadness because they were developing something beautiful together even though it would be short-lived. And disheartened because Tace was transforming into someone more confident in her abilities and value—deservedly so—but Berit wouldn't be around to see how amazingly far she was able to go.

"So, what are you going to do?" she asked. She shifted until their legs were touching.

"I guess I'll talk to Chris. I've mentioned the brewery, but I haven't really told her how excited I get about being there. She'll understand, and she can fill out loan applications, in case I can't make enough to cover tuition for next term." Tace shrugged, as if these words were simple to say, but Berit understood their true weight. "I'll stay with the brewery for now, as long as I eventually can find a way to cover my expenses without needing to work two full-time jobs."

Berit frowned. She believed Tace was making the right decision, even though she still didn't believe in her chances of success. "You have such low expectations. When you're selling beer to a bar manager, you're more confident, but when you talk to me or—I'm assuming—when you talk to yourself, you don't seem able to really see what potential you have. You should be bursting with pride at what you've done so far, and you should be ready to fight for a better future than just getting by," Berit said, her voice rising at her frustration with Tace's inability to believe in herself. Berit knew how clever and capable she was. Even Chris and Kyle had no trouble depending on her for everything. Why couldn't Tace see the same strength everyone else did? "The only options you let yourself see are bleak. Either you run the brewery and you're poor and struggling, or you knock yourself out at a job you dislike for the rest of your life. Why can't you envision something better for yourself, and then go get it?"

"Don't try to turn me into you, Berit," Tace said, her voice low.

"I'm not." Berit felt the sudden rift between them. Tace had let her butt in to her family life, and listened to what she said about Chris's loans, but she'd somehow crossed an unseen boundary. "I'm just trying to make you see—"

"You're the risk taker. I'm not. I'll try to make this job work on my own terms, and if that means my goal is breaking even or running the brewery as a hobby while I work at the store, then that's what's right for me. Like you said before, you need to aggressively promote your work in war-torn countries or to wealthy universities," Tace said, her voice sharp with anger. Berit didn't know if it was aimed at her, or at Tace herself. "I can take some suggestions and use them to sell beer, but I'm not going to turn this brewery into the next Anheuser-Busch. It's not who I am."

"Okay," Berit said. She felt stunned by Tace's speech. What nerve had she hit? The academic one again? Was Tace still convinced she was less a person because she didn't have Berit's credentials or her degrees? She pulled her hand away from Tace's. "I don't know what else I have to do to convince you that you are every bit as smart and worthwhile as I am, no matter how much money your brewcry makes or how many credits you have in school. But if you want to keep telling yourself you don't matter, go ahead. Just don't say it to me because I don't want to hear it anymore." Berit stood up, leaning so heavily on her cane that the tip sank into the soft ground. "Keep going with what works for you—aim low enough and make plenty of excuses beforehand, then you won't be surprised when you fail."

Tace watched Berit walk away with an open mouth—she wasn't sure whether it was because she was shocked by Berit's words or because she wanted to call her back. She stayed silent and closed her mouth. She wasn't making excuses before she even failed. She was being realistic, given her lack of experience and schooling. She wasn't used to making choices or living for herself because she always had to take care of...

Two adults who were perfectly capable of making their own mistakes and earning their own achievements.

Tace felt the hot pressure of tears in her eyes. How long she'd spent expecting so little. And when she finally held passion in her hands, she'd looked for any reason to let it go.

Did she mean Berit or the brewery? She wasn't sure. She bent her knees and hugged them tightly to her chest. If she listened to Berit—and she'd moments before told her she was the only one speaking for Tace—then she had to admit how much she wanted to succeed. She wanted to see her beer winning contests and in bottles on store shelves. She wanted to make enough money to travel and see the world. Visit Berit wherever she went next.

Tace rubbed her suddenly sweaty palms on her jeans. Could she admit she wanted those things and then try wholeheartedly to get them? Without whining about her lack of a degree or how mean the college bullies had been? Or about how hard it had been to be a parent when she was still a child? Because she could go get a damned degree now if she wanted one. And she wouldn't trade the love she'd shared with Chris and Kyle for anything.

Could she acknowledge her desire for success with the brewery and face possible failure with no excuses? Maybe. Could she acknowledge her hunger for more of a life with Berit, even though the differences between them were too deep to bridge? Tace shook her head. No.

She got up and started walking after Berit. She'd apologize for her outburst and together they could strategize about the brewery. She didn't want to waste a single night fighting with her. Tonight, she'd hold her tightly in bed. In June, she'd let her go.

CHAPTER TWENTY-ONE

Tace pushed the swinging door open an inch and peeked through the narrow slit. She still couldn't believe she was here. Margaret's large, open tasting room was crammed with rented tables and folding chairs. Fine china and sterling flatware graced every place setting on the starched white tablecloths. The one hundred tickets to her beer challenge had sold within hours, and every seat was full.

Tace closed the door again. "I'm going to be sick."

"Me, too," Joseph agreed. He wouldn't even look out at the crowd, preferring to hover near his kegs like a nervous mother bringing her child to the first day of preschool.

"You're not going to get sick," Berit said. "Here, have a drink. It'll calm your nerves."

Tace looked at the sparkling glass of merlot. "Are you kidding me? Whose side are you on, anyway?"

Berit just grinned and took a sip of her wine. "This is Margaret's, not Campton's."

Tace shook her head and peered out the door again. She could trace tonight's fiasco directly to her talk with Berit after their spat in Pioneer Park. They'd sat down together and discussed Tace's plans for the brewery, brainstorming ideas for conquering the wine-loving town of Walla Walla. Tace had reminded Berit about the first wine tasting they'd been to, when their server had suggested pairings of wines with fine-dining options. She admitted she'd internally matched her beers against the fancier wines, and the discussion had led to a plan to challenge a winery to a taste-off.

Finding a willing competitor had been tough. She'd arranged to have the competition at Margaret's—neutral territory—and then she had called over twenty wineries to issue her challenge. None had accepted—instead they'd been variously condescending, amused, or dismissive. In the end, she'd called Campton Estates— the site of her first humiliation—because they regularly hosted wine-and-food pairing events. She'd talked to the husband and wife owners, and they'd agreed to battle her during the spring release week, when Walla Walla was filled with tourists and the wineries held a variety of different promotions for them.

Tace paced back and forth between the door and the kegs. In keeping with the casual tone of her beers, she was wearing dark jeans and a green button-down shirt. Joseph was wearing—of all things—a bowtie with his flannel shirt.

"Have you ever eaten at the restaurant that's catering?" she asked him. He looked at her as if she'd asked whether he regularly walked across hot coals. "I guess not. Maybe we should have gone and tasted the food before we agreed to this."

Berit put her arm around Tace's shoulders. "They made a special menu for tonight, so you wouldn't have been able to try the dishes anyway. You had to go with your instincts, just like the winery."

Tace sighed and looked at the menu card she'd been given when she arrived, with its calligraphy and decorative swirls. She'd gotten the same menu a week ago, printed in a plain font, and she and Joseph had read the descriptions and made the decision about which beer to serve with each dish. Matching taste with words. What if the night was a complete failure?

She pushed the thought away. She had been confident when she made her choices, and Kyle and Joseph had hauled the kegs over here. There was no going back now. She'd either be humiliated in front of the large crowd of wine enthusiasts or she'd prove her beers were as delicious and nuanced as an expensive glass of wine.

She sniffed the air, smelling the hint of herbs. They were almost ready to begin, if the appetizers were already on the stoves in Margaret's large kitchen.

As if she'd summoned her, Margaret appeared and called Tace out to the tasting room. Berit grabbed her arm before she went out.

"Believe in yourself," she said, giving Tace a kiss. "You know I do. Your beer is wonderful, and everyone will love it."

"That really means a lot when your lips taste like wine," Tace teased, but she hugged Berit in gratitude. Berit's confidence in her gave Tace the courage to walk through the door and stand in front of the elegantly dressed crowd, even though she wanted to run out the front door and back to her brewery. She'd curl up behind a fermentation tank with Suds, and no one would be able to find her.

Instead, she smiled when Margaret introduced her and explained the judging criteria for the friendly competition. She traded jokes and playful jibes with the Camptons. She somehow made it back to Berit, even though her knees were trembling.

"Apps are first," she said to Berit. "This is our IPA."

"My first morning in your home." Berit brushed the back of her hand over Tace's cheek. "I'll never be able to smell lavender again without thinking of the taste of your beer and you on my tongue."

"Please stop," Kyle said, making a gagging noise. "I'm going to hurl."

"Not on the diners," Tace said. She grabbed Berit's hand and kissed it. "I think that would reflect badly in our score."

Joseph carefully filled the small tasting glasses with the summer IPA, and Tace, Kyle, and Berit carried trays of them around to each table. According to the rules Tace, Margaret, and the Camptons had elected, she was allowed to use any of her beers, seasonal or regular, but she couldn't create something new for the occasion. As soon as she'd read the description of the appetizer, seared scallops in a butter sauce with herbes de Provence, she'd known the ale would be a nice pairing. The lavender and basil would complement the herbs, and the sharp hoppiness of the IPA would make a pleasing contrast with the creamy, sweet scallops.

Tace tried not to feel discouraged at the sight of her simple glasses next to the delicate wineglasses with a pool of pale gold in the bottom of each one. She kept her mind focused on the next course, and it seemed they'd just finished serving the beer when it was time to collect the empty glasses.

The salad course was next. Tace had gone with another seasonal, the autumn amber ale, because she thought the added local flavors would appeal to the subtle palates of the tasters. Field greens with berries and young sweet onions, dressed with a balsamic-raspberry vinaigrette. The citrus from the amber's orange flavors combined with the nutty, anise undertones should be refreshing enough so the beer didn't overpower the freshness of the salad. Tace hoped. She thought the winery had an edge here, with a chilled mourvèdre.

"I think I did the best I could with the pairings," she confided in Berit while they waited near the kegs for the people to finish their salads, "but I don't think we'll be able to beat the wines. They've got some excellent flavor profiles."

Berit took her hand and pulled her over to the swinging door. She held it open and gestured toward the full tasting room. "What do you see out there?"

"A lot of pretentious wine lovers," Tace said.

Berit pinched her arm. "Try again."

"Ouch." Tace rubbed the sore spot. "Fine. I see people who seem to enjoy good food and drink. And I see an absolutely beautiful setting with candlelight and a welcoming atmosphere."

"Much better. And what do you hear?"

Tace smiled at Berit, keeping her eyes on the woman she loved instead of looking into the tasting room. "I hear laughter and conversations. The clink of glasses and silverware on plates. Soft music."

Tace moved Berit away from the door and it swung shut again. She held Berit's face between her hands and kissed her softly. She loved her. Loved the taste of her and the feel of her. Loved the way Berit made her feel inside. She couldn't say it out loud because their relationship was too complex and, at the same time, too simple in its finality to complicate it even more with those words. But it felt good to admit them to herself.

She carried the warmth of her acknowledgment into the next course in the competition. She'd taken a risk in the entrée round by choosing her only non-seasonal beer of the evening, the porter. This had been her least favorite beer when she first took over the brewery, but now it was one she loved. Maybe because she'd been involved in the long process of testing and reworking it until she and Joseph were happy with the result. The porter was delicate and a little sweet, with dry-hopped floral notes, but it had a toasty acidity because they conditioned it with subtle flavors of coffee and chocolate. She'd never tried it with anything like the smoked Copper River salmon and roasted asparagus, but she hoped she'd made the right choice.

By the time she'd emptied her tray of glasses, she no longer cared if she'd made the perfect choice or not. She saw the room from a different perspective after Berit made her really look and listen. People were having a good time and enjoying the meal. She received compliments, handed out her new business cards, and made plans with the Camptons to offer her beers in their tasting room. The evening was a success, no matter what the result.

The chef's choice of dessert was deceptively simple, just a brownie, but Tace's mouth had watered when she read the description. Premium dark chocolate topped with a layer of vanilla-bean-scented crème brûlée. She'd immediately paired it with her newest seasonal, the spring stout. It was the least-adorned of her seasonal beers, with only a mild hint of edible wildflowers to add sweetness and lightness to the strong flavors of roasted malt and coffee.

After she'd delivered the last of her beers to the diners, she carried an extra plate of dessert to the back room. "You have to let me know if they work together," she said to Berit. She fed her a forkful of the brownie and watched Berit sigh in ecstasy as she chewed.

She cleared her throat and handed Berit a glass of stout. The evening was going well, but Tace wanted to be home and alone with Berit. She was jealous of any event—even one this important to her—that kept them from spending precious time alone. She raised her hand and brushed a crumb of chocolate off Berit's lower lip, groaning when Berit's tongue darted out to lick her thumb. "I want you home, in bed, naked, now."

"Soon, darling," Berit said. She took a sip of the stout. "Mmm. Creamy mouthfeel. Perfect for dessert." She kissed Tace, letting her tongue linger against Tace's lips. "And the beer's good, too."

Tace stared after her as she walked away, heading into the dining room to collect dessert glasses. Tace followed behind, hoping her flushed cheeks and glazed eyes wouldn't be too noticeable in a room full of beer and wine drinkers. Margaret and her staff counted votes while the tables were cleared, and all too soon Tace found herself standing in front of all the people again.

"The vote was extremely close," Margaret said, holding the etched beer stein Tace had chosen as the prize. "The two contestants were neck and neck until the dessert round, when one pulled in front. The winner of the first annual Bike Trail Brewery Pairing Challenge is Stacy Lomond."

Berit and Kyle cheered in the back of the room while Joseph silently lifted his fists in the air in victory. Tace felt a silly grin on her face while she thanked everyone and acknowledged her brewmaster. The event had been planned as a fun way to get publicity, but winning was a thrill. She'd challenged the supremacy of the wineries and had made a statement about the quality of her beers.

The rest of the evening was a blur to Tace as she helped dismantle the room and load the near-empty kegs into Joseph's truck. Once they'd finished and Kyle went with him to help unload and to pick up his car at the brewery, Tace finally had Berit alone.

"I knew you'd win," Berit said, pulling the seat belt across her chest. "Everyone was raving about the flavor profiles of all the beers."

"It's a great feeling," Tace admitted. She hesitated before telling Berit about the plan she'd been forming all evening. "I feel like I've accomplished something special with the brewery. I was tempted to quit along the way, but you were always there to encourage me."

"You've discovered a real talent here, Tace. I just didn't want you to give up before you gave yourself a chance."

"And I didn't." Tace drove along the dark road, her headlights flashing across fields at every curve in the road. "I didn't quit when I doubted myself, or when it seemed to interfere with my obligations to Chris and Kyle. I wouldn't sell the brewery for any of those reasons, Berit, but I might sell for the most important reason of all. You."

"What are you talking about?"

Tace reached over and took Berit's hand. "I got an amazing offer on the brewery from the Camptons tonight. More than I'd ever expected. I could sell to them and come with you when you leave. I love you, Berit. I enjoy working at the brewery and I love my town, but none of it matters without you."

"Tace, you can't stop now. This is just a step along the way for you. You'll be winning more awards and developing new beers. You'll be expanding and turning this into a highly profitable business."

Tace glanced over at Berit with a frown. "I thought you wanted this. You said you hoped I'd go to Baja with you, and now I can."

Berit stared out the window. "I accepted a job in Syria, near Aleppo. It's an amazing opportunity."

Tace felt the distance growing between them and Berit hadn't even left yet. Her own voice sounded cold and hollow. "When were you planning to tell me?"

"I didn't want to ruin tonight. I was waiting until after…but what does it matter where I'm going? We both knew I was leaving.

Once I'm beyond the city limits I'm gone, no matter what my destination is."

"I guess I was starting to hope. I hoped I'd be able to come visit you where you're working. Or that you'd come back for a while between jobs." Tace felt her dream of a future with Berit begin to crumble. She'd told Berit she loved her and felt only her withdrawal in response. "Tonight I really believed I'd be selling the brewery for the right reason. I took a chance on myself and turned it into something special. I wanted to take a chance on us."

"You'll always be someone who is grounded in place, no matter where you live. You dig roots, you connect with the world around you. I don't. I pull up tent poles and move somewhere new."

"Then why can't I be grounded in Syria, with you? I can connect with different places, not restrict myself to this one place."

Tace offered everything she was. She'd move, she'd adapt. She just wanted to be with the woman she loved.

"I can't take you with me to Syria, Tace. It's a warzone, and the site is restricted to a small team of archaeologists. No families or anyone else. I'm sorry, but I think it's for the best. I'll be going back to my old way of life, and you'll be here, starting an exciting new chapter in yours. We have another month together. Please, let's make the most of it."

Tace saw only emptiness ahead. Berit's words made even her broken shards of hope turn to dust and blow away. She wanted to say yes to another month with her. They'd both accepted the time limit on their relationship, but everything had changed for Tace.

She pulled her hand away and put it on the steering wheel. "I'm sorry, Berit, but I can't. I can't pretend I don't want more, and I won't accept any less."

CHAPTER TWENTY-TWO

B erit sat in her office with the door locked and tried to pull herself together before she had to face her next class. The past week, while she and Tace had cohabitated in silence, had been torture. They avoided each other if possible—Berit had spent most of her time in her office here at Whitman, and she heard Tace leave the house before dawn and return well after dark. The few times when they had crossed paths, they'd done so with downcast eyes and muttered hellos. Berit had considered moving into a hotel until the semester was over. Then Tace could have her room and her life back. But Berit had hung up the phone every time she dialed the hotel's number. Even with the strain and evasion, she couldn't bear to leave Tace's house.

Berit had been so proud of Tace on the night of her pairing challenge. Not just because she had pushed beyond her comfort zone by stepping into the spotlight and pitting her beers against a well-known and popular winery's offerings. And not just because she had publicly tested herself against the very winery in which she'd once been treated as someone inferior.

Most of all, Berit had been proud and impressed because Tace had made damned good beer and excellent choices in her pairings. Berit had had a chance to sample the different dishes with the beer in between servings, and she'd marveled at the skill Tace had acquired in such a short time. Her taste combinations were sophisticated. Bold in some areas, like the IPA, and exceedingly subtle in others, like the fragrant hint of wildflowers in the stout.

Berit crossed her arms on her desk and rested her forehead on them. She loved the memory of the competition, but she wanted to cry when she thought of the horrible car ride home. She'd just been marveling over Tace's gifted palate when Tace said she wanted to sell the brewery for Berit, because she loved her. Berit should have rejoiced to hear those words because they were echoed in her own heart, but instead they caused her pain. Tace had given up too much for love in the past. Now, when she finally had found her calling, she was ready to walk away from her new life and into Berit's old one. Berit couldn't possibly take more of Tace's soul than she'd already given to others.

Berit raised her head and looked around her office. Even in here, where most of the mementos and photos were from digs or trips abroad, Tace's presence was tangible to Berit. She remembered Tace helping her unpack those first, meager boxes. And Tace refuting her pretense of not caring about her classes or teaching. All the books and papers and visual aids Berit had acquired since their trip to Pullman were because of Tace, too. Berit had completely changed her teaching style after their talk.

Funny how her relationship with Tace had deteriorated as rapidly as her comfort as a professor had grown. Berit had found her teaching legs, thanks to Tace's comments, but Berit had lost her grip on Tace. She missed her.

She'd miss her even more once all hope of even seeing her in the kitchen or passing her on the street was gone. Berit had panicked at the thought of Tace giving up her world to enter Berit's. She wouldn't be happy with the decision for long, Berit knew. Eventually Tace would grow resentful. She'd miss her home and hate the long hours sitting in the desert while Berit pursued her career. She'd miss her brewery, Joseph, Suds the cat, her brother and sister. Most of all, she'd miss the experience of creating something uniquely her own. Tace was the very definition of an artisan, and Berit wouldn't let her give up her craft.

So she'd made up the story about Syria. Not completely, of course. The job was one of the potential offers she'd been considering, but she hadn't agreed to join the team. It wasn't even certain the project would get off the ground. But she hadn't been able to think of any other way to make Tace stay behind.

Berit gathered the materials she needed for class and walked down the hall. She barely limped anymore and she hadn't used her cane for a few weeks. She was ready to move on. To Syria or some other site many time zones away. Far from the temptation to call Tace and tell her she'd changed her mind. Tell her to sell the brewery, pack a bag, and come to wherever the hell Berit happened to be.

Berit set up the projector and brought up the presentation on her laptop while she waited for her advanced Greek students to arrive. The difference between this semester and the last one was startling to her. She felt sorry for the students who had endured her pained lectures in the first term, and she felt inspired by the excitement of the current crew.

"Hey, Dr. Kat." The first student to arrive called her by the nickname she'd been given about the time her teaching style changed. It had been the first of many affirmations that she was doing something right.

Berit took a deep breath and forced thoughts of Tace to the back of her mind. She couldn't bear to let them surface while she was working, or she'd break down in the middle of class. Get control, get through the next hour. She'd cry in her office after class was dismissed. "Hi, Leslie. How's your final paper coming?"

They chatted for a few minutes until the rest of the class arrived. Berit dimmed the lights and showed the first slide, of a fragment of a tablet. She stared at it for a moment, forcing herself to breathe deeply and slowly. She'd gotten the idea for today's class from Tace, who had asked about Berit's first experience on a dig. Berit had shown her these same photos, and they'd spent three hours talking about ways of interpreting the past. Berit hoped this class would be just as inspiring to the students as Tace's input had been to her.

"Since we've finished translating *Herakles*, I thought we could do some exercises in epigraphy, the study of inscriptions. If you look at the writing on this tablet, you'll notice there aren't any punctuation marks or breaks between words. In many cases, it's clear where the breaks should be, but sometimes there are several possible ways to interpret the meaning of the inscription."

Berit pointed at the missing corners of the tablet. "The stone here is badly damaged, leaving little text behind. My colleagues and I worked on this puzzle for over a month, and we came up with several very different translations. Usually in archaeology, we're restricted to the small pieces of information we find. We need to make inferences and guesses about the rest, and sometimes we never know if we're correct or not." She walked away from the screen and perched on the edge of the table. She had to remain focused on her class instead of dwelling on the indecipherable and unsolvable puzzle of her and Tace's ill-fated relationship. At least this archaeological conundrum had been answered to her satisfaction. "The fascinating thing about this story is what happened three months later. We actually discovered a more intact and legible tablet with the same writing. We were able to see the missing parts and determine how much of our conjecture had been right and how much was very, very wrong."

Berit raised the lights and handed out sheets of paper with the incomplete inscription on it. "We'll start working through this today in class, and I want you to finish translating on your own over the weekend. We'll compare our versions next week, and then compare those with the inscription on the later find. Aaron, where would you put word breaks in the first line?"

Berit led the students through the difficult task of translation, giving them clues along the way and listening to them defend their choices when other students disagreed. She wanted to go home and share the experience with Tace, but instead she walked back to her office as soon as class was dismissed. She shut the door again, hoping a little peace and quiet would ease the tension headache she was beginning to feel behind her eyes, but she heard a sharp knock on her door as soon as she sat down. Kim opened the door and came in without an invitation, sitting in the chair across from Berit.

"What the hell is this?" she asked, tossing a paper onto Berit's desk.

Berit picked it up and scanned it. "My evaluation of Professor Trying Too Hard. Who wears tweed jackets with suede elbow patches in a video like this? What's he trying to prove? Maybe the more important question is, what's he trying to hide?"

"Nothing!" Kim said. She sounded annoyed, like she usually did when she broached this subject. Berit figured she was cranky from lack of sleep, with a newborn baby boy and all. "He's a very accomplished professor. And I know plenty of people who wear jackets like this."

Berit raised her eyebrows and kept silent.

"Well, I know a few people who wear them. At least one." Kim sighed. "My point is, you keep coming up with the most ludicrous reasons to reject every candidate we've had."

"I do not," Berit said. "I'm merely noticing some small but important details."

"You haven't said something positive about any of them."

"I did so," Berit said. She rubbed her temples. Anytime she had to discuss these applicants she got tense, and the feeling was compounded by the way she and Tace had been circling around each other at home. She missed having her in bed. For sex, of course. And for cuddling and talking. For feeding each other dinner from take-out containers...

"Name one," Kim said.

Berit sighed. She wanted to sit alone in the dark and feel sorry for herself, not have this same discussion with Kim. "I recall mentioning that Professor Hasn't Washed Her Hair in Months had an interesting map on the wall behind her."

Kim leaned forward and braced her hands on her knees. "I can think of two possible reasons for you to be this contrary. One, you aren't taking your place on the hiring committee seriously. If so, you should excuse yourself from it."

"What's the other reason?" Berit asked, interested in spite of herself. She wasn't quite sure why something about every single candidate seemed to jump out and irritate the hell out of her.

"You want to stay, and you're subconsciously sabotaging anyone else's chance of getting the job you want."

Berit snorted. "Unlikely."

"I don't know," Kim said, studying Berit with a shrewd expression. "I've heard some interesting reports about your classes this semester. It seems your students are actually enjoying them and are learning something. Maybe you've discovered you like teaching more than you expected."

Berit rolled her eyes and gave a dismissive wave. She couldn't come up with any other gestures to show her contempt for Kim's suggestion. Yes, she was enjoying her classes more than she had last term. Yes, she felt proud when her students came up with original and interesting ideas because of her questions and prompts. But she only had to be here for another month. Would she be nearly as enthusiastic if she knew she'd be doing the same routine every day for the next thirty years? Not a chance. She was happy to be doing a good job, and she'd be relieved when she didn't have to do it anymore.

"Well, we're going to make a decision this week, whether or not you agree with our choice. You can decide if you want to treat this committee appointment with respect or not. If you do, we'll be glad to hear your input. If not, resign."

Kim left, and Berit picked up the evaluation form again. Kim was being ridiculous. Berit was one of the best choices for this committee because, after last semester, she considered herself an expert in bad teaching.

She sighed and tossed the form in the trash. She was finished with classes for the day, but she didn't want to go to Tace's house and hide in the bedroom. She could go for a walk, but everywhere she went she thought of Tace. She got a book off her shelf and opened it to the next day's assignment for her Greek 101 class. Maybe she could find some way to make the material more interesting for both her and her students.

She tapped her fingers on the desk while she went through the chapter. This work wasn't the same as fieldwork. The excitement of a find, the grit in her teeth, the change of scenery every few months or so—she missed them all. But she couldn't deny that she'd been happy here, too, first-year Greek and all. When she'd been able to go home to Tace at the end of the day, when she'd had Tace to hold all night, she'd been…content? No, not the contentment she'd always dreaded because it led to stagnation. Tace had given her a sense of peace without tedium. She'd intrigued and captivated Berit, never bored her. Somehow the hours spent with her had made Berit's entire day brighter, because she was always with Berit even if she wasn't in the same room.

Berit still didn't believe she was cut out to be a teacher. She was improving on the job, and she had moments of pure enjoyment while doing it, but she wasn't convinced she belonged here. But if staying here meant having Tace in her life, *then* could she stay here and teach, day after day? Berit wasn't sure, but she'd better figure out the answer before she packed up and moved to the ends of the earth.

CHAPTER TWENTY-THREE

Tace went into the small bathroom at the brewery and peeled off the gloves she'd been wearing while she cleaned and sanitized the cold-side equipment. She'd never realized how important these chores were until she started learning about all the contaminating organisms just waiting for a chance to sample her wort and beer. From the start, Joseph had been vigilant about cleanliness, and Tace gladly joined in the labor-intensive process. She sometimes thought they spent more time cleaning between batches than actually brewing.

She washed her hands and splashed cold water on her face and arms. The temperature had risen into the eighties, but Tace didn't mind the heat. She'd been working harder than ever since she and Berit had split—although with Berit still living in her house, they weren't separated enough for Tace's comfort. Every time she saw the glow of light under Berit's door or passed her coming in or going out, she felt the nearly irresistible desire to rip down the barrier she'd put between them and take Berit into her arms. Tace was hurt and sad—the emotions she wasn't supposed to feel because she'd known from the start Berit would leave. So she threw herself into the physical side of the brewery, heaving sacks of malt and scrubbing tanks until her arms were limp. Then she'd go outside and work in the yard, pulling weeds or dragging sacks of fertilizer across the yard.

She was falling into bed late every night, nearly collapsing under the stress of hard work and a broken heart, but she nevertheless tossed and turned while sleep eluded her. She was going to need to get past this, and soon.

Tace dried her hands and walked through the sparkling clean brewery, mentally rehearsing the words she'd use when she began doing official tours next week. She had shot glasses with her logo on them for visitors to take as a souvenir after their tastings. Stacks of T-shirts were neatly folded in the brewery office, with the labels of their regular beers on the front. She wanted to get seasonal items made eventually—sweatshirts for the winter beer and tank tops for spring and summer. She was getting new ideas almost daily now, but she wasn't sure how much of her flurry of effort was due to her interest in the brewery and how much was just a desperate attempt to forget about Berit.

She stopped next to a mash tun and tried to remember what she was supposed to say at this stop on the tour, but all she could think of was the taste of Berit's lips after she'd sampled the extract. She was in the malt room, too, with her hand cradled in Tace's palm while they tasted the grains. She was everywhere in this building, in every ingredient in every beer. In every place in Tace's heart.

She needed fresh air. And work. Tace headed outside to mow the already short grass. She had to find some way to sweat Berit out of her pores. She stepped through the door and saw Kyle's car parked next to hers. He'd been helping at the brewery in exchange for room and board. Tace didn't know how long his enthusiasm would last, but for now he seemed willing to help Joseph. He wasn't supposed to be working today, so Tace scanned the yard, looking for him, but when she turned around she saw Berit instead. She was sitting by the old woodpile—Tace couldn't bring herself to get rid of it—and flicking a piece of grass for Suds to chase.

Tace wanted to turn and run the other way, but she forced herself to walk toward Berit. They'd spent so much time being intimate and close, it was difficult to reconcile their ease in touching and kissing with the new tension between them.

"Hi, Tace," Berit said when she got close.

Tace sighed at the sound of her voice. She'd missed it. She'd missed everything about Berit. "What are you doing here?" she asked. She sounded curt, but she couldn't be anything else. If she opted for something softer, she'd lose her control.

"Kyle let me borrow his car. I wanted to talk to you, and I couldn't wait until you got home."

Was she leaving already? Would she be gone by this evening? Tace's eyes felt wet, but she brushed at the tears with a jerky movement. "So, this is good-bye?"

Berit shook her head and glanced toward the brewery, as if expecting to see Joseph half-hidden in the shadows. "Is there somewhere more private where we can talk?"

Tace wanted to say no, to tell Berit to get out of this place because Tace wouldn't be able to bear it when she had left for good but reminders of her were everywhere. Even though Tace needed to protect herself, she couldn't resist the look in Berit's eyes and Berit's need to talk. She shrugged off her personal misgivings about being alone with Berit and started walking toward the river, toward her favorite spot on the property and one still untouched by Berit's presence.

Tace was careful to keep from touching Berit as they walked the short distance to the clearing on the corner of the brewery's acre. She had mown the grass yesterday, and the surrounding hawthorns and salal gave the area a sense of complete privacy. This had been her mini-version of the hikes she'd been missing, her one place to get away from everyone and everything. Now Berit was here, and her memory always would be. Tace sat on the ground near the meandering stream and hugged her knees to her chest.

She wanted to maintain some distance, but Berit refused to do the same. She sat behind her, with her legs on either side of Tace, and pulled Tace against her, so her back was pressed against Berit's chest. Berit had been silent on the walk from the parking lot, but as soon as Tace was in her arms, she spoke. "I took the job."

"I know," Tace said, trying unsuccessfully to pull out of Berit's hold. "Syria. You told me."

"Not Syria. I took the job at Whitman," Berit said. She loosened her hold and Tace was free, but she didn't move away. "I'll be teaching here next year."

Tace held perfectly still while she processed Berit's meaning. "But you don't like teaching."

"I like it more this semester. And I'm better at it. Who knows how I'll feel in another year or two."

"Bored stiff?" Tace offered with a humorless laugh. Berit was saying the words Tace hadn't dared hope to hear, but she didn't believe them yet. She didn't believe this plan—the one Tace wanted more than anything—would make Berit happy.

Berit shrugged and Tace appreciated the honesty of the gesture. "Maybe. Or maybe I'll like it more every semester. When we were together, I was happy here. I was inspired and interested—not just in my classes, but in you and in this place."

Tace wanted to celebrate, wanted to grab Berit and kiss her, but she wasn't convinced Berit was really staying. For how long? Were they only prolonging their inevitable and painful separation? "What if you like it less every month? What then?"

Berit wrapped her arms around Tace again. "Then we decide what to do next. Together."

Tace shook her head, but she put her hands over Berit's, sighing at the familiar feel of her.

Berit pulled one hand away and skimmed her fingers through Tace's hair. "I love you, Tace. I spent my life roaming, without a home, and I finally found what I didn't even know I'd been searching for. You're my home, Tace. Whether we stay here or eventually move on, I want us to be together."

"No running away to Syria?" Tace asked, resting her head back on Berit's shoulder, daring to believe that Berit was staying here for her. Knowing that in the future, if they decided it was necessary, she'd leave here to be with Berit. All that mattered to Tace was being with Berit, and she finally was sure Berit felt the same way.

Berit laughed. "I promise."

Tace turned her head and kissed her then, pressing her back flush against Berit's chest. She felt the familiar arousal Berit always ignited in her, but there was depth to the heat between them because desire was joined with gratitude and love.

Berit broke away from the kiss and whispered in Tace's ear, punctuating her words with flicks of her tongue. "I have one more very important question for you. Will you move back into our bedroom?"

Tace nodded, not trusting her voice because her throat was suddenly parched. She leaned her head back on Berit's shoulder again while Berit kissed her neck, drawing out the sadness and tension Tace had been carrying inside. Berit moved her hand from Tace's hip, under her shirt, and up her rib cage until she held Tace's breast in her palm. She massaged her gently at first, and then with short, rapid movements as Tace moaned and arched her back. Her response to Berit's touch was sudden and intense, and she spread her legs wider to give Berit easier access when she reached to unbutton Tace's jeans.

Berit's hand moved down her stomach and into her pants, and Tace knew Berit could feel how wet and ready she was. Berit groaned against her neck and bit her shoulder. Tace came hard and fast, without warning, and she trembled in the comforting circle of Berit's arms. As soon as she could catch her breath, she turned and eased Berit down to the ground.

Tace kissed her, moving from her mouth, down the tendons in her neck, across her collarbone, and back to her lips. She'd never get her fill of Berit, never get over the wonder of finding her and being loved by her. She braced her hands on the ground above Berit's shoulders and lowered her hips until they were pressing hard against Berit's.

She watched Berit's face as she started to move against her, rubbing against the crotch of Berit's jeans. Their hips moved together in unison, as if they were fused together. Tace lowered herself to her elbows, never breaking the contact or cadence of their lower bodies. She kissed Berit, long and slow in contrast to the ever-increasing movement of their hips, and poured everything she'd been keeping inside into the kiss. Fears eased, doubts removed, love returned. Tace dug her fingers into the wet mud, tangled them in the slender blades of grass, and the jerk of Berit's hips when her orgasm overtook her made Tace come again.

Tace rolled to her side and lay on her back next to Berit, twining their fingers together.

"I love you," Tace said when she had enough breath to talk again. "More than this town and more than my job here."

"And I love you." Berit turned her head and nuzzled Tace's shoulder. "I always thought I needed constant change in my life, but what I need is *you* as a constant in my life. I can stay in one place or travel the globe, as long as you're with me."

"Always," Tace said. She squeezed Berit's hand gently. "Here or anywhere. We're in this together."

CHAPTER TWENTY-FOUR

T his is how you pack?" Tace asked. She pulled small
bundles out of Berit's suitcase and laid the shirts and
pants on the bed, smoothing the wrinkles and folding them neatly.
"Everything is wadded up in here."

Berit sat on the bed and watched Tace tidy up her unruly
clothes. "I never saw a reason to bother. After four months on a
dig with no showers and only the same three unwashed outfits to
wear, you stop caring about a few wrinkles."

Tace put the clothes in a pile, large to small, and stuck them
in the suitcase. "Please tell me you're planning to use the hotel's
shower at some point while we're in Greece. Or are you nostalgic
for the authentic dig experience?"

Berit held up her right hand. "I swear I will take regular
showers. As long as you take them with me."

"Deal," Tace said.

"I can't wait to see Athens with you," Berit said. She lay
back and put one arm behind her head, staring at the ceiling and
picturing the places they'd visit. They were traveling for her work,
thanks to an offhand suggestion Tace had made one day. She'd
looked around Berit's office at all the bowls and trinkets Berit had
collected over the years and that she'd finally gotten out of her
storage lockers. *Too bad Whitman doesn't have a Classical Studies
museum*, Tace had said. *You could be curator and we could travel*

the world looking for things to exhibit. Berit had laughed at the idea at first, but then she'd given it more thought. Thought led to an official proposal, and now she had the chance to start her museum from the ground up. She wouldn't exactly be digging up the finds herself, but she'd still enjoy the search and discovery. Tace somehow—even without trying—made life better, in every way.

"And I can't wait to be there with you, seeing part of your world and going places you went with your grandfather."

Berit smiled. She'd feel closer to him there. She'd even be introducing him and Tace, in a way. "I'll like that," she said. "But we're going to make some memories of our own, too."

"Plenty of them." Tace grinned at her before taking a pair of shorts out of a drawer. "Am I packing too much?" she asked.

"Yes," Berit said. She yanked the shorts out of Tace's hand and tossed them on the floor. She grabbed her wrist and pulled her onto the bed. "I don't mind how much stuff you bring, but I do think you're spending too much time packing."

"Oh, really? Can you think of a better use of my time?"

Berit could, as a matter of fact. Ideas sprang immediately to mind. "To start, you could take those clothes off."

"Why don't I start with yours, and we'll see how things go." Tace used both hands to push Berit's tank top up her body and over her head.

The slow crawl of Tace's hands over her skin made Berit gasp as a shimmer of goose bumps followed in their wake. Berit felt her nipples grow hard even before Tace lowered her head to take one deep into her mouth.

Berit held Tace's head close to her breast and she squirmed as Tace sucked harder, exactly the way Berit wanted her to. Berit whimpered with pleasure when Tace kissed her belly, inching her way down her body.

Tace reached the barrier of Berit's sweatpants and she lingered there, licking hypersensitive skin and moving the pants over her hips one millimeter at a time until Berit was going to go mad for her touch. Tace finally pulled Berit's sweats down her legs and dropped them off the bed. She nestled herself between Berit's legs and caressed the skin of her inner thighs.

Berit watched Tace's long, slender fingers as they moved over her skin, touching everywhere with teasing lightness, but never going high enough to ease the growing ache between Berit's legs. Berit wanted to urge her to hurry—take her now and let her come—but other parts of her wanted to draw out the time she was with Tace, milking every ounce of pleasure and closeness she could get out of Tace's touch.

Berit closed her eyes and sighed when mouth replaced fingers in the exploration of Berit's body. The silky rasp of Tace's tongue was familiar to her now. Berit had always fought against familiarity, preferring instead anonymity and unpredictability. She knew every part of Tace's body intimately, but the knowledge only added to her excitement and pleasure.

Berit opened her legs farther at the insistence of Tace's hands, and then her back bowed upward when Tace touched her gently with the tip of her tongue. Berit moved with her, feeling her energy coiling inside her as Tace moved deeper. Berit hung on the cusp of an orgasm, calling Tace's name and asking for more, crying out with pleasure when Tace offered everything she was.

About the Author

Karis Walsh is the author of lesbian romances including Rainbow Award-winning *Harmony* and *Sea Glass Inn*, as well as a romantic intrigue series about a mounted police unit. She's a Pacific Northwest native who recently relocated to Texas with her goats. When she isn't writing, she's playing with her animals, cooking, reading, playing her viola, or hiking in the state park.

Books Available from Bold Strokes Books

Love on Tap by Karis Walsh. Beer and romance are brewing for Tace Lomond when archaeologist Berit Katsaros comes into her life. (987-1-162639-564-0)

Love on the Red Rocks by Lisa Moreau. An unexpected romance at a lesbian resort forces Malley to face her greatest fears where she must choose between playing it safe or taking a chance at true happiness. (987-1-162639-660-9)

Tracker and the Spy by D. Jackson Leigh. There are lessons for all when Captain Tanisha is assigned untried pyro Kyle and a lovesick dragon horse for a mission to track the leader of a dangerous cult. (987-1-162639-448-3)

Whirlwind Romance by Kris Bryant. Will chasing the girl break Tristan's heart or give her something she's never had before? (987-1-162639-581-7)

Whiskey Sunrise by Missouri Vaun. Culture and religion collide when Lovey Porter, daughter of a local Baptist minister, falls for the handsome thrill-seeking moonshine runner, Royal Duval. (987-1-162639-519-0)

Dyre: By Moon's Light by Rachel E. Bailey. A young werewolf, Des, guards the aging leader of all the Packs: the Dyre. Stable employment—nice work, if you can get it…at least until silver bullets start to fly. (978-1-62639-6-623)

Fragile Wings by Rebecca S. Buck. In Roaring Twenties London, can Evelyn Hopkins find love with Jos Singleton or will the scars of the Great War crush her dreams? (978-1-62639-5-466)

Live and Love Again by Jan Gayle. Jessica Whitney could be Sarah Jarret's second chance at love, but their differences and Sarah's grief continue to come between their budding relationship. (978-1-62639-5-176)

Starstruck by Lesley Davis. Actress Cassidy Hayes and writer Aiden Darrow find out the hard way not all life-threatening drama is confined to the TV screen or the pages of a manuscript. (978-1-62639-5-237)

Stealing Sunshine by Tina Michele. Under the Central Florida sun, two women struggle between fear and love as a dangerous plot of deception and revenge threatens to steal priceless art and lives. (978-1-62639-4-452)

The Fifth Gospel by Michelle Grubb. Hiding a Vatican secret is dangerous—sharing the secret suicidal—can Felicity survive a perilous book tour, and will her PR specialist, Anna, be there when it's all over? (978-1-62639-4-476)

Cold to the Touch by Cari Hunter. A drug addict's murder is the start of a dangerous investigation for Detective Sanne Jensen and Dr. Meg Fielding, as they try to stop a killer with no conscience. (978-1-62639-526-8)

Forsaken by Laydin Michaels. The hunt for a killer teaches one woman that she must overcome her fear in order to love, and another that success is meaningless without happiness. (978-1-62639-481-0)

Infiltration by Jackie D. When a CIA breach is imminent, a Marine instructor must stop the attack while protecting her heart from being disarmed by a recruit. (978-1-62639-521-3)

Midnight at the Orpheus by Alyssa Linn Palmer. Two women desperate to make their way in the world, a man hell-bent on revenge, and a cop risking his career: all in a day's work in Capone's Chicago. (978-1-62639-607-4)

Spirit of the Dance by Mardi Alexander. Major Sorla Reardon's return to her family farm to heal threatens Riley Johnson's safe life when small-town secrets are revealed, and love may not conquer all. (978-1-62639-583-1)

Sweet Hearts by Melissa Brayden, Rachel Spangler, and Karis Walsh. Do you ever wonder *Whatever happened to...*? Find out when you reconnect with your favorite characters from Melissa Brayden's *Heart Block*, Rachel Spangler's *LoveLife*, and Karis Walsh's *Worth the Risk*. (978-1-62639-475-9)

Totally Worth It by Maggie Cummings. Who knew there's an all-lesbian condo community in the NYC suburbs? Join twentysomething BFFs Meg and Lexi at Bay West as they navigate friendships, love, and everything in between. (978-1-62639-512-1)

Illicit Artifacts by Stevie Mikayne. Her foster mother's death cracked open a secret world Jil never wanted to see…and now she has to pick up the stolen pieces. (978-1-62639-472-8)

Pathfinder by Gun Brooke. Heading for their new homeworld, Exodus's chief engineer Adina Vantressa and nurse Briar Lindemay carry game-changing secrets that may well cause them to lose everything when disaster strikes. (978-1-62639-444-5)

Prescription for Love by Radclyffe. Dr. Flannery Rivers finds herself attracted to the new ER chief, city girl Abigail Remy, and the incendiary mix of city and country, fire and ice, tradition and change is combustible. (978-1-62639-570-1)

Ready or Not by Melissa Brayden. Uptight Mallory Spencer finds relinquishing control to bartender Hope Sanders too tall an order in fast-paced New York City. (978-1-62639-443-8)

Summer Passion by MJ Williamz. Women loving women is forbidden in 1946 Hollywood, yet Jean and Maggie strive to keep their love alive and away from prying eyes. (978-1-62639-540-4)

The Princess and the Prix by Nell Stark. "Ugly duckling" Princess Alix of Monaco was resigned to loneliness until she met racecar driver Thalia d'Angelis. (978-1-62639-474-2)

Winter's Harbor by Aurora Rey. Lia Brooks isn't looking for love in Provincetown, but when she discovers chocolate croissants and pastry chef Alex McKinnon, her winter retreat quickly starts heating up. (978-1-62639-498-8)

The Time Before Now by Missouri Vaun. Vivian flees a disastrous affair, embarking on an epic, transformative journey to escape her past, until destiny introduces her to Ida, who helps her rediscover trust, love, and hope. (978-1-62639-446-9)

Twisted Whispers by Sheri Lewis Wohl. Betrayal, lies, and secrets—whispers of a friend lost to darkness. Can a reluctant psychic set things right or will an evil soul destroy those she loves? (978-1-62639-439-1)

The Courage to Try by C.A. Popovich. Finding love is worth getting past the fear of trying. (978-1-62639-528-2)

Break Point by Yolanda Wallace. In a world readying for war, can love find a way? (978-1-62639-568-8)

Countdown by Julie Cannon. Can two strong-willed, powerful women overcome their differences to save the lives of seven others and begin a life they never imagined together? (978-1-62639-471-1)

Keep Hold by Michelle Grubb. Claire knew some things should be left alone and some rules should never be broken, but the most forbidden, well, they are the most tempting. (978-1-62639-502-2)

Deadly Medicine by Jaime Maddox. Dr. Ward Thrasher's life is in turmoil. Her partner Jess left her, and her job puts her in the path of a murderous physician who has Jess in his sights. (978-1-62639-424-7)

New Beginnings by KC Richardson. Can the connection and attraction between Jordan Roberts and Kirsten Murphy be enough for Jordan to trust Kirsten with her heart? (978-1-62639-450-6)

Officer Down by Erin Dutton. Can two women who've made careers out of being there for others in crisis find the strength to need each other? (978-1-62639-423-0)

Reasonable Doubt by Carsen Taite. Just when Sarah and Ellery think they've left dangerous careers behind, a new case sets them— and their hearts—on a collision course. (978-1-62639-442-1)

Tarnished Gold by Ann Aptaker. Cantor Gold must outsmart the Law, outrun New York's dockside gangsters, outplay a shady art dealer, his lover, and a beautiful curator, and stay out of a killer's gun sights. (978-1-62639-426-1)

White Horse in Winter by Franci McMahon. Love between two women collides with the inner poison of a closeted horse trainer in the green hills of Vermont. (978-1-62639-429-2)

Autumn Spring by Shelley Thrasher. Can Bree and Linda, two women in the autumn of their lives, put their hearts first and find the love they've never dared seize? (978-1-62639-365-3)

The Renegade by Amy Dunne. Post-apocalyptic survivors Alex and Evelyn secretly find love while held captive by a deranged cult, but when their relationship is discovered, they must fight for their freedom—or die trying. (978-1-62639-427-8)

Thrall by Barbara Ann Wright. Four women in a warrior society must work together to lift an insidious curse while caught between their own desires, the will of their peoples, and an ancient evil. (978-1-62639-437-7)

The Chameleon's Tale by Andrea Bramhall. Two old friends must work through a web of lies and deceit to find themselves again, but in the search they discover far more than they ever went looking for. (978-1-62639-363-9)